ADVANCE PRAISE FOR *DANCING WITH CHAIRS IN THE MUSIC HOUSE*

Quirky, funny and haunting.
—LINWOOD BARCLAY, *New York Time*s bestselling author

Caro Soles' book is an extraordinary piece of fiction. Haunting, and highly evocative, it deserves to find its place in the pantheon of the best of Canadian literature.
—MAUREEN JENNINGS, author of the *Murdoch Mystery* series

Author Caro Soles takes us on a captivating trip through late-1940s Toronto, its afternoon teas and general propriety, revealing a story rich in character and local colour. Our guide is young Vanessa, whose astute observations of her genteel family and the oddball tenants of a downtown rooming house keep the pages turning with hints of calamity to come. Great (and often witty) writing, love of music, and a wonderful sense of time and place mark this enjoyable novel.
—CAROLE GIANGRANDE, author of *The Tender Birds* and *All That Is Solid Melts Into Air*

Intimate, evocative and memorable, Caro Soles' *Dancing with Chairs in the Music House* holds the reader spellbound from its opening sentence — It's 1949, a brand-new year, and we're moving. Again. — to its heart-stopping conclusion. Vanessa Dudley-Morris, the novel's engaging ten-year-old narrator, kept from school by an eye condition that threatens blindness, is free to roam her new home, a rundown rooming house at 519 Jarvis Street. Vanessa is a keen observer of her world and through her, Soles gives us accurate and incisive portraits of Toronto and her citizens at mid-twentieth century. Remembering the way we were then is a gift, but the greatest gift in Soles' novel is her characterization of Vanessa. Like Henry James, Caro Soles is able to capture in words the experience of what it feels like to be growing inside.

—GAIL BOWEN, award-winning author of the *Joanne Kilbourne* series

DANCING WITH CHAIRS IN THE MUSIC HOUSE

CARO SOLES

DANCING WITH CHAIRS IN THE MUSIC HOUSE

CARO SOLES

inanna poetry & fiction series

INANNA PUBLICATIONS AND EDUCATION INC.
TORONTO, CANADA

OTHER FICTION PUBLISHED UNDER THE
NAME CARO SOLES

Marlo's Dance
Do You Know Me?
A Friend of Mr. Nijinsky
The Memory Dance
The Danger Dance
The Abulon Dance
A Mutual Understanding
Drag Queen in the Court of Death
The Tangled Boy

*In memory of my Mother,
whose middle name really was Boadicea.*

1. MOVING DAY

It's 1949, a brand-new year, and we're moving. Again. From a lofty height—from the tip-top branches of the naked elm trees that march along both sides of Jarvis Street, say—we must look like ants. Worker ants, of course, because we're each one carrying something. A long line of ants, carrying our possessions across the street to our new home upstairs in Rona Layne's big house at number 519. Ferrying our Lares and Penates across the River Styx, only we have to walk, so I guess that doesn't work.

Naturally I don't get to carry much because I could drop something, or stumble, or not see a car coming and get run over. Mother thinks it's likely I'll get run over more than anyone else, though I don't understand why. I'm not too small for them to see. I'm quite big, especially in my winter coat and hat—wider than Janet anyway, who's tall but skinny. And the driver would feel a tremendous bump if I were hit. But I won't be. I can see the cars plainly. It's all quite silly, but there's no use saying anything. No use at all.

The weather is cooperating by sending us the January thaw. The snow is mostly melted on the sidewalks, and the sun is shining. As usual, my big brother Jonathan is telling everyone what to do, even though he's not as old as Janet's big brother Francis, who came home from studying to be a priest just to help. Isn't that grand? Janet's family is Catholic, but that's all right, Mother says, because not all Catholics are bad. I know this already from history, but I don't say anything. And I still like to read *Foxe's Book of Martyrs*. So does Janet. She says it makes her feel all shivery. Janet is my best friend.

Daddy is over at the new house now, making sure everything goes in the right place. He helped move the piano and is probably tired after that and has to rest. Early in the morning, before the milk wagon clinked its way up the street, the Sullivan boys brought a wide board and a few things like long rolling pins covered with bits of carpet. Then they rolled the piano across the road, sort of like the way they built the pyramids, according to the *Book of Knowledge*. Jonathan stood with his arms outstretched in case some cars came along. Since Mother wouldn't let me cross the street, I don't know how they got it up all the wooden stairs at the back to the second floor where we're going to live. But later on, after breakfast—oatmeal again, with lots of brown sugar—I got to carry armfuls of cushions and then the footstool Daddy made last year as a Christmas present for Mother. There's a scratch on one of the curvy legs from where Mother threw it across the room that time a letter came saying we didn't get some money we were supposed to get from the government because of Daddy's service in the war—the Great War, not the one we just had. You don't notice the scratch if you turn the stool with that leg to the wall.

I love moving. We do it a lot since coming to this big city, sliding from rooming house to rooming house when people complain about the noise from Jonathan practising all the time or someone points out the unwritten *no children* rule. I barely remember all the places we've been. Something about this move makes my parents think we might stay here for a while, and that's what they long for. A haven. Perhaps it's because the piano is considered a good thing in the Music House and the owner has known about me from the start. She once said I have perfect pitch.

After months of nothing happening in my life, suddenly everyone is here with us. Everyone we know in Toronto has come to help, even Mr. Steels, the man who lived upstairs at Mrs. Alistair's place. He used to show me how to make animals out of pipe cleaners in his room until Mother found out and told me not to go up there alone any more. But he's here now, for a while at least. A few times he catches my eye and winks, and I feel a strange flutter in my chest and put my head down and flush. I am relieved when he leaves, touching the grimy peak of his flat cloth hat to my mother in a small salute before setting off down the street with his irregular jolting gait. He was in the Great War, too.

In my head, I think of the new place as the Music House. I have been inside lots of times because of the master classes in piano that Miss Rona Layne teaches to a Select Few in her studio. She is an *artiste*. She has toured Europe and played for the Crowned Heads many times, and now she takes on only the brightest and best ... and my brother, who is studying to be a concert pianist when he isn't busy doing high school things. Twice a week we climb up the four smooth steps and go through the heavy front door into the gloom of the square hallway. Stairs wind up sedately into the dust-filled sunshine that floods in from the frosted windows on the landing. I am curious to know what they look out on, what the sun on the other side of the windows would shine on, but I never have the nerve to take a look. I always sit as if glued to the black oak of the bench with the griffins carved on each end. When I was younger, I was afraid the great creatures might attack me if I left them, breaking the promise I made to my brother to stay on the bench. I could almost hear their enormous wings beating as they took to the air to hunt me down and drag me back in their great talons. So I sat there, swinging my legs in their long black stockings, trying to hear what was going on in the studio. But the door was down a corridor and covered by a thick velvet curtain, and nothing penetrated to the dim hall. But now that I'm ten and I'll be living here, I can find out about the sunshine. I can come down from upstairs anytime I like, and the griffins won't even know I'm there. Isn't that grand?

Standing now on the other side of the street guarding a pile of bedding in a basket, I look at the Music House, trying to imagine living there in our two rooms and tiny kitchen (which is really just a closet) on the second floor. Going in the front door as a matter of course, crossing the wide hall, climbing up the long flight of stairs through the dust motes. *Good morning, how do you do? Yes, I live here now. I live in this mansion.*

From here the house looks a little like the profile of a giant beast, crouching on the lawn behind the ornamental wrought-iron fence, showing us its profile. The one-storey studio wing would be the paws, stretching off to the left, while the head towers up to the third-floor gables and the back swoops down to the *porte cochère* on the right. It seems heavy, sinking into the ground with the gravity of its own importance, rather like Mrs. Craven, the landlady at the house before last.

Our old place is just a big house. As I turn around and look at it now, it makes me think of a fat old lady, the verandah her full skirts spread around her on three sides, resting on the snow-covered lawn. Mrs. Bowther often sat there, watching the world go by from under lowered lids, her hands clasped over the big bible spread across her capacious knee. Mother often said she would do better to read it than to try to absorb it by osmosis. Then she explained how if Mrs. B. were a plant, it might work a lot better, and Daddy explained how osmosis works in plants. Most of my lessons are like that. It's better than school, I imagine, though sometimes I long for the company of others my own age. Mrs. B. is out there now, watching us, no expression on her face, her eyes like raisins sunk into her unbaked cookie-dough face.

Finally I get to help Janet carry the basket across the street while Jonathan walks beside us, a rolled-up rug on his shoulder as if it were nothing more than a long rolled-up music score. It occurs to me for the first time that playing the piano must make you strong. Thumping with both hands on the great black

Steinway that crouches in Miss Layne's studio, making it growl and whimper and shout, would take the kind of strength that makes it easy to carry our rug as if it were nothing. I feel a thrill of pride in my brother that all his musical accomplishments have never aroused in me before.

By noon everyone has gone, and we are officially living in the Music House. It feels so different here; everything is on a loftier scale: the halls are wider, the rooms bigger, even the ceilings seem higher. Daddy is very tired, but he has already put up the big metal double bed in the bedroom where he and Mother and I will sleep. Mother has made it up with clean sheets and the bleached pillowcases made of sugar bags, and he is now lying down, resting, boxes and baskets piled up waiting on the floor around him. The rest of us are across the hall in the living room where there's a daybed for Jonathan to sleep on. It is the first time we have had a real living room. Jonathan says we had one in the apartment when we first came here, the one that was broken into and the police came and told Mother this was no place for a lady. We moved a few days later. Pity I can't remember it.

The living room seems huge. It has a working brick fireplace with several ornamental painted tiles. A truck brought our old dining table and chairs from storage sometime during the morning. It brought the wing chair, too, which is now sitting in the cupola where the windows curve out almost like a ship. The tall expanse of small leaded panes reflect the light unevenly. When I stand there, I can almost see the street and the roof of the *porte cochère* where Taffy, Miss Layne's fat cocker spaniel, is waddling around sniffing in the yellowed snow. As I watch, I can tell by the slope of her back what she is about to do, and I turn away, embarrassed for the poor thing.

"Taffy. What a disgusting name for a dog," I say, thinking of the wonderful butterscotch flavour called up by the word, the way it would melt on my tongue, the contrast with the squatting ugly dog.

"That's a bit harsh, isn't it, dear?" Mother is putting books in our new bookcase that is built into one wall under a row of small windows, but I know she isn't really paying attention.

"If I ever have a dog, I'll call him Vercingetorix," I say, rolling the name off my tongue with pleasure.

"No, you wouldn't," says Jonathan. "Don't show off."

"I'm not!" I exclaim, indignant. But I feel a tremble of uncertainty, a cool wash of hurt. Often I am unsure why I say things.

"I think it's a fine name," Mother says.

"Make yourself useful." Jonathan heaves another box onto the table. He has just brought several boxes across the hall from the room where Daddy is napping, and he forgot to close the door, so anyone walking down the hall can look in. A wizened old woman lurches by with a small paper bag clutched in one hand. This is the second or third time she has come down the hall and out to the back porch where the icebox and garbage cans live. As she goes by, she turns her head and stares at us, her beady eyes bright like tiny searchlights, before turning away abruptly. Mother gets up and closes the door, the latch clicking softly in the silence.

Jonathan makes a choking sound. I clap my hands over my mouth to keep from exploding in rude laughter.

"What a nosy old bag," Jonathan says. "Not very subtle, is she?"

Mother smiles, her grey eyes sparkling with mischief. "Poor thing is just a bag of bones."

"All she has to do is knock on the door and introduce herself, like a civilized person." Jonathan is unpacking the dishes and laying them out on the table. I begin to fold up the paper. Everything in our family gets used many times. Some of this tissue paper is so soft from wear, from being used to wrap Christmas presents and birthday gifts, creased from packing dishes and glasses and cups, that it makes no noise when I fold it.

"Baggy Bones," Mother says softly, and we all burst out in muffled laughter.

Suddenly I feel very happy. It happens sometimes, when we're doing things together like this, when Mother is laughing, Jonathan is smiling, and I feel a real part of something.

I push my glasses up on my nose. "Baggy Bones," I whisper.

2. THE MUSIC HOUSE

DAYS GO BY, AND I AM STILL EXCITED about living in the Music House. For one thing, there's the kitchen, even though it's very tiny. Infinitesimal, really, and there's no window. Mother says it was probably a broom closet for the maids in the former life of the house, but we don't care. There's a sink with a cupboard over it and beside it a small table with a shelf underneath. Last week Daddy bought a stove for the kitchen. It, too, is tiny, almost like a toy, but it's way better than a hotplate. Daddy says it's a table-top model, and sure enough, it just fits on top of the table. It has two burners on top and an oven just big enough to get our eight-inch square cake pan inside. Mother made a sponge cake with chocolate sauce to celebrate the move, the kitchen, our new life here. I mixed the margarine in its bag with the colour bud until it was bright yellow all the way through, then helped Mother spoon it into the crystal butter dish. When we are both in the kitchen, we can just close the door.

When Mother gets tired and depressed, she says our new place is nothing but three rooms in a glorified rooming house, but mostly she calls it a flat. If that's the same thing as an apartment, even I know this isn't right. Everyone on the second floor uses the hall that separates our rooms—two on one side, one on the other. Anyone can walk down past the tapestry, past our kitchen, our living room, and our Everything Room. You never know who you're going to meet when you open one of our doors, but mostly it's just Baggy Bones pretending to take a small paper bag out to the garbage cans on the porch. We think of it as our porch because it's outside the windows of the room where Mother and Daddy and I sleep in the big brown metal bed with the shiny silver-blue spread. Mother's two wardrobe trunks sit open along one wall, serving as dressers. The table Daddy made last fall from cast-off wood juts into the room at a funny angle, and the laundry basket sits under it. Mother bought the basket from a Gypsy woman who came to their back door one day down East. A week later, when they brought me home from the orphanage, that's where I slept, under a blanket crocheted by some Anglican nuns Mother knew from church. One of them is my godmother, but I've only seen her a few times. Mostly I remember the brown habit that almost swept the ground, the wrinkled wimple framing a wrinkled face. Mother said she was thrown out of her old order so she started her own. I guess she decided to wear brown to be different. I would choose pink, or perhaps bright green like the grass.

Daddy is going to make window boxes so Mother can have a garden this summer. She used to have a wonderful garden in the big house on the corner lot out West, when my brother was still a baby and we still had lots of money. I wasn't even born then, but I've heard so many stories about that house I can see it in my mind's eye: the gleaming hardwood floors, the bay window in the living room, the big entry hall with its black-and-white marble tiles, the sweeping, curved staircase.

The Music House may have hardwood floors, too, but most of them are covered by the long runner in the hall. There's only us, Baggy Bones, and Mrs. Smyth on this floor, not counting Miss Layne and her housekeeper Miss Jones, of course. They live in a totally separate *real* apartment at the front of the house, right at the top of the stairs, and we rarely see them. I don't know how many rooms they have. Up on the third floor, there's a Miss Tyndall whom we've never seen; the Englishwoman, Mrs. Dunn; and a new couple, mother and son, who will be moving in this weekend. I overhear Baggy Bones tell someone called Marie this bit of news through the door that she leaves open a crack so as not to miss anything.

Mother likes Mrs. Dunn. They met in the hall and Mrs. D. introduced herself.

"This is my daughter, Vanessa," Mother said scooping me up against her with one arm, as if she were a bird gathering me under her wing.

"How are you, dear?" said Mrs. Dunn, shaking my hand gravely.

"I'm very well, thank you, and I hope you are," I said, as I was taught, trying not to make it a singsong. I've never heard anyone else say this, but Mother always insists. Everyone is invariably pleased.

Mrs. Dunn smiled even more broadly and invited us to tea on Thursday. Maybe in England, where she comes from, this is what people say to one another. I've never been to England. Neither has Mother, but she is always pleased when people assume she is from there, as they often do.

"Our family goes back to William the Conqueror," she tells me, looking fierce and proud as she works the bellows to make the fire come to life in our brick fireplace. Daddy sighs, the sound light as a feather floating up to the ceiling. "If my grandfather had followed his head instead of his heart, we'd still be there in Hadleigh Hall where we belong!"

One time Mother showed me a picture of Hadleigh Hall, a huge place that makes the Music House look like a cottage. The whole stately pile is surrounded by formal gardens where fountains used to play and a rose arbour blazed with colour in the pale sunshine.

Sometimes when Mother tells the story, it's as if she is still angry at the man who followed his heart instead of his head and was exiled because of it and became a remittance man. Sometimes she tells it to show how her grandfather was, in reality, a man of principle, of honour. He chose to marry the woman who otherwise would have been ruined. She was a school teacher. She worked with children just like Mother and Aunt Dottie.

"We were at Agincourt," Mother goes on, shaking the poker. "We were at the Boyne!"

"On what side?" Jonathan asks, suddenly interested.

Mother scowls. "Charles the First may not have been much of a leader, but he was the king, after all."

"He liked dogs," I say.

"So did Hitler," Jonathan remarks.

My father grunts and makes a face. Although this recent war was not his war, any mention of it reminds him of the years of hell that ruined his health and made him unable to work, of the poisons that still secretly crawl though his blood just under his pink skin, erupting now and then and putting him back in torment. He is never completely free of it. Somewhere on his body, there is always a hot patch of itch and pain, and at times of stress, the poisons erupt through his skin. Then he spends hours every morning, every night, washing down the sores, spreading on the tarry-smelling ointment, wrapping himself in bandages to keep his clothes free of stains. When things get really bad, he disappears for weeks at a time into Sunnybrook Veterans' Hospital, and Mother visits almost every day. But when he's home, he always dresses in a shirt, jacket, and tie, although he wears slippers in the house now, a concession to his swollen ankles. I'm not sure if he wants to dress this way or if it's to please Mother, to whom proper dress is very important. "We may have fallen on hard times," she says, "but think of who we are."

I often think of who we are. I wonder about it, about how I fit in. I was born into such a different background. Not that I know much about my real background, except that it was French. The knowledge of my adoption is in my mind like the shadow of a memory, a faint exotic perfume from another world, but when we talk to people, I never say a word. I let

Mother spin her story of where we've come from, why we're here. Jonathan and I each have a part in that story, both of us shining examples of Mother's handiwork. He's adopted, too. We are the chosen ones. I listen, and every time I marvel at the power of her words. How her view of who we are changes our world. She keeps us going, holds us all together. She is indomitable, my father says, like Boadicea, her namesake, the warrior queen. Of course that's only her middle name, but the indomitable part's still the same.

I am looking forward to tea with Mrs. Dunn. I don't often get to visit anyone, even Janet, who goes to school, takes violin lessons, and has to practise and do homework. She's a year older than I am, but we have a wonderful time playing together. One of our favourites is the Trojan War game, and I carefully explain to her what our roles entail. We make wristbands and greaves for our legs out of brown paper decorated with black and red crayon in the kind of Greek designs we find in Janet's encyclopedia. We scale walls in her garden and indulge in hand-to-hand combat with short swords made out of sticks. I used Daddy's supply of sandpaper to make them smooth. One time we built the Trojan Horse in her living room, using overturned chairs, two small wicker baskets, and a brown chenille bedspread. Her mother was not pleased with this, and I couldn't go over there to play for two weeks. Mother wasn't cross. She's the one who's reading me the *Iliad*, after all, so I guess she feels a little responsible. "Just wait till we get to the *Odyssey*," she says, laughing. "You'll be building ships then." I love going to Janet's, but we've only been to tea once.

At three-thirty on Tuesday afternoon, we go upstairs to Mrs. Dunn's. Mother is wearing her Liberty-print dress, with the tiny blue flowers all over it, and she has her pale-blue sweater draped over her shoulders. I can smell the dash of 4711 cologne she has splashed on her wrists and her earlobes. Under it lies a faint memory of the lavender from the sachet she made to hang in the wardrobe trunk where she keeps the dress and her suit from Ada Mackenzie and the hat made to match by Rose Broderson. I'm wearing the usual: white blouse, navy blue tunic, long black stockings. Both my blouses are getting tight, but Mother has sewn an extension on one side of the placket and moved the buttons over so there's more room. You can't see this adjustment under the tunic, but I know it's there.

The stairs up to the third floor are quite different from the others. They're enclosed and narrow and dark, and although there is a small window on the landing, its tiny diamond-shaped panes are dirty and streaked, letting in little light. The carpet on the stairs is thinner too, but our footsteps are still muffled as we rise higher and emerge into sunlight streaming in through the glass part of the door that leads onto the roof. I am delighted. I can see the top of the iron ladder that leads from our porch down below, looping gracefully into the air before swooping down to attach itself to the edge of the roof. I hadn't had a chance to climb up from below yet, so I didn't know where it ended up. It's a great discovery, enlarging my world in a way I can't explain.

Mother pays no attention to this, but is looking at the brass numbers on the doors. We are number 6 and 7. Mrs. Dunn is number 9. *Engine, engine number nine, steaming down Chicago line,* I think, beating out the rhythm with my hand against my thigh before I can stop myself.

"Hush, dear," Mother says, and she knocks on the door.

Mrs. Dunn is large, with silver hair piled into a bun on top of her head, tortoise-shell hairpins like my grandmother's attaching it all firmly in place. She is wearing a grey skirt, a silky cream blouse with a ruffle down the front, and a lacy black sweater that looks hand-knit. My grandmother knits all the time, so I recognize the pattern. Mother smiles, and her face lights up, as it does for company. They stand for a few moments talking in the middle of the bright room, and I notice Mother is using the interrupted step, her hands clasped, her head on one side. She has tried to teach me to stand this way—feet together, one slightly in front of the other—but when I try, I find it hard to balance, and she laughs and says there's plenty of time to learn more grown-up, ladylike ways.

Mrs. Dunn brings a tray with tea things on it over to a small table by the window and sets it down. The cups and saucers rattle slightly. The cups are touched with gold around the rims, and all three have a different flower pattern. I wince, thinking of the similar cup and saucer I received last year at Christmas from an ancient great-aunt whom I have never met. Opening that present was such a disappointment, but I smiled and smiled and said, "How lovely." Also on the tray is a plate with a doily on it, with Peek Frean biscuits arranged around the edge in an exact circle. We don't have this kind except on special occasions. Jonathan bought a package last week for Daddy's birthday. Daddy has a sweet tooth, like me. When we take our walks and he talks about nature—how trees grow, how reforestation works—we sometimes stop in the store where they sell penny candy. Last time I bought a marshmallow mouse and he bought a licorice rope. It's our secret.

We're sitting now: Mother on a small armchair, me on a hard chair so high my feet barely reach the ground. I'm trying not to look at the biscuits. I'm drinking my tea slowly. It's half milk, and Mrs. Dunn has put sugar in it, which I'm not used to. Finally our hostess offers me the plate. I glance at Mother who gives me a small nod. There are only two chocolate ones, and I feel guilty taking one of them, but my mouth is almost watering, I want it so much. I take it and don't look at Mother again until the biscuit is gone.

"I'm so sorry about Vanessa," Mrs. Dunn is saying. I've been so involved in the chocolate biscuit issue, I've missed the "curtain may fall any time" speech, where Mother quotes the big-name eye doctor we came to Toronto to see. I push my thick glasses up on my nose and take refuge in the sickly sweet tea. It's cold now, but I don't care.

"What grade are you in, dear?" Mrs. D. asks now. She

obviously hasn't heard the whole speech, or Mother hasn't gotten to that part yet.

"I don't go to school," I say.

"She can't see well enough," my mother says, and her hand flutters over to me and covers mine convulsively. "The doctor told us to keep her at home. Have her rest her eyes every day. We spend that time reading to her."

"I'm sure you'll learn more with your mother than at school anyway," Mrs. Dunn says, smiling at me a little too long, a little too hard. I duck my head, feeling the unwelcome blush.

Mother talks for a bit about the tutors who have come to the house to teach me. Most of them are Mother's "Lame Ducks," as Daddy calls them, but this doesn't come up in Mother's version. She finds them everywhere she goes, talks to them, finds out if they have some knowledge that could be useful to me. I've had a smattering of Greek and quite a bit of Latin from a man who speaks only in whispers—a British soldier suffering from shell shock. He was an Oxonian, with a doctorate in classics. I loved lessons from Mr. Thompson too, who arrived on two crutches, his body twisted from two years in a POW camp in Japan. He was a linguist, and he taught me French and Geography. Now I have Mrs. Dane, a pinched woman Mother found at church, who used to teach in a convent school and now teaches me penmanship and Canadian history. I expect she won't be coming back though, ever since Mother discovered she was getting some of the history wrong. Mother will send her away with a flea in her ear now, I expect. I wish Miss David could be a tutor. Her real name is something like Davidovitch, but David is easier so she uses that. She's always so happy and enthusiastic about everything. I don't think she knows she's a Lame Duck. Perhaps she could teach me some of her language, though I'm not sure what it is. Mother seems rather vague about it.

Mrs. Dunn tells us about some of the people who live in the Music House. Mrs. Smyth used to teach music at a girls' school, but Jonathan has already found that out. He has talked to her a few times, has even been in her room. Mrs. Dunn says she has an urn of her husband's ashes on the mantelpiece.

"So that's who she's talking to," I say without thinking.

Mother frowns.

"I imagine so, dear," says Mrs. Dunn. "She doesn't have anyone else."

As we are leaving, we meet a tall woman and a boy about eighteen or nineteen, around Jonathan's age anyway, standing in the open door of the room looking onto the roof. These must be the new people Baggy Bones mentioned.

"How do you do?" Mother says. "We live downstairs. I'm Lillian Dudley-Morris and this is my daughter, Vanessa."

The tall woman is wearing a fur coat with a long filmy dress the colour of violets underneath. She smiles distractedly, shakes our hands, and tells us her name is Alice Pierce. "And this is Brian," she says, gesturing to the boy.

I stare at Brian Pierce. I've never seen anyone so beautiful, like a Renaissance painting in art books from the library. His face is a perfect oval, and his skin is very pale. His eyes are green, his hair a mass of careless blond curls.

"This is Vanessa," Mother says.

Mutely I stick out my hand and shake first one, then the other.

"Hello," Brian says with a smile.

I just nod and duck my head. I can feel the heat from Brian's hand on mine all the way down the stairs.

3. JANEY DREW

SNOW LIES DEEP ON THE GROUND NOW, and every morning our windows are laced with frost like big doilies. We have been in the Music House for weeks. Suddenly everyone has a job. Mother says my job is to be good and do my lessons and rest my eyes. Not very exciting. Daddy has had his job for a while now, something he does at night at the Windsor Arms Hotel, but he doesn't talk about it and neither does Mother. Whatever it is doesn't make him happy the way he is when he's making things out of wood. I think he should just make things and sell them, but no one listens to me and most of what I think I don't say out loud anyway. Mother is going to teach part-time at a private kindergarten. She is filling in for someone who is in the family way. She is happy about her job and has worked at this school before, but she's sad when she has to leave me. Daddy is supposed to be looking after me, but he is tired and sleeps most of the day now. Jonathan is at school. He goes to Jarvis Collegiate and does some babysitting and tutoring, too, and he even has a job for when summer comes. He'll be going up north to some tree-planting place. He won't actually be planting anything, though, which is good because I don't think he has a green thumb. He'll be supervising, which means telling everyone else what to do, I guess. He'll be good at that.

"Wish me luck," Mother says, pausing at the door one more time. She is wearing the tweed skirt with the blue flecks and the sky-blue cardigan over the white blouse she bought at the

May Company on sale. Every night she will wash that blouse in the kitchen sink and iron it early the next morning. I know this because this is what she does every time she has a job. The only difference is this time we have our own kitchen and a tiny dressing room with a wash basin attached to the Everything Room, where we can hang things to dry overnight. Daddy has strung a line on the porch, too, where we can hang wet things during the day. When everything is dry, we just unhook the line and reel it in as if it's a fishing rod, and it stays there all curled up inside its black case until we need it again. We are all pleased with this invention. Mummy says he should get a patent for it, but he just smiles and shrugs. Now every time I look at it, I think, patent pending.

"Good luck, good luck!" I sing to Mother, the chant making it more potent, like a charm. I can tell she doesn't want to go, even though she's happy to get the job and have more money for food and Jonathan's lessons and everything. "Can I go to Janet's house when she gets home from school?"

"'May I,'" Mother corrects, checking her purse to make sure she's remembered everything. "We'll see when I get home."

She buttons up her Persian-lamb coat, gives me a quick hug, and finally leaves, blowing one last kiss before she turns and goes down the staircase.

I stand very still, waiting to see if Baggy Bones will poke her head out. Sure enough, after a moment she peers out, checking the hall. I smile. She makes a *tsk* noise and pulls her scrawny neck back inside like an old turtle. I go down the hall, pretending I need to go to the bathroom near the stairs.

The bathroom is palatial, with a huge tub raised high on gnarled claws on one side, a white sink on a pedestal on the other, and of course, the throne. It is so much better than the tub we had three houses ago—a rusty old tin thing with a wooden rim all around the top, in the dim basement. Mother kept worrying about germs. We didn't stay there long. Here everything sparkles with whiteness. Along the far wall is a chrome stand for towels, but of course, no one leaves anything there anymore. The whole thing is tiled in tiny black-and-white octagonal tiles on the floor and large square ones halfway up the wall. Octagonal means eight sides. The room is a lovely place to sing because it echoes most satisfyingly, but Mother never lets me anymore, not since that time there was a sharp knock on the door when I was on the fourth verse of "Barbara Allen." I flush the toilet, wash my hands, and wipe them on my tunic. I imagine Baggy Bones listening, frowning, nodding her head, her sparse curls quivering like scrawny baby birds. As if she knows anything.

On the way back, I pause and study the enormous tapestry that covers one whole wall, leaving only enough space for Mrs. Smyth's door. In the dim light, the woven picture seems to grow, reaching back into the wall, drawing you in. It is a medieval hunting scene, and if you look closely, more and more animals become visible in the dark forest, lurking in the shadowy trees as the hunters, one blowing a curved horn, pursue their prey. I stop and look at it every time I pass by, and each time I notice something else. The air here is different. Far above my head, the trees sigh in a ripple as the breeze stirs the duke's standard. The dogs bark as they surround the wounded quarry. For the first time, I realize the young man holding the banner looks like Brian from upstairs. I feel that funny little flutter again in my stomach. I turn and run back to our living room, not sure if what I hear behind me is coming from the tapestry. It could be Mrs. O'Malley, the caretaker, toiling up the stairs with her cleaning things. I sit under the dining room table for a while, catch my breath, and recite the kings of England all the way up to William and Mary, where I get stuck.

After a while I come out, look up the rest of the kings in our *History of England* and memorize them, saying them over and over, making it a song, giving it rhythm so that it stays in my head. As I do this, I sway back and forth in time to the musical accompaniment in my head. This is the way they used to memorize those long messages in the olden days, visualizing different rooms for each section, everything filed away to be unloosed with a symbol, a sign, a special motion of their body. I'm building my own memory palace, but so far I have only memorized things lasting about four pages, like "The Shooting of Dan McGrew." But the *Iliad*? "The two Aiantes fell like twin pine trees, and they bit the dust, and their armor clang upon them," I declaim. I only remember bits and pieces, colourful phrases that gleam in my brain like shiny pebbles catching the light.

I sit down at the big desk that Mother says has probably lived in this room for many years and wonder about all the other people who have used it. Mother says this house was built by an old Toronto family in Queen Victoria's reign, just before she (Mother, that is) was born, which was in 1900. The house next door is now Ryan's Art Gallery, but it was built by the Massey family, too. I guess they all loved each other and didn't quarrel and blame each other for things turning out badly, the way Mother's family does. Families are all different, Daddy says.

Seth strikes ten-thirty from his new home on the mantel. The clock is an original Seth Thomas mantel clock, one of the few things rescued from the big house out west where Mother and Daddy used to live before the Crash. They brought it with them as they drove all across the USA in the Model T Ford in the middle of the Great Depression, my brother in the back seat throwing his teddy out the window now and then and making them stop to pick it up. That's one of the family stories I love to hear over and over. "Teddy gone," he would say, and then Mother would pause and smile, and Jonathan would sigh, and I would laugh and laugh, picturing my serious brother as a chubby baby doing naughty things.

I get out the duster and the lemon oil and clean the table and chairs, remembering to do the rungs. Always do the rungs first, Mother says, even if you don't have time for much else. People notice these things. I wonder why. I polish the desk and all the little carved things on the drawers. The whole room smells the way it does when Mother cleans. Outside the door, I hear Mrs. O'Malley. She is cleaning, too, pushing her mop about the hardwood floor that shows on either side of the carpet, running the carpet sweeper, humming tunelessly under her breath. Sometimes she ties a rag around the mop and attacks the cobwebs hanging from the corners of the ceiling. I watch her through a crack in the door. I wonder if Baggy Bones is watching, too. I don't like the idea that we might be doing the same thing, so I stop watching.

I sit down at the piano to practise. I'm supposed to do at least half an hour every day, but it hardly seems worthwhile since I don't have a music teacher anymore. All the music money goes to pay for Jonathan's master classes with Rona Layne, but Mother says maybe next year. I don't really mind.

When Jonathan does scales, they swoop and sing and growl. When I try, they clump and thump and stumble. No matter how hard I practise, it doesn't get much better. Sometimes I hate the thing. All my life it has been with us; a big, solid upright grand following us everywhere, constantly a bone of contention to movers, neighbours, landlords. Sometimes a friend, sometimes like the albatross in "The Rime of the Ancient Mariner." It stubbornly refuses to disclose its secrets to me; the smooth ivory keys it is my job to clean every day resist all my efforts at the powerful chords my brother coaxes from it so easily. I hear the music inside me clearly, but I feel now that I will never be that good, that talented, that special—not like Jonathan. I feel the tears coming as my hands slide into the Mozart minuet, the notes I know so well. The melody sings so loudly in my head, though what I play is only a pale imitation. Just last night I sat and listened as Jonathan's long fingers made this same music pour out into the room, and I knew I would never win anything like he did at the Kiwanis every time he entered, and I ached so hard inside that it was all I could do to keep from crying. I had to lie and tell Mother my legs were hurting again, and she sat and rubbed them until I calmed down and told her it was better.

Daddy is still asleep. I creep in, and he doesn't even stir. I put on the heavy navy-blue sweater-coat Grammy knit me for Christmas and slide out the door and down the hall, being careful to walk on the left-hand side of the runner as I pass Baggy Bones's door. It doesn't squeak on the left side. Sunshine pours in through the frosted windows on the landing. No one is around, so I walk over to the glass door and try to open it, but it is locked. Even pressing my nose to the door, I can't see anything through the milky glass that keeps out everything but the light. Disappointed, I turn back and continue down the stairs, moving slowly through the dust motes, one hand on the wide wooden banister. I'm in a castle; I'm the chatelaine drifting down the main staircase. Maybe today I'll count all the rooms in my domain.

I stop at the bottom, aware of someone else in the hall. Janey Drew, the child prodigy, is sitting on the bench between the griffins. I wonder how much she practises every day. She's wearing white knee socks and patent leather Mary Janes. She has a white blouse with yellow flowers embroidered on the collar and a pleated red skirt with straps over the shoulders. Mother told me she's one year older than I am. Eleven is way too old for straps. Really.

I go over and sit down beside her. I rub the toe of one shoe along the back of my leg, trying to clean it on my sock, make it shine like hers, even though mine are scuffed Oxfords.

"I'm Janey Drew," she says. "What were you doing up there?"

"I'm Lorna," I say. Lorna, the chatelaine of the castle, who can go wherever she likes, do whatever she wants to do.

Janey turns towards me and folds her arms across her chest. "You are not," she says. "You're Jonathan Dudley-Morris's little sister."

I sit up very straight and stare back at her. I feel a faint tingling of fear, as though I'm slipping down an unknown slope.

What is she doing? Why? "That doesn't mean my name isn't Lorna," I say, a little too late.

She flounces away from me on the bench. "You're weird!" she says, tossing a long braid over her shoulder. My braids are too short to toss.

I can't think of anything to say now, so I just sit there, waiting. I wonder where her mother is. She's usually not alone like this. I look at her hands, her slender fingers, clean fingernails. I try to imagine them on the keys of the great black Steinway in Miss Layne's studio. I saw a picture of her on the studio wall when I was there last year with Jonathan and Mother. It shows her making her debut at nine years old with the Toronto Symphony Orchestra, a tiny girl in a pink dress with puffy sleeves and a big sash, bent over the piano, elbows out, one braid hanging free as she attacked the keys.

"I'm going to be in the Kiwanis Festival," I say, pushed by her silence, by her utter disinterest.

Janey laughs. "I used to do that when I was little," she says. "That's for babies. Now I'm preparing for my debut in Carnegie Hall in October."

"So's Jonathan," I say. I think of all the talk that's been going on lately at the dinner table, in front of the fireplace: discussions about what this entails, how much it would cost, whether it would be worth it or whether he should go to university instead. "It's good to have a second string to your bow," Mother says. I don't really know whether he's going to Carnegie Hall or not, but loyalty stirs. "He's going too."

"Really?" She turns and stares at me again with those cool blue eyes, and I stare back, willing myself not to turn away. Then she laughs. "Fibber," she says. She gets up and shakes out the wrinkles on her skirt.

"Hah," I say. I get up too and watch her, my face burning. We are the same height. "Shows what you know." She doesn't respond. "Aren't you too old to be wearing a skirt with straps? That's for babies." I turn around and flounce out the front door and down the steps. Too late I realize it's winter outside. I pause, looking along the path past the wrought-iron fence to the street beyond. I'm not allowed to go there alone. I turn around and head for the back where I left my skipping rope this morning. There is hardly any snow on the concrete under our porch, and I start to skip. My heart is racing and there are tears on my cheeks, but I'm not cold. I'm so upset it takes a few minutes to get a rhythm going with the skipping rope. I begin to chant, "*Janey Drew, Janey Doo, Janey pooh, pooh, pooh*," over and over again.

4. THE PROMENADE

JONATHAN AND I ARE IN THE PROMENADE Music Centre on Bloor Street. We are sitting in a small booth with glass windows all around, listening to records so he can choose the one he likes the best. Records are one of the good things in life that Jonathan says we should have, no matter what. We've been here quite a while.

"Did you hear where the theme came in?" he asks. "It's carried by the violins this time. Listen. Here it comes again."

"I hear it," I say, but I'm not really sure anymore. We've been here for hours, and I'm tired and I keep thinking about the long walk home. I try not to fidget.

Jonathan selects one more record, and as he plays it I'm sure he forgets I'm sitting on this hard chair. I think about the different ways to listen to music. When I listen with Mother, she talks about seeing pictures, imagining things the music brings to mind. Jonathan's way is harder. You have to think a lot and I'm not sure thinking and music go together for me. Maybe you can listen both ways, depending on the mood.

I'm startled by the door opening and Jonathan talking to the salesman. Finally he has made his choice and buys one record. We walk outside and head towards home.

"Put on your mittens," Jonathan says. His breath smokes in the air. It's cold, but the snow is all shovelled away.

"Do you know everyone who takes lessons with Rona Layne?" I ask, thinking of Brian.

"Most of them. We meet at recitals and concerts mostly. And there aren't that many of us."

"She only takes Special People, doesn't she? Like Janey Drew?"

He laughs. "We're not special. We just want one thing very much and have spent far too much time trying to get it."

"But if you want it badly, and you work hard, then how can you say—?"

"It's complicated. Some of them have no life. Take Janey, for instance. What choice has she had? What kind of childhood?" He is walking faster now, and I have to take running steps to keep up with him.

"But she wants to play concerts more than anything," I pant.

"She thinks she does, yes, but what else does she know? What I mean is, there should be some variety in life. Some balance."

I stop and want to burst into tears. I'm out of breath. My chest is tight.

Jonathan stops and goes down on one knee like Mother does when she's worried about me. "What's the matter? Are you all right?" His face is on a level with mine, and his clear grey eyes stare into mine disconcertingly. "I'm sorry the Kiwanis isn't going to work out for you this year. Maybe you can enter next time. I could be your teacher and—"

"No! I don't care about that! I just can't walk that fast!" I push my glasses firmly in place.

He takes my mittened hand and rubs it as if that will cure what ails me. He stands up. "All right. We'll saunter," he says. "Let's window shop."

It's not as good as with Mother, who has stories for everything we pass, but it's better than running and trying to talk and getting worried about what he is saying. Once we turn down Jarvis Street, there are no more windows. We walk under the naked elms, and he talks about history and how neighbourhoods change over time. This one has apparently gone way down in the world. I let the words flow past and enjoy holding his hand and the soft feel of the sidewalk under my shoes. It's different from the sidewalk on Bloor Street or Wellesley or Church, where we go to buy milk and vegetables and sometimes a chicken or small Sunday roast for special occasions.

When we're almost home, he looks down at me and says, "While I'm out tutoring this afternoon, you can play the new record, but only if you're very, very careful."

I'm so surprised I just nod my head. Then as we go up the front steps I ask, "May I play the old records, too?"

"Sure," he says, "but woe betide you if you break any."

Daddy has gone to his doctor's appointment, and Mother is meeting someone about a job helping a family with their difficult child this summer. I'm not sure what this means, and Mother isn't sure either, which is the reason for the meeting, I guess. Everyone talked about it last night at the dinner table, and Daddy didn't like the idea. Jonathan kept insisting she charge more so they realize she's not just a glorified nanny. It seems these people will be away, so they'd like Mother to take charge of everything, including the difficult one. All this would happen after her teaching job is over, of course. I was hoping she would come home afterwards and stay with me all day, but meanwhile Daddy is feeling tired at his job and may have to stop soon and Jonathan's tutoring money isn't that much. All this flows around me but doesn't seem to touch me directly. There's nothing I can do to help except look after myself and not break records or bother people in the Music House.

Before she leaves, Mother says, "Don't use the telephone." Her voice is so stern I wonder if she's found out about my telephone games, when I dial a number and talk to whomever answers. "I am bedridden," I say and make my voice all quavery. "I need to talk to someone!" Sometimes they stay for a while and I make up stories about my terrible lonely life and my life-threatening illness, but she doesn't mention any of that so I guess she doesn't know.

When everyone is out, our space feels different. I talk to my invisible friend Gem, who has been with me for a long time. Sometimes she's a girl and sometimes a boy, but mostly just a friend I can talk to and tell what's going on in my world, although she knows already, I'm sure, being with me all the time and seeing everything over my shoulder. I dress the chairs up in my old blouses and a few colourful scarves Mother gave me to play with and drag them around in an awkward, bumping dance. I put on a record—"The Emperor Waltz", my favourite—and pull my dashing partner around the floor again. The Count is smiling just for me, dressed in a regimental scarlet tunic, a sword at his side. He has green eyes and blond hair, and he looks only at me. I am the centre of his universe. "La, sir, so kind of you to send me flowers. Orchids! My favourites."

"My only wish is to please you," he says, and I tilt my head to one side and smile, and fan myself with the folded lined-paper fan.

When the record stops, I am tired. I throw the bedspread over the dining room table and sit underneath, sulking in my tent like Achilles. Sulking is restful but it isn't much fun, and I wonder how he managed it for so long. I decide to do some exploring. I fill Daddy's old army canteen with water and hang it from one shoulder so the strap crosses my chest. The water always tastes a little musty, but that has become part of the atmosphere that makes my adventures real.

There are many parts of the Music House I haven't seen yet. One of them is beyond the frosted glass door on the landing on the main staircase. I creep down and try the door, but it's still locked. Defeated, I climb the stairs back to my own space, put on my coat, and wander outside onto the porch. To my right is the wooden staircase leading down to the frozen garden. To my left is my horse, Bucephalus. He's a very uncomfortable sort of horse because the railing that forms his back is only about four inches wide. The post that goes to the roof forms his long proud neck, and Daddy has put a small nail here to attach his reins. His rolling eye looks back at me as I climb into the saddle, an old rag rug that has lost its colours. Sitting here holding the reins and looking out over the porch railings across to the garden behind the coach house, I can see forever. On one side is our icebox; on the other is the back door. Today I begin to worry that Baggy Bones might make one of her frequent trips to the garbage can in the corner by the stairs, and I find I can't let my mind loose or force any adventures to happen in my head. I get down and put away the rope that makes my stirrups and the bit of leather from an old belt that Daddy made into his bridle. The saddle goes on top of the icebox.

Daddy has made the window boxes so Mother can have her own garden this summer. Later on, there will be flowers all along the railing and maybe some runner beans. Then we can sit here feeling hidden from the world. It will be my job to watch over the seedlings and be careful not to water them too much, but so far there is nothing in the boxes but the crusty remains of the last snowfall.

At this end of the porch is the iron ladder going up to the roof on the third floor. One side is loose. At first this scared me, but today I am an intrepid explorer. I take a small drink from my canteen and begin to climb. The ladder shivers, and I stop to catch my breath. Looking down, I realize for the first time that the Music House is shaped like one huge gigantic backwards L, with the Secret Garden enclosed on two sides by the house and the other two sides shielded by fence and bushes. The tenants' plain boring garden begins at the top of the L and stops at the fence where the coach house is. Behind this wooden barrier lies another hidden garden, but this one looks overgrown and wild, not that I can see much from my perch.

Straight down below lies Miss Layne's tiny formal space, its red brick paths chipped and uneven, the fountain in the middle silent and streaked with lichen and the frozen black water that makes the small drift of snow look dirty. This garden is outside her studio (the jutting-out bottom of the L) and is off limits to everyone, guarded by high thick bushes and a locked wrought-iron gate. This is the first time I've got a good look at it, since it's hard to see from our porch or the rest of the garden because of all the bushes. The backyard we all can use is barren of anything but grass, which is now sleeping under the snow. Rona Layne's is a real Secret Garden, like the one in the book Mother read to me last year before we started that awful *Pilgrim's Progress*. It's obvious even to me that no Dickon has been working in this one for a very long time.

The ladder shivers again, and I close my eyes for a moment, but only one side is loose so I keep on going. Now I can see the flat roof outside the window of the new people. It's like a more dangerous sort of porch, dangerous because there are no railings and the floor part is just pebbles on tar under a thin layer of snow. Brian is huddled in a camel-hair polo coat with a hood, his back against the brick wall by the bay window of their room. He's holding a cigarette in one gloved hand, staring down at the Secret Garden, and he looks so sad. I freeze, afraid that any breath, any movement will give me away. Perhaps he'll think I'm spying. Sometimes I do, I admit, but not this time. It's upsetting when people think you're doing something you're not. It makes me feel nasty.

A breeze springs up, and his curly hair stirs as the hood slips back. He turns and looks right at me. I stare, unable to move, to speak. Count Brian. My chest tightens, and it's hard to breathe.

He winks.

A bubble of laughter rises inside, and panic flutters in my stomach. I imagine laughing so hard my hands slip off the cold iron ladder and I fall, twisting in the air, crashing through the bare bushes into the Secret Garden.

Nothing happens.

He lays a finger against his lips and points towards the window. I nod. Mother would be cross if Jonathan smoked, even if he did it outside. Hooking my left arm around the ladder, I lift my right hand and wave. His smile follows me back down to my own porch. I sit there for a while, trying to catch my breath. The memory of that smile keeps me warm.

5. NOBLESSE OBLIGE

SNOW FLOATS LAZILY PAST OUR WINDOWS, sparkles in miniature drifts on the windowsills, clings to the branches of the great tree outside our living room window. I have been in the house for days. All the library books are read, but we can't go out for new ones. It's a long walk to the library through treacherous slippery streets, and no one has time to take me anyway.

Jonathan is doing homework, so I'm supposed to be extra quiet. I am looking through old scrapbooks at pictures of Hadleigh Hall that Mother cut out of a magazine. I wonder if it ever snows like this in England. It must be cold in a stately pile with no central heating, trying to keep warm huddled over all those fireplaces, wrapped in steamer rugs and wool shawls from Jaegers like the one Mother has in her special drawer.

I wonder what it would be like if Mother's grandfather had not "done the right thing" and married the village schoolteacher, ending up in the colonies as a remittance man with nine children. If he had been less honourable, it would have been better for Mother, surely. She would have grown up in the stately pile and wouldn't have to worry about money, ever.

I say this to Jonathan, but he laughs. "You want to add the bar sinister to Mother's troubles?"

"But maybe she wouldn't have been born at all?" I suggest.

"Then where would *we* be?" Jonathan asks.

Where would we be? I don't want to think about that. I look out the window and wonder if there are any stately homes in my real family, if my real father or grandfather had lived in one, been disgraced, and moved to Canada as a last resort. Or maybe he was a modern sort of *coureur des bois,* never staying long in one place, always seeking adventure. I think of the famous Canadian poem: *De place I get born, me, is up on de reever, Near foot of de rapide dat's call Cheval Blanc.* Was my grandfather like the poem's Little Bateese? No. I shake my head and make a face. I take off my glasses and clean them using the shirttail of my blouse. I'm sure he was not like Little Bateese or his ilk.

Mother is always trying to lend a hand to the less fortunate. *Noblesse oblige,* she says; blood will tell. This worries me occasionally, but most times I just agree. Daddy calls the people Mother helps Lame Ducks. People tell her the most intimate details of their lives. She lends an ear, a helping hand, and sometimes a little money. When Daddy hears about this last part, he sighs and closes his eyes.

We hear about some of the Lame Ducks when Mother tells us their stories at dinner time: people she meets waiting for the bus, or someone who fell on the street and she helped them up and took them into Murray's to get them something to eat. She's a great storyteller. She hires the educated ones to be my tutors for a while, like Mr. Jackson, but I'm not sure if he is a *bona fide* Lame Duck. He is certainly lame, not that we ever mention that or even notice his two canes and twisted legs. I pretend he walks just like everyone else. He never talks to me about his terrible experience in the Japanese POW camp. I wonder if he ever talks to other servicemen. "He's a proud man," Mother says. "He has dignity." Like Daddy, I think. Daddy would never be a Lame Duck.

Miss David, on the other hand, is a real Lame Duck. Mother met her at the Scott Mission where she was rooting through clothes at their thrift shop. "She's a diamond in the rough,"

Mother says. "Not much education, poor soul—she never had a chance—but a hard worker with a heart of gold."

Miss David lives in a one-room basement apartment she shares with five cats. Mother shakes her head when she talks about the time she visited the apartment. She had dropped by to bring Miss David some important papers she had picked up for her at some government office because Miss David, who holds down two jobs, couldn't get there before closing time.

"Total chaos," she says. "Everything's higgledy-piggledy."

"I imagine all the cats mess things up a lot," I suggest.

"They certainly don't help," Mother agrees, shaking her head. "But the place is pretty clean, all things considered."

Miss David comes over one day to get help filling out some other papers. She's applying for citizenship. She brings a big box of chocolates as a gift.

"My brother, Stefan, he work in candy factory," she says, smiling her gap-toothed smile.

I hope she comes again. I never get candy! Sometimes as a special treat, Daddy makes fudge, but that hasn't happened in a while, and anyway, it's not like real chocolates.

Mother and Miss David settle down at the dining room table to work on the papers while I keep on arranging the books we took out of the bookcase this morning, dusting them with a damp cloth and putting them back again in the proper order. Miss David is odd-looking. The first thing you notice is her impossibly red hair, the colour of a Raggedy Ann doll. The profusion of tiny sausage curls all over her head reminds me of pictures of Shirley Temple in my scrapbook, but Miss David's face is wrinkled and old. Only her eyes are young: bright and twinkling. She is short and wears odd clothes that don't quite go together. Today, it's a green jacket, a mauve blouse, and a black skirt that's too short. Under the skirt, her legs look like inverted drumsticks, and as she sits at the table, her feet, in her funny little lace-up boots, barely touch the floor. She is always smiling.

Miss David has been in Canada for ten years, but it's hard to understand her until you get used to her accent. David isn't her real name, which is difficult to say. Her brother has a different last name, which is also difficult. Maybe they are half brother and sister. Maybe her father died a horrible death fleeing the Germans on the Russian Front and then her mother married someone else in desperation. When I told Janet about her, she suggested Miss David's brother might be wanted by the police for war crimes and so had to change his name. But that's too scary. I don't want to think about that.

"We save to buy house," Miss David says as they put away all the papers. "Stefan and I, we save every cent for this, our dream."

I see the wistful look on Mother's face and wonder if she thinks she could do that, too, if it weren't for piano lessons, trying to save for Carnegie Hall, paying tutors for me, and "key money" to find a place to live that will have me and the piano. I look down and notice Miss David has short stubby fingers. Peasant hands, Mother would say, but not to her face, of course. I'm glad that my fingers are slender, my feet small, my instep high, like a lady. It makes me feel like a real part of the family. I wonder if being a peasant will help Miss David to actually get her house someday. Being a lady does not seem to be doing Mother much good.

Finally, it has stopped snowing. Jonathan is practising now, and Mother and I are going to the shops to get eggs and margarine, Kraft dinner and bread, and maybe peanut butter. I am pulling on my long over-socks that Grammy knits for me, several pairs every winter. They are all strange colours. This pair is a deep heathery purple. I love the colour but wish it could have been a pullover instead. I hate that I never see anyone else wearing over-stockings. Mother says this makes them special, but I don't want to be special all the time. Not like that. I want to be special because I'm brilliant. Or talented. Or because I can climb higher than anyone else. I yank the stockings over my Oxfords and up my legs, fastening them with the garters that hang down under my navy bloomers. I pull my rubbers over the stockings, the Oxfords, everything. I pull on my navy coat and round hat.

Mother holds out her hand, and we leave. With her other hand, she is fastening her Persian-lamb coat at her throat with the large ornate black button. On the stairs we pass Mrs. O'Malley, but Mother doesn't stop, just waves hello and sweeps down the staircase, past the griffins, and out the heavy front door.

Outside I can see my breath. As we walk along, I pretend to be a dragon, breathing fire and smoke with great snorting noises and thinking of dire curses until Mother gets annoyed, almost as if she can hear what I'm thinking. But she can't. Not really. I let out a big puff of air in relief. She's worried about the job taking care of the difficult child.

It was all we talked about last night at dinner. "The poor thing spends her life in bed, her muscles not coordinated enough to move around, and she's barely a child at all. She's eighteen if she's a day, but she has the mind of a four-year-old."

"Hardly what you're trained for," Jonathan says.

"She must be very heavy to handle," Daddy points out. "You aren't strong enough."

"They need a male nurse," Jonathan suggests.

"They tried that," Mother says. "There was an ... unfortunate incident. Now she's afraid of men she doesn't know."

Daddy shakes his head sadly. "Shameful," he mutters. "Just shameful."

"But ladies can do shameful things too," I suggest.

They all turn and stare at me. "I hope you never know what she has been through," Mother says sternly.

They go back to discussing the pros and cons of accepting the job and ignore me. I help myself to a usually forbidden second helping of scalloped potatoes. Nobody notices. In the end, Daddy puts his foot down. There will be no job with the difficult child, in spite of the money it would bring in.

I can tell Mother is still unsure this is the right decision. She is to call them with her answer this evening, so there is still a chance she will change her mind and convince Daddy it will be all right once it's a *fait accompli*. Mother is a great believer in the *fait accompli*.

The greengrocer's is busy. Mother has brought the wicker basket that Aunt Dottie sent last Christmas filled with goodies, and we make our way to the dairy section near the back, looking for half a dozen eggs and a bottle of milk. We are almost there when Mother sees Mrs. Pierce inspecting a head of lettuce. We all shake hands.

"How are you settling in?" Mother asks, pulling her glove back on.

"It's a little cramped, but the convenience makes it worthwhile," Mrs. Pierce replies. She takes one more look at the lettuce and drops it into her wire basket. "The only thing is, it's a bit far to the Conservatory for Brian's practise sessions. Not that he ever complains," she adds quickly. She gives us a sharp look as if we might be about to accuse Brian of being a whiner.

"If he needs a piano to practise on, he's welcome to use ours," Mother says, always quick to help. "It's an upright grand, not quite a Steinway, but a Heintzman, which is close enough. It has a wonderful tone and is in perfect tune."

"That's very kind of you." Mrs. Pierce seems to be completely present now, really focusing on Mother for the first time. "Thank you for the offer, but it isn't necessary. I don't mind spending money on Brian's music. That's why we're here."

"Of course, and that's why we're here, too. But it's an expensive business, launching a career, isn't it?" Mother goes on. "Our piano is just a suggestion."

"Thank you. Most kind. I'll keep it in mind."

They nod at each other, smiling. The feathers on Mrs. Pierce's hat quiver and sparkle with droplets from the melting snow.

The beady little eyes of the silver-fox fur around her neck sneer at me.

Then Mrs. Pierce looks off into the distance for a moment, as if thinking. One hand goes to her throat, fingering the cameo brooch she wears on her scarf. She looks down at me as if suddenly remembering my existence. "And do you play, too, dear?"

I cringe.

"Vanessa is quite good," Mother answers for me, taking my hand in hers. "Miss Layne offered to take her on as well, you know."

"Really?" Mrs. Pierce smiles and lifts an eyebrow.

"At the moment, though, we're concentrating on Jonathan. We expect Miss Layne to pick him for the June recital. And Brian, too, no doubt," she adds quickly.

"Oh, I expect so," Mrs. Pierce says. She is paying for her groceries, tucking them away in her string bag. "You must come to tea sometime."

"Thank you," Mother says at once. "We'd love to." But I wonder about "sometime." Why doesn't she say when? To me it sounds like another version of "We'll see."

I watch Mrs. Pierce turn off her smile before she turns away, hurrying out the door into the snow.

I usually enjoy our forays along Church Street, but today I am too full of thoughts of Brian in our living room. *When will he come? What will he play?* I see him on the roof, huddled into his camel-hair coat, smoking. I see his finger to his lips, his secret smile. Just for me.

That night at dinner, Brian is discussed at length. Mother points out we will have to have a major cleaning effort if Brian takes us up on her offer. "I don't want him telling his mother what a terrible housekeeper I am," she says.

"But you're not," I object. "And anyway, she didn't say he would come."

"Obviously if he does, it will have to be when I'm at school,"

Jonathan points out. I'm glad to see he's taking it seriously. "Make sure it's at a definite time, with a definite time limit. If I do get picked for the recital, I'll need to practise a lot myself."

"And Vanessa must stay in the other room while he's here," Mother says.

My heart drops with an unpleasant thud. "Why?"

Mother's mouth goes into that hard line that means a battle is coming up. Her grey eyes blaze as she looks around the table. "You cannot be alone with him. Understand?" Mother leans towards me, the heat of her gaze crackling. "Is that clear?"

I nod miserably, but it's not clear at all.

"I don't think you have much to worry about with Brian Pierce, dear," Daddy says unexpectedly. He takes Mother's hand and pats it, and the fire dies out of her eyes.

As it turns out, Brian slips a note under the door during the evening, thanking Mother but saying he prefers to practise in the Conservatory for now, so all the fireworks were useless. I'm disappointed, but I suppose it doesn't really matter. If I can't be in the room, watching, listening, just being there, what's the point? I wait for the invitation to tea. It doesn't come. That's just rude.

We're not the only ones talking about Brian and his mother. Later that week, I am standing in the shadows by the third-floor landing when I overhear Baggy Bones talking to her friend Marie. It's easy to hear her because she always leaves her door open a few inches. "Ventilation," she told Mother one day, popping out unexpectedly when we were on our way back to our rooms from the bathroom. "It's best to keep the air moving, you know."

"You're quite right," Mother said briskly, and we didn't laugh until we were inside, behind the closed door of our living room.

Now Baggy Bones is telling Marie about the noise from the room above, where Mrs. Pierce and Brian live: bursts of wild laughter, shrieks in the middle of the night, and pushing heavy furniture around. "And as if that's not bad enough, there's the constant tinkle of that spinner or whatever it is. It sounds like a giant music box."

"That must be annoying," Marie says, her voice soothing, her knitting needles clacking steadily. Although I've never seen her, I have a picture of her in my head. I imagine that she's always wearing a hat and galoshes with furry tassels like Mother's.

"And talk, talk, talk, all the time, nattering away," Baggy Bones goes on, in her shaky voice. "And it never occurs to her to wear slippers in the house. Click, click, click. It's enough to make my head ache."

"Shall I get you some tea, dear?" Marie asks, and the knitting needles pause.

"Never mind. You stay put. I'll get it."

I can hear her sigh as she gets to her feet; then I hear her moving around, the rattle of the kettle on the hot plate, the sound of tea cups on saucers.

"Between that pair upstairs and those people at the end of the hall running up and down to the bathroom at all hours of the day and night, it's a wonder I get any rest. My nerves can't take it, I tell you."

"Is it that bad, dear? I didn't notice."

"You would if you lived right beside them, let me tell you. Now, Marie, you know I don't have anything against children, but that girl is downright—"

What I am is lost as the kettle whistles shrilly. I push my glasses up on my nose and creep back home.

6. JANET GETS VIBRATO

"JANET'S FATHER IS A KNIGHT," I tell Mother as she braids my hair, pulling it back till I wince. "He's Sir Kelly and her mother is Lady Margaret. Isn't that exciting?"

Jonathan snorts in derision, a sound I know well. "He's just a Catholic knight, Piglet."

"So was Sir Lancelot," I say, my voice rising.

"*He* was a Knight of the Round Table," Jonathan sputters, "not a Knight of Columbus."

"He was *so* a Catholic," I shout.

"Hush, dear," Mother soothes. "Before the Reformation, everyone was Catholic, including the knights."

I glare exultantly at Jonathan, but he is still grinning annoyingly as he packs his books into his satchel. He's going to tutor some boys who are having trouble with Latin and English. He says they are so bad I could probably tutor them. I'm not sure this is meant as a compliment, but I pretend it is.

It's Saturday, and Daddy is sleeping. He's going to work tonight because someone else is sick and can't come in. Mother tried to talk him out of it because he isn't very well either, but he was adamant.

Adamant. I like that word.

Mother and I are going over to the Sullivans' to hear Janet play the violin. She called on the telephone to invite us yesterday. She was very excited. She says she now has vibrato. If she had managed that sooner, she might have done better at the Kiwanis, Jonathan says. I don't really understand this. I just want to go to a party.

The Sullivans have a big family. Janet is the youngest, though she's a year older than I am, just the same age as Janey Drew, in fact. But Janey's an only child. Janet has two sisters and three brothers. Two other children died years ago. Janet never really knew them, but she's always sad when she mentions it, as if they were best friends. She says they're with the angels. Not sure I'd like that. All those feathers. Today, only the sisters will be there and maybe some neighbours. Janet is very nervous. She told me so this morning when I called her on our telephone to make sure of the time.

"You shouldn't goad your sister like that," Mother says to Jonathan as she ties the yellow ribbons into bows on the end of my short braids. I wish I had long ones, like Janey Drew, so I could toss them over my shoulder, but every time they get almost that length, Mother pulls out the scissors and chops them off. After that, they look like paint brushes, the kind you paint houses with, not landscapes.

I'm wearing my good dress, the yellow one with the brown and red smocking that Grammy did for me three years ago. Mother has let it out a few times, but it's still a bit tight. If I don't make any sudden moves, I can wear it a little longer. My winter coat is getting tight too, but Mother says it's almost spring so it can last a few more weeks. It's so short now that my dress shows underneath a couple of inches. I'll be glad when spring comes.

We walk to the corner to cross with the lights. When I'm not with them, Mother and Jonathan cross right in front of the house. So does Janet. I know. I've seen them from the window. I don't say anything because I know the reason I can't. It's always the same. My glasses might fall, leaving me helpless in the middle of traffic, or some other version of disaster.

Mother is reviewing the rules of etiquette as we turn the

corner into Janet's street. I smile and nod and wonder if Sir Kelly will be there. I secretly admit that the name doesn't have the grandeur a knight should have, like Lancelot or Gawain or even Percival, but I suppose modern-day knights have to have modern-day names. And he isn't really grand anyway. He's a brown sort of man: his eyes, his hair, his suit, his shoes. He's short; even Jonathan is taller. And he has small darting eyes and a busy anxious look that is disconcerting. I feel my palms getting moist, and I swallow.

Janet's house is tall and dark and narrow, with a big arched window overlooking the ragged front lawn. On one side is the laneway that leads to the back door, which all the children use unless it's a special day. On the other side, it's attached to someone else's house. I don't know who they are. No one ever mentions them. Maybe they're peculiar.

Janet opens the door. "Come in, come in," she cries, making wide beckoning motions with her whole arm.

"Thank you, dear." Mother shepherds me in before her, as if I might not be able to get through the door without her help. She hands over our hostess gift of English marmalade, and Janet's mother coos and clucks as if she's never seen any before. In fact, she may not have for some time. Neither have we, as it's hard to get since the war. I wish we could keep it for ourselves, but of course, I never say this. Mother used our luxury money from her small lacquered box. Now there's not enough left to buy the new dessert spoon we've been saving for.

Janet's face, usually long and pale, is pink and animated. My grandmother would say she has roses in her cheeks. It's not something I can say. I just grin at her and whisper good luck.

"We have marble cake," she whispers back.

I try not to lick my lips.

Their living room is filled with people I don't know. The names slide by me as Mrs. Sullivan introduces us. I recognize the names of the two old sisters, dressmakers who live at the end of the street; Mrs. Moore, the mother of the annoying little boy named Mingy who lives across the street; and Janet's grown-up cousin Patrick, who's staying with them. Mother folds me against her as we share a high-backed padded chair from the dining room.

Janet's big sister Kathleen sits on the piano bench, ready to accompany her. She's in high school, like Jonathan, but she goes to the Catholic one. She doesn't look a bit like Janet or Magda, the sister who's one year older, or their mother. She is dark-haired and rosy-cheeked, and always seems about to burst out of the plain white blouses she wears with her homemade skirts, except when she's in her black school uniform with the starched collar and cuffs. Today, in honour of the occasion, she's wearing a bunch of violets pinned to her collar, and a purple ribbon ties back her long shining hair. I wonder when the marble cake will appear.

Janet finally joins Kathleen at the piano, picks up her violin, and announces what she is going to play: part one of some concerto by Mozart. The numbers used to name pieces of music never stick in my head, sliding out just like water slipping through my fingers. I'm nervous for her now, hoping she gets through it without mistakes. I tense against Mother, and she pats my hand. I think she is nervous, too.

I have never seen Janet play before. As I watch, I envy the smallness of the instrument, the intimate way she tucks it under her chin and draws the bow across the strings, swaying her thin body back and forth, her long pale curls swinging in silent accompaniment. She's much more interesting to watch than someone playing the piano. The violin is less intimidating, too, its size easily handled with one quick look, not like the long sliding look you need to take in all ten feet of a gleaming concert grand.

But as I listen, I decide a violin is a treacherous instrument. Its looks are deceptively friendly, but it is clear there are many pitfalls involved in mastering it. The bow squeaks and the notes waver and slip off pitch from time to time. I try not to wince.

I drop my eyes and wonder if my playing sounds this painful to others. I feel like a traitor even thinking this, and I remind myself of what Mother said. It's about progress, not perfection.

"I've got vibrato!" Janet had sung over the telephone. "I finally got vibrato!"

I look up again, hearing the improvement as she gains confidence. I glance at the music on the piano. Janet is speeding up as she nears the finish line, dragging Kathleen with her. I smile. I do the same thing. And then I hear the vibrato. My smile widens.

Everyone claps, and Magda brings in the marble cake and some homemade pinwheel cookies.

"That was really good," I tell Janet, and she blushes and takes a slice of cake. I take one, too, and eat it in tiny bites, making it last as long as I can. Then I help Janet carry the teacups to the kitchen, and we sit on clean brown paper bags on the back stairs and whisper to each other.

"I got the strap Monday for talking in class," Janet tells me, her voice so low I have to lean close to hear. She holds out her hands, palm up, telling me how it stung, the noise it made coming down on her skin.

I stare at her hands, searching in vain for evidence of her pain. I shiver, but there's a strange thrill of pleasure in it somehow that makes me uneasy.

"Did you tell your mother?"

She shakes her head, the curls at the ends of her long blonde hair swinging. "I told Magda. She said not to mention it 'cuz Mother might get all upset and flustered before the party."

"Oh." We sit in silence for a moment. I am trying to think of something bad happening to me and not telling Mother. Finally I say, "I talked to Janey Drew." It's my only news that's not the really big news about Brian, which I don't want to talk about yet, but it seems flat after her startling announcement.

"Really? What's she like?"

"She's rude," I say, flushing as I remember her words. "And stuck up, too."

"Well, that's not very nice," Janet says. She takes my hand and squeezes it.

I suddenly feel very happy, and at the same time I want to cry. I blink back the tears and begin to chant very softy, "Janey Drew, Janey Doo, Janey pooh, pooh, pooh."

Janet lets go of my hand and claps hers over her mouth, her grey eyes filled with shocked laughter. "How about *Zaney Du, Zaney, who? Zaney poo, poo poo.* Or, *Xanadu, Xanapoo, Xanaduu do, dee, doo!*"

We're giggling now, but I nod my head vigorously. Her way is secret, more exciting. No one gets into trouble spouting nonsense rhymes.

Suddenly she leans closer, the laughter gone. "Did you see that boy again? That Brian?"

I stop laughing too and look back at her. For a moment, I wish I hadn't told her about the boy upstairs. Now he's not mine anymore. I nod my head. I feel a little hurt as I feel her interest shifting from me to someone else. I'm glad I didn't tell her about the Brian in the tapestry. He's still all mine. "I saw him on the roof," I whisper.

"Tell me, tell me."

"He was wearing a camel-hair coat and his hair was blowing all over the place in the wind. And he was smoking."

"Lots of people smoke," she says.

I hear Mother's voice coming closer, talking to Mrs. Sullivan, collecting our coats, saying goodbye. I'm relieved.

"I'll tell you the rest later," I whisper. I get up and hand Janet the folded bag I had been sitting on. "Thank you for a lovely time," I say in my normal voice.

"Thank you for coming." Janet stands up and slips both paper bags back into their drawer in the kitchen before following us all down the hall to the front door.

There is a moment of confusion as we put on our coats and

crowd through the inside glass door into the small vestibule. I shake hands with Mrs. Sullivan, and Mother and I go outside and down the stone steps. Mingy Moore is outside with his sled, but I pretend not to see him. I'm thinking about watching the light change in Janet's grey eyes as she asked about Brian.

7. HORATIUS AT THE BRIDGE

WALKS WITH DADDY ARE FREE TIME. Free of words. Free of "need to": *need to know, need to be an example, need to behave like a Dudley-Morris*. It's a gentle time, a safe time, a silent communication of affection. Now and then Daddy stops and smiles and points out a type of tree, describes the kind of wood that comes from it, the kind of thing you can make from it. He shows me birds and flowers but doesn't expect me to memorize it all; he just wants me to enjoy it the way he does. Most of the time I can't really see the birds he points out, but I never admit this; I nod and say "Yes, yes," wondering where it is, what it really looks like. I used to say "Where? Where?", but he would never stop trying to get me to see it and I never could, so I gave up doing that.

Lately, he's been talking about Newfoundland joining the Dominion of Canada, making this big snowy island our tenth province. He says some harsh things about Joey Smallwood and shakes his head, and then he's silent for a while. I think about adding the new province to my map of Canada, using a colour other than pink. I wonder what the Newfoundlanders think about not being their own boss anymore. Of course, they always had the King, so I guess not much has changed. I like King George. Daddy said he was very brave during the last war. I have pictures of him and all the royal family in my scrapbook. I have the Dionne quintuplets there, too, and pictures of the royal corgis. The Queen is the same age as Mother.

Today, Daddy stops and looks at the remains of an old bookcase that someone has left in the alley behind Ryan's Art Gallery, which is a shortcut we sometimes take to Wellesley Street. It's missing the top shelf, and one side is badly stained.

"It's walnut," he says wonderingly. He reaches out and runs his hand over the good part of the wood. It's as if he can talk to it, feel what it was once, what it could become again. "I could fix that," he murmurs. "What a shame."

"Maybe you could rescue it," I say. "Come back when it's dark and bring it home. It's not far."

"We'll see." With a final pat, he turns away, and we continue our walk to Allan Gardens.

When we get home, Daddy is tired. After lunch, he lies down on the bed and covers himself with the quilt Grandmother made from old dresses many years ago. Mother tells stories about the dresses sometimes. The one with the tiny blue flowers that Grammy wore to the picnic with the church ladies the time Granddad put whiskey in the lemonade. He was always trying to "liven up the stick people," as he called them. The one with pale red stripes that Aunt Dottie wore to the job interview; she had been careful to back out the door so no one would see the burn mark made by the iron when Mother tried to do her a favour and press it just before she left. There was even one of Mother's dresses there, a crinkly material with navy blue polka dots. Looking at the quilt is like opening a book of family history, each piece a story. But it's a book only Mother can read.

Daddy is asleep almost at once, his mouth slightly open, his breath sighing when he breathes out. I spend some time tidying up the table and the wardrobe trunk, both the top and the drawers. I find Mother's box of jewellery. There isn't much. All the really good stuff is gone, along with the big house and antique furniture, the paintings and silverware. "Gone like smoke," Mother says, her voice thin and distant as she remembers what used to be. Something I never even saw. I slip on her silver link bracelet. Jonathan bought this one for her birthday a few years ago, saved up his money for a long time from his first real job. It's big for me, heavy on my wrist, but it feels good. I push it up over the cuff of the navy pullover Grammy knit for me last year. Daddy catches his breath and sighs, turning on his side in his sleep. I creep out the door and go out on the porch.

Clouds scud across the sky, but I'm warm in my sweater. Looking over the back fence, I see the untended yard behind what used to be the coach house—the grass long, like emerald hair. I wonder what treasures lie buried under those green waves. I look at the high wooden fence. In the corner of our yard, partially hidden by a large lilac, is the one place where I have been able to climb to the top of the fence. So far, I haven't tried to get over it; instead I clambered up on the garage roof, which is beside the coach house. That roof is lower. Janet showed me how to get up. When we play there, we call it Mount Olympus. But today, Janet is at school, everyone is working, and I am all alone.

I run down the stairs, across the quickly melting snowy lumps of our yard, and into the corner. I push behind the lilac bush and find our log undisturbed. Janet and I have wedged it against the fence to give us a step up. It's harder to climb the fence on my own, but I finally pull myself upright and stand on the narrow wooden beam that runs along the top, holding on to the bush for balance. I look down and it seems a long way to the ground. I look up quickly. When Janet's here, we usually put one foot on the corner post and take a big step over the yawning chasm below onto the garage roof. But today, for the first time, I look to my left and realize the coach house building is very close. I can almost see into one of the windows on the ground floor. The glass is dirty, the putty falling out from between the panes. Faded yellow paint peels off the wooden frames. If I lean closer, I can touch the beam of wood that runs across from the fence to the building as support. I guess there used to be a gate below it, but that's gone now, and a sheet of metal blocks the way in from the ground.

I take a deep breath and start to edge across the beam. With every step, I can see more of the window below me. But what catches my interest now is the wide ledge above it. From there it would be easy to climb onto the roof. What an adventure that would be to tell Janet! What a great view I would have! I could see what lies behind the coach house and the garage and everything that has been hidden up to now. My secret kingdom would be huge! I imagine lying in bed, running through all the new pictures in my head. "The curtain may fall any time," the doctor said. And Mother says, "Fill your head with wonderful images." So we go to art galleries and museums. "Remember everything," she says. I will remember this.

I am across the chasm now, both hands resting on the soft yellow bricks around the window frame. If I bend down, I can see inside, but it's so dark and dusty in there I can't make out anything clearly—just long tables and piles of junk on the floor. Someone said this place used to be an artist's studio—after the horses and coaches left, of course. Maybe there are stacks of canvases against the wall, undiscovered masterpieces, but I can't make out anything clearly.

Climbing up on top of the window isn't easy. I scrape my right knee badly, and for a minute I feel dizzy, thinking of my blood smeared on the rough wall. But at last I make it. I am standing with both feet on the wide lintel, flattened against the bricks, higher than I have been before, but still not on the roof, which I can now see: a lumpy expanse of tar and pebbles just above my head. I look down. It is a big mistake. My knees begin to wobble, my legs shake. My fingers dig into the rough uneven brick as panic sweeps over me. No one is around. No one will hear me if I fall. No one will come. Below me, the broken concrete of the walkway will crack my skull, tear my flesh. I think of Horatius at the bridge in the brave days of yore, of the Spartan youth letting the fox gnaw at his entrails, of Daddy and his men going over the top at Ypres into the deadly cloud of gas. This is nothing.

Gradually I force myself to loosen the grip of my right hand and reach for the rain spout. This high up, it curves into the building from the eaves above, and I am counting on it to get me the rest of the way. If I move my left foot to the brick that sticks out a few feet up, I can use the crook in the spout as support. *Don't think. Do it!* "Hold that bridge," I mutter.

With my left foot up, my right foot swings into place. I heave my weight onto the right foot and push. There is a creak—a tearing, rending sound—and the pipe begins to tremble under me. I clutch the edge of the roof and scream, pulling myself desperately forward onto the pebbled tar. The drain pipe crashes to the broken concrete below. I pull one knee onto the roof and slowly haul myself up the rest of the way.

Relief floods through me, so sharp and sudden I start to cry. *Thank you, God!*

After a few moments, I calm down and look around. I am higher than Mount Olympus. I can see part of the garden behind the stables, neglected and overgrown—not a garden at all but more like a place to dump old unwanted things. Broken dishes litter the ground under the window as if someone has thrown them there, one by one, in a rage. Rusted bedsprings lean at an angle across one corner, and vines are beginning to climb through the trellis of fractured metal, disguising the ugliness. By midsummer, the view from here might be quite different. I wonder if anyone will even be able to see these broken, useless things.

When I stand up, the branches of an old elm tree almost touch my head. From this angle, the lilac bush in the corner of my garden blocks the view of the Music House, but if I move over, closer to the emerald green of the stables' yard, I can see it all. But there are few windows facing this way, only our own from the Everything Room and the small leaded panes from up high over the built-in cupboards in our living room. There is a dormer window on the third floor, which I guess must be Mrs. Dunn's, but the other windows are hidden by the wild growth of the bushes protecting Rona Layne's secret garden. No one can see me. I smile in satisfaction.

The clouds are so close now that they are tangled in the trees. I bend my head back and stare up through the shifting pattern of greenery into the pewter sky. I shiver. For the first time, I realize it is getting colder. And there is rain in the air. My right leg twinges, as if the realization has reminded it to start hurting. It's time to go home.

I take one last look around my secret kingdom and walk over to the edge of the roof where the gutters are broken. I will have to find a new way down since the drain pipe is no longer there. I make a circuit of the roof, looking for another drain pipe, crawling under the low hanging branches of the elm, but there isn't one. The eaves are rotted away in several places, but how will that do me any good?

I crouch on the edge, looking down on the surface of Mount Olympus. It's not that far down, but there's a walkway between the stables and the nearest garage. I try to calculate how far away it is, if I could make it by taking a running leap. But what if I miscalculate? Or slip on the takeoff?

The first drizzle of rain streaks my glasses. Panic flutters. I can't risk the Great Leap now. Everything is blurred. My secret kingdom suddenly changes into a prison. I am a cursèd maiden doomed to spend the rest of my days on an invisible island. My right leg is beginning to hurt; I can feel the slow twist of pain that often comes in the dampness and cold. But I won't give up.

I button up my sweater and lie on my stomach on the roof, reaching down over the edge with my right hand, feeling around for something to grab onto: a foothold, a stout vine, anything! Nothing. Tears spill out, making it even harder to see. I wonder if Horatius was cold and wet when he was holding the bridge.

My knee is bleeding now, and as I sit up, I realize with horror that Mother's bracelet is no longer on my arm.

"No!"

Panic claws at my stomach, and for a moment I think I may throw up. I look around me on the roof. Take off my glasses and dry them on my shirt. But they are wet again almost at once. I crawl around the whole roof, looking for the bracelet, running my hands over every inch of the rough pebbly surface. I pray to Saint Anthony. Janet told me about him, how he helps people who have lost things, even if you're not Catholic. I often pray to him now, but never so fervently as today. My hands are getting numb. I blow on them and keep crawling. Nothing.

And then I know. The bracelet isn't on the roof. It's somewhere on the broken concrete down below. It must have slid off my wrist as I was feeling around for a way down. I can't stop the tears, and now I am completely blind. I hug my knees and let myself cry. It doesn't matter anyway. No one can see. No one will find me.

I hear Mother's voice in my head: "Never give up, 'tis the secret of glory!" I wipe my nose and get to my feet. I look through the cloud of drizzle at the Music House. Jonathan won't be home for ages. Neither will Mother. Daddy always sleeps for a few hours, and he was extra tired today after our walk. I wonder if Mrs. O'Malley is home. I shudder at having to call her for help, but I don't see any sign of her anyway. In case someone might glance out their window, I wave my arms above my head and jump up and down. But who would be looking? Why? And how could they see in all this grey dullness? I sit down again and huddle in misery.

"Vanessa?"

I freeze, afraid to look.

"It's me. Brian."

I wipe my eyes and swivel around on my bottom. Brian's head and shoulders appear at eye level, through the mist. Tiny droplets of water glisten on his blond curls.

"It's all right," he says, holding out his arms. "I'll help you down."

I can't speak. My teeth are chattering with nerves. Cold. Fear.

"Come on." His arms are reaching out to me.

Count Brian. My knight in shining armor.

I crawl over to him and slide into his arms, and he lifts me to the top of the fence, holding me steady till I get my balance and climb down the way I usually do.

"Thank you."

He smiles and brushes off his trousers.

I tell him about Mother's bracelet, and he jumps over the fence as if it was nothing, finds it among the cracked concrete, and climbs back again. I thank Saint Anthony silently, then Brian out loud. Twice.

"I was on the roof getting some air," he says, and I know he means smoking. We're walking up the stairs to the porch. He's holding my hand. "I saw you climbing. That was pretty brave. Bad luck the drain broke. I went inside for a while and didn't realize you couldn't get back down until I saw you jumping up and down, waving your SOS."

I hiccup. "I wasn't supposed to be up there."

"I figured as much," he said. "I wasn't supposed to be entertaining a friend either. Or smoking, for that matter, so we're both guilty. It'll be our secret. Deal?" He held out his hand.

I nodded. "Deal." It sounds very grown up. I've never said that before.

"No one will ever know," he whispers. "Cross my heart and hope to die."

I shiver as I watch him run down the hall backwards, a finger to his lips. Then he turns and disappears through the archway to the third-floor stairs. "I'll never tell. Never," I say to myself. Then I go into the Everything Room to put the bracelet back where it belongs. Brian and I share a secret. I feel warm inside in spite of the rain.

8. JANET'S PROJECT

ON SATURDAY, MOTHER DROPS ME OFF at Janet's house on her way to buy groceries. I haven't seen Janet since I told her about my great adventure on the roof. I didn't mean to tell, but somehow it all came out. I couldn't help myself! Anyway, she promised she wouldn't tell anyone, so I know Brian's secret is safe too. It's been more than two weeks, and I'm excited. All this time I've been thinking of her spending time with Mary Margaret, her friend at school, picturing her walking along Bloor Street with her big sister Kathleen to the Royal Conservatory for her violin lesson, wondering what it must be like to have sisters and friends. The downside seems to be rarely having new clothes, always being stuck with hand-me-downs that need to be shortened because Magda was born tall. It seems a small price to pay for companionship. I look down at my own clothes. Although they were new at one time, they are always bought a size too large so I can grow into them. Now most are a size too small. It makes me feel awkward.

Janet is wearing faded red shorts with wide legs and a striped T-shirt that looks like a boy's. Maybe it belonged to one of her brothers. She finishes drying the dishes from lunch, and I help her put them away. Her kitchen is big, the only room in the house that seems bright, maybe because of the yellow paint on the walls and the cupboard doors the colour of the orange I get in my stocking at Christmas.

I usually choose the game, but right away Janet announces that the adventure today is gardening. "This summer we're going to have flowers and tomato plants and maybe some potatoes," Janet says with enthusiasm, taking off the big apron she is wearing and hanging it up behind the door. Upstairs, I can hear her mother's sewing machine whirring steadily. "Come on. It's warm outside. We don't even need a sweater." Her narrow face is flushed with the possibilities. She turns and races down the back stairs into the yard. She calls it a garden, but it's really just a square of beaten-down earth surrounded by a wooden fence and a few scraggly bushes straining towards the sunlight. A lilac struggles into bud in one corner. The rest of the bushes look dead. I think of the Secret Garden over at my house.

Janet is standing, hands on hips, looking at the yard. "It just needs fertilizer," she says firmly. "I read all about it in our encyclopedia."

"How do we get that?"

"Simple. We'll just follow the milk wagon around, and when the horse does its business, we'll bring it back here. See? Nothing to it."

"Are you sure?"

"Come on! He always comes around this time on Saturdays." She thrusts a shovel at me and grabs one herself, along with a burlap bag she flings over her shoulder. She must have laid things out earlier. I follow her along the lane out to the front and watch as the horse-drawn cart clops into view. I hang back against the fence as the milkman hops off, swinging the metal basket with four bottles rattling in it, their fat little necks filled with cream. He exchanges three full ones for the empties left on Janet's front step and goes next door with the fourth. I glance at the horse, standing patiently in the shafts in front of the Silverwoods Dairy wagon, shaking his head as if he knows what we want and has decided not to oblige.

"He's not doing anything," I whisper.

"He has to eventually," Janet says. She sits on the bottom step beside the milk, elbows on her bare knees, cupping her chin in her hands. I sit beside her, the stone cool against my bottom, and together we watch the slow progress of the milkman as he clinks his way down one side of the dead-end street and up the other until he stops opposite us at Mingy Moore's house. Mingy's younger than us and boring to play with. He doesn't know how to play our kind of games or plan special projects like this one. All he wants to do is play board games like Parcheesi and Snakes and Ladders, which is all right if you're really desperate, I suppose. He lives with his parents above the garages where two gleaming ambulances lie waiting for some disaster to set them into motion. Sometimes when I think about it, it makes me tense.

I'm still thinking about Mingy Moore when Janet punches me on the arm. "He's moving again," she says, jumping to her feet and heading for the corner.

I follow her, feeling nervous as we turn onto Jarvis Street. It's the first time I've walked on the street on my own—without Mother or Daddy or Jonathan I mean—but I don't want to admit this to Janet, who walks all the way to school alone and is always running errands for her mother. I'm getting more and more anxious as we amble along, getting closer and closer to Wellesley. I've been told over and over that I'm not supposed to cross the street. I'm wondering if being with Janet would count as an excuse, when the horse finally obliges with an odoriferous pile that makes Janet caper with joy.

"But look where it is!" Panic makes my voice squeak. The lumpy piles are in the middle of the road. "If cars come, it will be flattened. If we try to shovel it up, so will we."

"Don't be silly." Janet pushes her hair behind her ears and takes a firm grip on her shovel. "You hold the bag. I'll run out and get some when the light's green."

"I don't think—"

But the light has changed. She darts out and is already on

the way back with a steaming load while my mind stutters to find words to stop her.

"Easy peasy!" she crows. "Hold the bag open."

I do as she says, and she makes three more trips. It takes two light changes to get it all done, and between us we drag the steaming sack back up the street, around the corner, and along the lane into her yard.

"Now all we have to do is dig it into the ground," she says.

We are trying to do this when Jonathan arrives to take me home.

He doesn't say anything until we get to the corner. "You stink." He looks at me disgustedly. "What were you playing this time? Stable hand?"

For the first time, I notice my shoes and socks are streaked with horse pooh, and there are traces of brownish yellow on my wrists and the front of my dress.

"We were preparing the earth for planting," I say, trying to make it sound important, but it comes out in short bursts as he grabs my hand and pulls me across the street unceremoniously.

By the time we arrive on the back porch, where Mother is watering the window boxes, I am out of breath.

"Look at her!" he exclaims, throwing out his hand to indicate my state. "Covered in horse dung!"

"I am not covered," I say. "And anyway, it was for the garden!"

Mother looks me up and down, wrinkles her nose. "Of all the unladylike activities," she scolds, peeling off my shoes and socks. "Does Janet's mother know what you were doing?"

"I don't know." I am suddenly miserable at the thought of getting Janet in trouble, perhaps being forbidden to play with her again. "It was just gardening!" I exclaim, knowing how much she longs for her own garden.

"Poor girl won't ever get anything to grow in that dank patch of mud. Go inside and get undressed. You need a bath."

"A real bath or a sponge bath?" I ask.

"We'll see."

Usually I look forward to having a real bath, but it takes organizing in this house. Mother doesn't want us holding up the bathroom when others might need it, so right before dinner and right after dinner are out. It's late afternoon now, so I have to make do with a sponge bath in the small dressing space off the Everything Room. This tiny place is always filled with the sharp medicine smells of Daddy's ointments and the lotions he uses to dull the pain and itching of his ruined skin. It is like a tiny hospital in here. Two shelves are covered with bottles and jars and tubes, several pill bottles, and rolls of bandages in different sizes. I imagine him in here in the evening, slathering himself with lotions in an effort to smother the flames, wrapping his arms, his legs, his waist with the bandages like an Egyptian mummy. Only under his clothes does he look like a casualty of war. I think of Janet's dad, who was in the latest war. He wasn't a casualty, at least not that I know of. But maybe he, too, has a secret wound that eats at his flesh or maybe his brain. It's a new idea, and it fascinates me.

"Vanessa!"

I push my glasses up on my nose and realize that Mother has been talking all this time. This is not good. She is examining the clothes I stuffed in the laundry bag. "Have you any idea how hard it is to keep clothes clean? Any idea how my hands ache after washing out your blouses and shorts and undies? Come here. Look at these socks!"

I stare down at the streaked yellowish socks and push my glasses up on my nose. "I'm sorry."

"Wash them." She fills the sink with water and plunges in the socks. "Rub the soap into them and keep scrubbing until they're clean. Completely clean. Do you understand?"

I nod. She hands me the bar of yellow laundry soap and leaves me alone.

It takes a long time. I have to keep stopping to wipe the tears off my glasses so I can see. The socks still don't look really clean like when Mother does them, but I hang them up on the line on the porch and hope for the best. My fingers are all wrinkly. I go into the living room, where Mother is talking to Daddy. "I'll set the table," I say quickly.

"Please do," says Mother, and she gives me one of her piercing looks as if trying to see through my skull into my thoughts.

I am sent to bed early. I lie in the Everything Room, pressed against the wall on my part of the bed. The wallpaper is coming away from the wall along the seam here, and I try not to pick at it. There are bunches of purple flowers on the paper and purple curtains on the bay window that look as if they have been here for a long time. Mother took them down when we moved in and hung them over the porch railing. Clouds of dust wafted out when she hit them with a broom. Mother ripped up old lace curtains and remade them to go under the purple ones; it brightens the room a little in the daytime and makes it so you can't see in very well from the porch.

I can't go and see Janet for at least another week. It's not clear whether this is because of the horse dung incident or the fact that I have fallen behind in my schoolwork. Mother blames herself for the latter and is spending this evening in the other room, working out my new schedule of studies. She hasn't had the time to find any more tutors for me, so I am on my own for a while. I don't mind this. I get to read by myself, as long as I don't do it for more than half an hour at a time. We have a kitchen timer to set so I don't forget.

I am finally drifting off into a bright dream world where Brian and I are mounted on a silver horse, setting forth on a wonderful adventure, when I feel the bed shift and Mother bends over me. I squeeze closer to the wall, but she rolls me over and brushes the hair off my forehead.

"Midnight surprise," she says. "Get up. Put on your dressing gown."

Sleepily I roll out of bed and pull on the old kimono Mother cut down for me.

Daddy is home. He and Jonathan are sitting at the dining room table with a gargantuan bowl of ice cream in the middle. There is a bowl at everyone's place.

"Ice cream?" I say, wondering if I am still asleep after all. We never have ice cream.

Daddy is beaming. He is still in his street clothes, but Jonathan is in pajamas. He sleeps in the living room on the daybed.

"I don't think she should have any after what she did," Jonathan says.

"It's for everyone," Daddy says. "Eat it all up. It won't keep in the icebox, you know."

I sit down and see that Mother has put the new silver spoon she just bought with the money from her new job at my place mat. I feel a rush of joy and pick it up and look at her. She's smiling. Everything's all right.

"This will make the ice cream taste even better," she whispers. She is now the only one without a silver spoon.

9. THE MISSION

JONATHAN HAS BEEN CHOSEN as one of the four performers at the big June Recital in Eaton Auditorium. He has started practising already, although it is only May. Mother is very excited. "This is the first step," she says. "This is the beginning of great things!" But Jonathan seems depressed.

From my perch on top of the low built-in cabinets where we keep the books and some china, I listen as I work on my project for Mother's birthday present. Her birthday isn't till June either, but it will take a long time and I want it to be special, like Jonathan's performance. I've called it *Proverbs and Strange Sayings Illustrated by Vanessa Dudley-Morris*. So far, I have done "Birds of a Feather," "Hammer and Tongs," and "Raining Cats and Dogs" I'm working on "Hoist on His Own Pétard," but it's turning out to be harder than the others. I'll have to look up *pétard* in the *Book of Knowledge* so I know exactly what it looks like. I think it's a dagger of some sort, but I'm not sure. Jonathan's not sure either. I want to get it just right.

One of Bach's partitas sparkles in the air around me. From where I sit cross-legged in my aerie, I can see Jonathan's long fingers dancing over the keys, striking each note with precision and force in spite of the fast tempo. When I try this, I'm told not to thump. *How does he manage?* I remember listening to hours of scales and swooping, rattling-fast exercises from the yellow book. I have no patience for boring scales. When I'm alone, I try to reproduce what he does—the pieces, not the exercises—playing mostly by ear what he plays, but with quite different results. I don't have a music teacher at the moment, but I'm still supposed to practise.

Mother often tells the story about the first time she took Jonathan to Rona Layne's to audition. When she tells it in company, I feel a strange mixture of embarrassment and pride. We'd just arrived in Toronto then, and I was only five, but I went with them since Daddy was either at work or in the hospital—I forget which. Everyone was very nervous. Getting Jonathan a superior music teacher was part of the reason we had come to this big city—that and seeing this well-known doctor for my bad eyes—and he had been practising his audition pieces for weeks. While he played, I watched Rona Layne, fascinated by this tiny woman dressed in a long-ago style; her feet, not much bigger than mine and crossed at the ankle, were clad in beaded velvet shoes with tiny curved heels. She looked like Queen Victoria before she got fat.

As they talked afterwards, I wandered over to the great Steinway and began to play my version of what Jonathan had just played. I still remember the sudden silence and how I stumbled to a stop, thinking I had done something wrong. Rona Layne came over and pushed the cushioned piano bench closer to the keyboard, adjusted the special wooden contraption that allowed short legs to reach the pedals, and asked me to go on.

At once, I froze.

"Play whatever you like," Rona Layne said. "Or would you like to see the music in case you forget something?"

I shook my head. Although I knew the notes one by one, I couldn't sight-read very well. I haven't improved much since then.

She smiled and sat down close by. "That's fine, dear. Choose something else. You can play whatever you like. Pretend I'm not even here." She folded her hands.

She was impossible to ignore. I wanted to cry, but I didn't. I looked back at Mother. She nodded encouragingly, and I started again. A moment later my fingers stumbled and I jumped down and ran back to Mother, hoping the floor would open and swallow me, the curtains would tumble and cover me, the sky would fall, and I wouldn't have to know what happened next.

"She plays by ear?" she asked.

"She just copies what I do," Jonathan said dismissively.

Miss Layne went over to the piano and stood in front of the keyboard, striking one note after another, asking me to name the note. I did, whispering it to Mother who repeated it.

"She seems to have perfect pitch." Rona Layne came back and leaned close to Mother with her small doll smile. "You may have two of them."

Whenever Mother repeats this story, she looks at me fondly and I cringe. I know I am not anywhere near as good as Jonathan. I know I lack that special something he says you need, what he says Janey Drew has, that special something they all have who gather around Rona Layne—her Special People. Like Brian. I am not one of them.

"Why don't you dust while you're up there, Piglet," Jonathan says now. He is putting the music away in the piano bench, except what he's taking with him to his lesson. "Make yourself useful." He throws the dust cloth up to me, and I begin to clean off the top of the cupboard, the sill of the small leaded pane window that looks out over the back stairs, the window frame.

Jonathan puts on his cardigan and combs back his straight dark-brown hair with his fingers. It's getting a bit long and one side flops down over his high forehead. "Try not to get into trouble," he says, standing at the door, his music case in one hand.

I climb down, run to the door, and watch his back disappearing down the dim hall. When he's gone, I wander after him, past the tapestry. I catch the sound of whispered words, and I freeze, thinking it's the hunters muttering amongst themselves in the woven forest. But it's just Mrs. Smyth talking to her husband in his urn. I retreat back to the porch and look out over the grass and fences behind the house and wonder what's in the garden behind ours, the one I saw plainly the time I was stuck on top of the coach house. Mother says it's a crying shame the place is so neglected and allowed to go to rack and ruin, with the housing shortage the way it is. She gets that dreamy look in her eye as she describes how we could live there, what we could do with the space, the curtains we'd hang, the colour we could paint the cupboards in the little kitchen (she's sure there's a little kitchen in there somewhere), and the high polish we could put on the wooden floors. We could bring our big rug out of storage, the one with the tree of life pattern that matches the smaller one we have now in the living room. Mother is always imagining what things might be like in some other place. Daddy just smiles, lies back in his chair, and closes his eyes.

Daddy is sleeping now. Again. He hasn't been back to work since the midnight ice cream feast and I can sense Mother getting more and more worried, but nobody says anything. I run down the back steps and cross the driveway to the gap in the fence between our house and Ryan's Art Gallery. I'm filled with the energy of a new idea and slip through the thin part of the hedge and turn left, following the driveway till it veers into a lane going out to Wellesley Street. This shortcut will take me to the place Daddy and I saw the old wooden bookcase. It could still be there. Maybe.

I keep to one side of the lane, hoping no one will notice me against the bushes. Jonathan's lesson will take an hour at least, maybe more, plenty of time for my adventure. I almost turn back when I feel someone watching, but I think of Daddy, his hand patting that wood, and I keep going. Out of the corner of my eye, I glimpse the rows of windows of the apartment building looming above the unkempt bushes along one side of the alley. They look blank, burnished gold from the afternoon sun—but behind this innocent shield, who is lurking? Watching? Waiting to pounce? Whispers follow me in the bushes as I start to run.

The lane slopes suddenly downward, and I am on the street where I often walk with Daddy. I stop. Take a deep breath. I've missed the wood. The people and cars and sudden rushing confusion startle me. I turn quickly, push my glasses firmly in place, and trudge back up the slope of the driveway. I'm walking slowly along the other side of the alley now, keeping the whispering menace at bay as I look from side to side. I spy a piece of wood behind the back porch of the Art Gallery where the garbage cans are. In a pile of discarded things, I find two broken chairs, a battered old suitcase missing a handle, a pail with a big hole in the bottom, and the bookcase. It seems to be more damaged than it was before, but there's still enough left to make something. I wish Janet was here to help, but she's in school and I won't see her till Saturday so I have to do it myself. If I wait, someone might take the rest or break it even more. I wish Brian would come along. I blink and see him there, right there on the porch, smiling, the sun in his hair, his hands in his pockets the way he stands sometimes. "It's all right," he says. "I'll help you." I sigh. He doesn't go to school, but I suppose he's at the Conservatory now, practising.

I knock one shelf loose, using a rock for a hammer, and slide the top shelf under my arm. I can't carry more than two pieces at once. I begin my trip back to the porch. I have to keep stopping because the shelves are heavy and slip out of my grasp, but I'm happy I'm rescuing the wood for Daddy. All the time I keep imagining what he will make, how pleased he will be.

After two trips I'm tired, but there is more wood still there so I go back. I look at the remains of the bookcase. The bottom part is nailed firmly together, and it's too big for me to carry. I think about the old wagon we saw on one of our walks and wish I had one here. There's nothing to do but go home, leaving the rest behind.

I'm piling the shelves up neatly beside the icebox when Jonathan bursts out the back door, his face red.

"Where the hell have you been?" he shouts at me.

I stare at him, speechless. I've never heard him swear before. What is he doing back so soon anyway?

"I've been looking for you for ten minutes!" He sees the wood and looks from it to me. "What's all this?"

I tell him about my plan to cheer Daddy up with the wood he admired a few days ago. "There's more, but I can't carry it," I finish. "I tried."

"Hell," he says again. "Show me."

I turn and run down the stairs and lead him to the remains.

"All right," he says. "Okay. We can do this, but you have to help. And you have to promise you won't disappear like that again. Tell me!"

I nod, hoping that will do. He shifts the awkward piece into his arms, and I help balance it as we make our way home, me skipping sideways like a crab.

Jonathan makes lunch of vegetable soup and a peanut butter sandwich, and then he has to go back for afternoon classes at Jarvis Collegiate. He gives me a lecture before he goes. I look meek and nod my head a lot and say, "Yes, yes, Jonathan." I am very glad he helped, but it's good to be quiet again. I'm used to quiet now.

I take out the map of Canada that Mother traced for me and fill in the borders of the provinces and the capital cities from memory, remembering to add Newfoundland. Daddy was pleased when they joined the Dominion in March. He said there were some Newfoundlanders in his unit in the army and they were "good men." I colour the provinces green and yellow and blue and burnt sienna with the new coloured pencils I got for my birthday. I list the premiers, correcting the one I got wrong last time, and write down what each place is famous for. Seth strikes the half hour. I go to the kitchen and put the kettle on.

"What are you doing in there?" Mrs. O'Malley appears at the half-open door, leaning on her mop. She shouldn't be here in the afternoon, I think, but I just stare at her, confused by her sudden appearance. She licks her lips and pushes her frizzy hair back from her face. "You should be doing school work," she says.

"I am," I say.

"Then what are you doing here?"

"It's recess." Janet told me about recess. They have it in Parliament, too.

Mrs. O'Malley leans back and roars with laughter. It's insulting. I feel my face getting redder and redder. I think of closing the kitchen door but can't quite bring myself to do such a rude thing. The kettle boils, and I mix the cocoa and sugar in our mug with St. Paul's Cathedral on it, wishing she would go away. She watches me, but she's moving the mop around again in tiny circles on the narrow band of wood on each side of the hall runner.

"You should be at a real school," she says now, all her laughter gone.

I don't answer. I take my mug, turn out the light, and push out the door, closing it carefully behind me. I feel her eyes on my back as I go into our living room and close that door, too. Then I slide my back down the door and sit on the floor, sipping my cocoa as I listen to Mrs. O'Malley humming and mopping on the other side. I have the unpleasant feeling she knows I am just sitting here, right against the door.

At last she goes away. I sit here for a long time, listening to the Music House breathe around me. In my head, I recite the states on the other side of the Canadian border, then the provinces from sea to shining sea.

Seth is striking the quarter hour when I get up and go outside to the porch. The window boxes are filled with soil now, ready for the seeds Mother has bought: nasturtiums, marigolds, baby's breath, and sweet peas. One small box will be full of runner beans. We can't plant anything until after May 24, but already Mother has started some of the seedlings indoors. They're stretched out in egg cartons along the windowsills in both rooms and look spindly and frail, like invalids.

I can't go downstairs since I promised Jonathan not to, but he didn't say anything about going up. I smile in secret triumph and skip along the porch to the ladder. I feel more confident climbing it now. Halfway up I pause, swing around so my back is against the brick wall and look out over all three gardens. The secret one is directly below, almost hidden in overgrown bushes, now fragrant with lilacs and orange blossoms. Straight ahead, just beyond our own boring square of close-trimmed lawn, I can see over the back fence into the long grass of the abandoned yard behind the coach house. No one has mowed there for a long time. It has a derelict air, forgotten, unloved. If I could climb the fence and explore it, I'd be the first one to set foot there for many years. My footprint would stay there, imprinted in the soil like Friday's on the sand, a testament to me being there. But that will have to wait. I swing around again and climb higher.

No one is on the roof today. For the first time, I climb all the way up and tiptoe over the pebble floor to the door. It is locked. Disappointed, I turn away and look around. I am beside the wide bay window of the room where Brian and his mother live. Brian is one of the ones chosen for the Recital too. I guess now he and Jonathan are rivals. Maybe they always were.

I slide down and listen. From inside comes the tinkle of an instrument. Not a piano. A harpsichord! I recognize the plucked string sound from some of our records, where Wanda Landowska plays Bach anytime we want.

I slide to my knees and slowly inch my face closer to the window. I want to see the harpsichord. The only ones I've ever seen in real life are at the museum in the ancient instrument section. No one ever plays them.

I can see inside now. Brian is playing a small spinet to the right of the window, facing my way. His eyes are on the keyboard, watching the black keys and the white sharps and flats. His mother is standing behind him, her hands slowly rubbing his shoulders. As I watch, Brian's long hands slow, pause, stop altogether. He leans back against her, and Mrs. Pierce slides her fingers down inside his shirt. She rests her head on his and keeps rubbing. I can see the movement, like mice under the white material of his open shirt as her hands slide lower and lower.

I pull back, feeling curiously warm and short of breath. I think of Jonathan and Mother. She often watches him play, often caresses his cheek or touches his hair, just as she does with me. She rubs my legs when they hurt. Maybe Brian's chest is hurting. I take another quick peek. Brian is frowning now, pulling away. He turns towards her with angry words I can almost hear but not quite. The sudden change in the atmosphere frightens me, and I jump back, shifting along the roof on my bottom until I reach the ladder. Quickly, I climb down and run inside.

Daddy is standing in the living room, fully dressed, his small brown leather suitcase open on the dining room table. When he sees me, he closes it and sets it on the ground.

"I have to go to the hospital now," he says. "Be good. Do what you can to help your mother. She's a brave woman."

"I will, Daddy. Are you coming home soon?"

"As soon as I can, dear." He kisses my forehead and cups the back of my head gently, the way he always does when he goes away.

I take his fingers carefully in mine and squeeze just a little, in case it might hurt. I go with him to the front door. As he walks down the path and out the curly iron gate, I am desolate. I think of the wood I gathered for him as a surprise, and I almost run after him to tell him about it, but he is already far away from me in his mind. I can tell by the way he is walking:

carefully, steadily, his face set. Mother says he still walks like the soldier he once was, marching with a swagger stick tucked under one arm, many long years ago. "It was another world then," Mother says.

I run back upstairs and into the living room. Everything is emptier with Daddy gone. I take off my glasses and burst into tears.

The rest of the day is subdued, as if the colours have faded from things around me. I go to bed early. Late that night, I wake up with a scream as a white horse crashes through the window, a man on his back with blond hair like Brian's, only longer. I tell Mother about the horse (without mentioning Brian) in between sobs, and she rocks me back and forth, back and forth. It takes a long time to get back to sleep.

10. THE ICE MAN

J ANET IS VISITING SOME COUSINS for the weekend, and I am all alone on Saturday afternoon. I've been looking forward to seeing her all week, and now I feel restless and upset and sort of angry all at once. I can't find words to tell all this to anyone, so I stamp around the living room until Jonathan tells me to stop. He's studying. Mother is trying to do accounts, and she doesn't notice when I go outside, wanting to slam the door but afraid of what will happen if I do. I don't want that kind of attention. I just want someone to play with.

Outside, the sun has disappeared and the sky is a dull heavy grey. Humidity hangs over everything like wet drapery. It's not quite June yet, but we're in the middle of an early heat wave, Mother says. I wish we could go down to visit Grandmother by the Bay of Fundy like we did last year, but we don't have enough money for train fare now. And Mother doesn't want to leave Daddy in the hospital all alone anyway.

I hang over the railing of the porch, staring at the grass below. It's already beginning to brown at the edges, like a cake that's been in the oven too long. Mr. O'Malley mowed it a few days ago, pushing the mower over the ground quickly, as though he was in a race with some unseen demon, missing bits here and there. Sloppy worker, Daddy says, and shakes his head. Daddy doesn't like sloppy workmanship. For a moment, I wish Daddy was with me here. We wouldn't even have to talk; we could just sit together, looking at the grass. I'd like that. But Daddy is in Sunnybrook with some other sick veterans. Mother is going to visit him tomorrow afternoon, but I'm too young. It seems I'm too young to do anything interesting.

Heavy footsteps are coming up the stairs. I straighten up and brush my hands off, push my glasses up, smooth my hair. It's the ice man in his sweaty white T-shirt and dark-green pants. Balanced on a leather pad on one shoulder is a big block of ice that he holds in place with a sharp spiky pincer thing. Water drips from the ice, but it doesn't bother him.

"Hi, kid," he says, opening the wooden door of the top compartment of the icebox and heaving the block inside. "Hot enough for you?"

"It is quite warm," I say.

He leans back, hands on his kidneys, and laughs. Then he pulls an ice pick out of the case on his tool belt, chips off a piece of the ice, and hands it to me. "Have a cool one," he says, slinging the giant pincer things over his shoulder. He waves and lopes down the back stairs, his knees loose and easy.

I follow and watch him take another block of ice from his truck, heave it onto his shoulder, and make his way to the O'Malley's back door. There's a girl standing there, holding the door open for him. She's taller than me and lumpy. Her face looks like unbaked dough, and her arms, what I can see of them under the long sleeves of her lacy cotton cardigan, are scarred, the skin tight and red. Her neck is scarred as well. But her hair is thick, black and shiny, curled carefully all around her face, and she's wearing a crisp green dress. I feel like a tomboy in my Saturday shorts. I hesitate, wanting to go up and change, but knowing Mother wouldn't let me wear my good dress. Besides, I might miss finding out who she is.

The ice man goes in twice. They must have a big icebox. He seems to know the girl and calls her Patricia. Then he waves to me as he gets back into the truck with *Lake Simcoe Ice Company* printed on the side in loopy lettering. He leaves behind a bit of wet sawdust on the driveway.

"You shouldn't eat ice," the lumpy girl says, watching me. "You'll get germs."

I shove the sliver into my mouth and watch her. "Who says?"

"My mom." Patricia leans against the doorframe.

"I doubt that it will kill me," I say, biting off the end.

"You talk funny," she says.

Overhead, thunder rumbles and she jumps. I grin, feeling superior. "You want to play double ball?" I ask, dropping the remains of my ice. "I've got two good hard bouncers upstairs. We can do Okie and the Kaiser."

"It's going to rain," she says. "I gotta go inside." But she hesitates, no longer leaning against the door but holding it open with one hand.

"It's nice and dry under the porch," I say. Now that she's backing away, I want her to stay. I don't want to be alone. "I'm Vanessa." I start to move towards her, holding out my hand, but she backs away.

"I know. I'm Patricia O'Malley," she says. "You want to come inside?"

"Sure!" I'm ashamed of my eagerness, but I follow her. "Why haven't I seen you before?"

She stops in the dim landing and looks at me. Her small dull eyes sharpen. "I've been away," she snaps.

It's clear she's not open to more questions. It's rude to pry, no matter how much I want to, so I look around. At the top of the steps to our left, there's a huge bank of square golden oak doors with the same kind of yellow metal handles as our icebox. My mouth falls open. "Gee," I say.

Satisfaction gleams from Patricia's smile. "It's real ritz, isn't it?" she says. "Of course, we don't use them all 'cause there's just me and Mum and Dad. They were for the whole house in the old days."

I try not to look at the puckered skin on her wrists and neck, but it's all I can really think about so nothing else occurs to me to say. We stand there in silence for a moment. Now that we're inside, she doesn't seem to know what to do next.

"It's hot in the kitchen," she says. "Mum's baking bread."

Outside, the thunder is getting closer. Mrs. O'Malley calls Patricia, who looks annoyed. "Wait here," she says, and turns and goes up past the great bank of empty iceboxes through the swinging door that must lead to the kitchen. There are shelves on the wall opposite the iceboxes, so I guess this used to be a sort of pantry. There are a few rows of pickles and relishes and some jams and jellies there now. I never thought of Mrs. O'Malley cooking, preserving, making bread. Having a family.

"I have to go in for supper soon," she says, suddenly appearing on the stairs.

"But it's just five o'clock," I exclaim.

Patricia shrugs. "Then I have to have a rest and do homework."

"What's down there?" I ask, pointing to where stairs go down to a door in the dimness beyond where we're standing.

"The cellar, of course."

"Can we go look?"

"There's nothin' interesting down there," she says, but she goes past me and leads the way down the stairs and through the door to the dim, cool cavern beyond. I follow close behind. She flips on the light. "See? Coal chute's over there and the furnace through there."

"Look at the treasure chests!" I exclaim.

"What are you talking about? That's just trunks, like for storing stuff the roomers don't want." She looks at me as if I'm mentally lacking.

I make a harrumphing noise but can't think of anything to say in the face of her total lack of imagination. Janet would have picked up the idea, and we'd have had a great game. Patricia is a bore. But she does show me where the other stairs to the cellar come up—right in the hallway leading to Rona Layne's studio.

"I'll go home this way," I say quickly, "so I don't get wet." Patricia shrugs, not caring what I do. She's ready for supper. She flips off the lights as she makes her way back to her kitchen. I watch, memorizing where the switches are, watching the shadows settle back into place behind her.

When the silence is thick, I'm sure she's gone. I creep back down the stairs and find the light. I flip it on, and the long cavern of treasures comes into view. Boxes and trunks, old lamps, a few chairs covered with dust. A lamp shade with a dusty fringe balances on a pile of magazines. *National Geographic*, going back a long time. *Life* magazine. Two piles. I move past them and finger the crystals of a small chandelier, which is hanging low from the rafters. Even in this dim cavern, it catches the light and breaks it into dusty rainbows. One of the crystals comes off in my hand. I try to fit it back into place, but the wire loop is gone. I hold it up to the light, watching the little rainbows come and go. I had a prism like this once, but it got lost in one of our frequent moves. I slip the crystal into my shorts pocket and move on.

As I walk slowly down the wide corridor crammed with its treasures, on either side I see doors that I didn't notice when Patricia was with me. I pause at the closest one. It's almost closed, and it sticks when I push it, but I get it back far enough to slip through into the dusty gloom on the other side. The room inside is tiny, not much bigger than our kitchen, and there is no window. One wall is made of makeshift planks nailed together every which way, and there are shelves along two other walls. Daddy wouldn't think highly of the workmanship. There isn't much on the shelves: only some brass candlesticks that need polishing, a bulging laundry bag, some boxes, and two old clocks. I open one of the smallest boxes and see jewelry. A gold bracelet is on top with one gold charm—a swan with a tiny diamond eye. I slip it on my wrist, then quickly drop it back in the box, squeeze out again, and pull the door shut.

Nearby, a trunk is partly open. The top is rounded like a pirate's chest, and it draws me to it as if I'm on an invisible cord. I open the top all the way and prop it back against the wall. Inside is a tray filled with small shoes and slippers, some wrapped in tissue paper, some tumbled untidily as if someone has been rummaging about. I pick a pair of rose slippers with curved satin-covered heels and a beaded design on the front. They fasten with a pearl button on the strap. "Rona Layne," I whisper. I sit down, take off my new tennis shoes, and shove my foot in. They're almost too small for me across the toes, but I can wear them. My feet look so different—dainty and old fashioned. I totter around the basement. Although the heels are not high, they still make walking difficult for me. I come back to the trunk and examine the rest. They're all about the same but in different colours with different beadwork. Perhaps she had them made to match her gowns when she was playing for the Crowned Heads. I try on a few more, then shove them all back in, thrusting my feet into my canvas shoes again, returning to the present day with a thump.

Further along, there's a clear space where several boxes are piled. Only a light film of dust covers them, as though they have arrived more recently, and I can see books poking through the top one. I reach in and pull one out. It's a history of musical instruments. On the inside leaf is written the name Brian Alexanian, with an address in Vancouver. We have lots of books from second-hand shops, so this is familiar to me, though we usually cross the original name out and write ours underneath. I reach in and pull out another book. The same name is written inside this one, too. And the next. And the next. They are all on music, one on building harpsichords. I think of Brian Pierce upstairs, playing the spinet, his mother's long hands moving under his shirt, restless, searching. These books belong to him. All the books in the carton belong to him. There is no other Brian in the house.

What does it mean?

The books aren't any fun to read and the light is bad anyway, so I pack them all back in their carton and dust off the seat of my shorts. Suddenly I know I have been here too long. It's as if the basement is accusing me of bad behaviour. I flick off the light and run up the stairs, only slowing down when I get behind the velvet curtain that covers the opening outside Rona Layne's studio. But no one is around.

As I go through the front hall and up the main staircase, a crash of thunder rattles the milky glass of the windows on the landing. I begin to hurry, rushing past the tapestry. The light here is odd today, yellowish. I finger the prism in my pocket—my new good luck charm. The people on the wall stare straight at me, watchful, appraising. An odd noise hums in the air. I burst into our room too suddenly, startling Mother. Jonathan isn't there.

"Did you get wet?" she asks. "You're out of breath. Are you all right?" She puts a hand on my forehead and holds it there a moment.

I concentrate on slowing my breathing. "I met a girl called Patricia," I say.

"There are so many girls called Patricia these days," Mother says. "I wonder why? In my day it was Mary and Betty, and flower names like Violet and Rose." She's spread folded flannel sheets on the table to protect it and is ironing shirts. "Here, let me show you how to do this. Might as well learn now." She smiles and I take her place at the makeshift ironing board. "Always start with the collar and then do the cuffs," she tells me and shows me how to do it, dipping her fingers in a bowl of water and sprinkling it on the dry shirt.

What seems so simple takes all my concentration, not to iron any more wrinkles into the thing, being careful not to scorch the material. I'm relieved when she takes over again. "You'll be doing this in no time," she says. "A quick study, you are."

I want to get back to Patricia. "That girl lives downstairs," I say.

"Mrs. O'Malley's daughter, I expect," she says, hanging the shirt on a wire hanger from the door handle and taking another one from the pile of clean laundry on the chair. "Poor thing. She's been through a lot."

"What happened to her?" I stand very still, waiting to hear the story, but I can tell she's running over in her mind how much to reveal. Her hesitation makes the details even more enticing.

At last she picks up the iron again and shakes her head. "Some people shouldn't have children."

"What happened?"

She begins to iron faster, her movements now short and jerky. "Mrs. O. says she left the child for only a second to reach for something and the baby rolled into a basin of boiling water. As if that makes sense! Imagine! Boiling water left near a baby! Scarred for life, the poor little thing."

"She's not very little," I point out, but Mother scowls at me fiercely and I wish I hadn't said anything.

"As if you can believe one word that woman says anyway," she goes on, more to herself than me. "I hope you were nice to the poor thing." She pauses and gives me another fierce look. "Don't ever stare at the afflicted!"

I nod, then shake my head and feel guilty about my earlier thoughts about Patricia. "She isn't much fun, though," I say, almost in a whisper.

"You wouldn't be much fun either if you'd been through what she's been through."

I wonder if this argument makes sense. In all the stories I've read, suffering makes you better, more interesting. On the other hand, I think back on all the pains I've had in my legs, coming suddenly and inexplicably, twisting me into tears and crying jags, lasting sometimes more than an hour unless Mother rubs them. I think about the long weeks spent in bed last year with rheumatic fever, about always being watched in case I get overtired. Has it made me better? Or just boring like Patricia? The idea worries me, but then I remember Janet and our long complicated games and feel better. She doesn't think I'm boring.

Mother snaps the wrinkles out of a sugar-bag pillowcase and irons it. She's still muttering about Mrs. O. "That woman has no moral compass," she says and spits on the iron to make sure it's hot enough for the pillowcase. "Would you like beans on toast for dinner?"

I nod. It's Daddy's favourite meal, and it makes me sad that he's not here to share it.

Mother seems to think of him at the same time I do. I see her smile sadly as she unplugs the iron. "Dear Ned loves his beans and brown bread," she says. "At his house, they served it every Friday, apparently, but not out of a can, of course."

I prefer them out of a can, but I don't say anything. I start to fold the flannel sheet while Mother puts away the laundry. I wonder as I often do about Daddy's home when he was a little boy growing up in a time when everyone had horses and carriages and ladies wore long skirts. We never talk about his life back then: his mustachioed father, his elegant mother whose name I bear, his older brothers and sisters, his cousins who live up the Saint John River in the large grey house on a point of land that bears their name. They are all frozen in time in our photo album, but he rarely talks about himself at all. "Your mother talks enough for both of us," he says one time when I ask, and he laughs his soft gentle laugh so I never know if he's serious or just playing.

"Why don't you set the table? Placemats will be fine tonight," Mother says. "We're having caramel pudding for dessert."

My mouth begins to water at the thought. Puddings are a treat in our house. I suspect Mother is trying to cheer us up now that Daddy's not here. As I go through the familiar routine of setting the table, I try to think of a way to bring Brian into the conversation without admitting how I found out his other name and getting into trouble. Then a possible explanation comes to me.

"Mrs. Pierce is divorced!" I exclaim. I hadn't meant to say this out loud, and Mother is looking at me strangely. "Like Mrs. Simpson," I add quietly. I begin to polish my serviette ring vigorously.

"You shouldn't listen to gossip," Mother says sternly. She gives me one last long fierce look and leaves the room. I collapse onto a dining room chair and blow breath out through my pursed lips. "Just like Mrs. Simpson," I repeat softly.

11. THE WHISPERING TUBE

It's hot tonight. During the day, the swineys were singing. Mother says they're cicadas, but I think my private name suits them better. I can't sleep. I wake up, and the sheet is damp and tangled. Mother has one arm thrown across my waist. Where our skin touches, everything is slippery with perspiration. She is breathing heavily, exhausted from her job. The damp air weighs me down, making me feel short of breath. Sudden panic surrounds me, and I wiggle out from under Mother's arm, crawl down to the end of the bed, and climb over the metal footboard. I glance at Daddy's side of the bed, forgetting for a moment that he is still in the hospital. I hope he's not awake, bathed in this strangling blanket of heat, feeling the sickness under his skin roil and swell and itch

Quietly, I put on an old T-shirt of Jonathan's and my one pair of shorts and creep out the door. In the hall, shadows cling to the wall, shudder along the tapestry. One pale light glows dimly outside the bathroom door, but it only seems to increase the darkness. Baggy Bones's door is closed. I imagine her in her cluttered room, curled up on her daybed, surrounded by her ratty shawls like a bird in its nest. I hesitate. I have never been out by myself at night. To my left, the porch door beckons.

Outside, I breathe more easily. The moon sails in and out of the clouds. Everything looks different, sounds different. Even the air feels different. I tiptoe to the end of the porch where the window boxes spill sleeping flowers over the balustrade.

The smell of orange blossoms lingers on the air, making me think of sunshine, of Mother and me sitting here surrounded by our flowers, Mother telling family stories about people I barely remember, while Daddy smiles and sands a piece of wood till it feels like skin.

Nighttime pulls everything closer together. I climb a few rungs up the ladder, leaning over to see what the Secret Garden looks like at this hour. The boy in the fountain is silver in the moonlight, the stagnant water around his feet black. Everything is bleached, the neglect hidden under the silvering effect of the moon.

As I hang there above the riot of greenery, a shadow moves. I blink and push up my glasses, trying to focus on the movement. Sitting on the other side of the fountain is Brian, one foot swinging back and forth. He is wearing tiny shorts and what looks like a white undershirt. His hair shimmers like a halo. I pull back, afraid of being seen. I wonder how he got all the way down there from the third floor. Perhaps it is cooler in the Secret Garden.

When I look again, another movement catches my eye. Someone is with him; someone is sitting on the red bricks, leaning against his legs, shadowed by his body. I can't see anything clearly from up here. I try to imagine Mrs. Pierce climbing over the iron gate in a long lacy nightie, the kind I imagine she wears. I pull back again, stifling giggles. The image in my head is funny, ungainly, impossible to believe. It makes no sense. I look again, and it seems that the shadow companion has dark hair. Not like his mother. Intrigued, I climb higher on the ladder, but the view from up here is no better. I still can't see the other person, just the two heads—close together now, bent, whispering. One dark, one fair. *A secret tryst!* Brian has eased down to the ground, his arms sliding around the one who must be his secret girlfriend. Why is she secret? Is she unsuitable in some way? Like Cousin Jim marrying the hatcheck girl in some jazz club in Boston five years ago?

I rest my chin on my arms against the warm metal of the ladder and wonder if I will be unsuitable in some way when I grow up. People seem to have a lot to live up to. I feel sorry for the girl down there, imagining Mrs. Pierce looking her up and down disapprovingly. I also feel annoyed with the girl, but I don't know why.

I'm just beginning to climb back down the ladder again when I sense yet another movement down below. The two figures are standing up now, arms around each other. They are almost the same height. I still can't see the girl, and now they are moving urgently towards the bushes, into the bushes, onto the ground. I strain into the shadows but can make nothing out. As I set both feet on the porch, I hear a rising moan from the garden that disturbs the air around me, makes me feel a rush of heat. The sound is cut off suddenly. Tears gather. I dash them away.

"Bugger all," I whisper, and head back inside. Suddenly I'm very tired.

Sunday morning, we go to church. We used to go to Saint Paul's, just up the street on Bloor, but now we go to Saint Mary Magdalene's. Jonathan insisted because of Dr. Healey Willan and the music. It takes a while to get there, but I'm glad we've switched. I love it. I love the incense and the lulling chants that sound like history for the ears. I like to think it's the same music Richard the Lionheart heard before he left for the Crusades. The same smells, too. The same words from the Bible that King James I listened to in Westminster Abbey in London during the reading of the Epistle. The only thing I don't like is there's not enough singing of hymns. I love singing hymns. And I don't like having to leave and go to Sunday school with the little kids. That part is boring.

After church, Father Wayne stands talking to Mother and Jonathan, one hand resting on my head as if I'm five years old. I hate that. I stand very still, feeling the weight of his hand, feeling the heat from his fingers in my hair. They are talking about the Corpus Christi procession and how I could be a part of it, scattering rose petals in front of the monstrance from a basket over one arm. I remember the procession from last year, although I didn't take part, and as I watch Mother's face, hoping she will say yes, I suspect she remembers too and doesn't like the idea. I'm afraid Mother might decide the procession with its statue, candles, and chanting is too much, too High Church, too Roman. I sense she is uneasy here sometimes, and I wonder if she thinks her stern Orangeman father, who I am told is often a marshal in the parade on the Glorious Twelfth, might not approve of this place that I think of as home—a place as close to my own secret identity as I can get, where I experience the scents and images of being French and Catholic without anyone knowing.

At last I squirm, and Father Wayne lifts his hand and gestures with it as he talks. I move quickly out of reach. Talk has shifted to other things, and he and Mother appear to have reached no decision on the Corpus Christi matter. If Daddy comes home in time, I can ask him. Or I can send a note. Mother will listen to what he says.

It's afternoon. Mother is going to the hospital to visit Daddy, taking my private note, and Jonathan is practising again for the big Recital. I spend a long time trying to get a page of penmanship good enough to show Mother when she gets back. Penmanship is not one of my strengths, Mother says. She writes in a clear, rounded hand, no matter how quickly she goes. Daddy writes in a stiff old-fashioned way, on a slant with curlicues here and there. Jonathan writes in funny crooked scratches. He says it's because he studies Greek and they have a different alphabet, so he can get away with it. I know the Greek alphabet too, but I don't do much writing with it.

I have an old penmanship book Mother got from Janet's mother, and she glued clean sheets of paper under the part Janet has written on and ruled the lines in. I've filled in most of it, but it doesn't look very good. No matter how hard I try, the pencil smudges, the lines wobble, and the loops go too high or too low. It's discouraging. At this rate, I may never get to write in ink. Today, in order to make things more interesting, Mother has suggested writing a page of memory work instead, but it has to have no erasures and only three mistakes. I've been working on it for a long time and am on my third piece of paper now. This time I think I have it. Mother said punctuation counts, too, so I hesitate a few times between colons, commas, and such, then take a chance. If I look it up, Jonathan might notice.

At last I finish the page of the opening lines of "I wandered lonely as a cloud" and put away my pencils and paper.

"Finished?" Jonathan asks, not looking at me.

"All done." I go to the door.

"Don't go out of the garden," he says.

"All right." I slip out into the hall and take a deep breath of relief. I'm not going to the garden. I turn toward the front stairs and see Baggy Bones outside her door, talking to Mrs. Tyndall. When she sees me, she scowls and hooks an arm around Mrs. Tyndall's narrow shoulders. "Come on inside where we can talk in peace," she says, scooping her in. She closes the door behind her. I stick my tongue out and think how rude she is.

I pause at her door, listening, but can't hear anything but the murmur of her voice. The archway leading to the third floor is nearby. As I stand in the opening, I catch sight of a round brass cup-like object sticking out of the wall next to the curtain just above my eye level. I never noticed it before, probably because the curtain usually covers it. I touch the brass, pull on it, and it comes out of the wall on a red velvet rope. I put it to my ear and hear voices far away. As I listen, Patricia whines, "But I don't want to lie down, Ma. I don't feel tired."

"You need your strength," Mrs. O'Malley says crossly.

"All I did was go to church and eat lunch!" Patricia complains.

"Twenty minutes." A door slams.

I listen for a few moments more, but all is quiet down in the kitchen quarters. I put the tube to my lips and make a long moaning noise. "Jesus, Mary, and Joseph!" exclaims Mr. O'Malley. I drop the tube and run upstairs quickly.

I push the door to my left and go out on the roof. It's sunny and the air is clear. I can see through the trees on one side, out over the fences, and into other people's gardens. Not much to see there really. I walk over to the edge and look down at the Secret Garden. It seems to sleep in the sunshine down there, so different from the time I saw it in the moonlight a few days ago.

"Don't get too close to the edge."

I leap back and whirl around, staring at Brian as if he has two heads. I feel an odd guilt, as if I had been talking about him behind his back, and I have, in a way—inside my head. I flush and stammer something that makes no sense.

He laughs. "Sorry, I startled you. Guess you were miles away."

I nod, but I'm not miles away—only down two floors, in the basement, thinking of his name in all those books I found, a different name no one here knows.

"It'll be summer soon," he says, looking out over the trees. "No more school, no more books, no more teachers' dirty looks." He laughs, but he doesn't sound happy.

"I don't go to school."

"In British Columbia, where I went to school, we only have twelve grades, not thirteen," he says.

This is so surprising I look right at him, at his silver-gold hair, his green eyes that seem to draw me inside them. I look away. If we lived there, Jonathan would be finished school, too.

"But Rona Layne lives here," I say.

"Exactly."

Brian slides down onto the roof, his back against the wall. I sit down, too, cross-legged, and start to play jacks with some pebbles.

"I met your brother a few days ago at the Conservatory," he says. "I really admire him."

I nod, feeling warm pleasure in the praise, as I always do, as if some of it is meant for me too, even though I know it isn't.

"What do you all think of his decision?" He looks at me suddenly, as if really interested in what I have to say.

I look back steadily, my mind racing as I try to come up with what he wants to know, but I can't interpret the question. Does he mean the summer job at the lumber camp? "The job will keep him in the outdoors a lot," I say, but I can tell this is not what he wants to hear. "Mother says it will be healthful."

He smiles and nods and says, "Yes, I'm sure it will," but something is missing in his words, and I know I have failed in my answer.

"It's hard sometimes, not knowing what you want to do, isn't it?" he says.

I nod, but I'm not sure what he means this time either. He's already doing what he wants to do, isn't he? I reach into my pocket and finger the crystal, my little rainbow maker, my good-luck piece.

"Have you decided what you want to do when you grow up?" he asks.

Vague panic clouds my mind as the question hangs in the air. When most adults ask this, I know they don't really want to know what *I* want. They expect to hear the usual answer, the approved one, the one that everyone agrees is right for me. Usually, Mother answers for me anyway.

But this time Brian really seems to want to know what I think, and it gives me pause. I have thought about it from time to time, but my plans are all much closer to the present. "I'm going to university," I say. That much I know. It's part of the approved answer Mother often tells me, so I feel on firmer ground now. "I like history," I say. "I like the stories of kings and queens and wars, and the way countries change and the borders swing from side to side. So sometimes you wake up and your official language is one thing. Then twenty years later, you wake up and it's another."

He smiles. "Maybe you should study languages so you'll be prepared."

"That only works in Europe, but I think I'll study languages too, anyway. That's a grand idea."

"Better to be on the safe side."

We sit in silence for a few minutes. "When I was your age, I wanted to drive a truck along the Trans-Canada Highway. I imagined pulling that air horn whenever I wanted, making people jump with surprise." He grinned.

"I want to be a singer," I say. It just bursts out. I have never told anyone before. "Or a dancer," I add, an even deeper secret.

"I love to dance." He jumps to his feet and holds out his hand to me. "May I have this waltz?"

I take his warm hand and stand up, suddenly feeling like Cinderella at the ball, but without all the preparation of ball gowns and coaches and such.

"Just follow along." He starts to hum something vaguely familiar, and somehow we are dancing, his hand firmly on my back, swirling me slowly in a circle. He smells like cinnamon. This is much better than dancing with chairs.

When he stops, I am dizzy. I touch the wall with one hand while he bows with a flourish, thanks me for the dance, and goes back inside. I hear music almost at once. He, too, I suppose, is practising for the Recital.

I sit there alone for a long time, my eyes closed, basking in the warmth left by his presence. Even though I didn't guess what he wanted to hear, it didn't matter. I told him the truth in the end. And we danced! *He is amazing. I don't care if his mother did get a divorce!*

12. A KNOCK AT THE DOOR

SOMETIMES I GET TIRED of hearing my own voice inside my head, of talking to the imaginary Gemma, of dancing with chairs. So I listen at the tube in the wall near Baggy Bones's door and hear Mrs. O'Malley scolding Patricia because she hasn't done her homework or her husband because he hasn't done something he was supposed to. Patricia talks back and whines a lot, but he doesn't say much at all. Patricia practises a simple piece over and over with heavy hands on their small upright piano. No wonder she didn't enter the Kiwanis way back in February.

I don't get to see Janet much these days. She's studying for exams. I'm supposed to be studying, too. Mother found a retired high school teacher last week while waiting in line at the butcher's on Church Street, and he is coming in to give me some tests in a while. I've been through this before, and it's not fun. Learning should be fun, Mother says, and usually it is, except for arithmetic. The numbers confuse me. They make no sense. Everyone has tried to help, to show me how simple it is, but each one seems to make it just that much worse. Daddy is the worst of all because he does the sums and problems differently from Jonathan or Mother or the way it says in any of the math books Mother found in a second-hand store. *If train A leaves the station at nine a.m., travelling at sixty miles an hour....* I am on the train. I feel it sway. I see the telephone lines dip and rise outside the windows, the way they do when

I go down to New Brunswick to visit Grammy. But by this time I have lost track of how fast it's going or when it gets to the other station. In my experience, trains are never on time anyway, so what's the point? And what is a number anyway?

Today is Thursday, and I've just finished helping Mother hang up the laundry on the line on the porch. She doesn't have to go to her job anymore, which is good for me, but Mother is very angry at being let go. She says it's because Aunt Rose can't find her diploma in the family house in Saint John. Mother raged when she got the letter. She says her family's neglect is like a conspiracy against her. "They can't even save my important papers!" she shouts. "One box! That's all I asked them to do for me, and now they can't find it. Dorothy's old essays from high school are carefully preserved, oh yes! But important papers of mine? Of course not! How important could they be if they're mine? And the school doesn't exist anymore so I can't get a copy. Everything is against me!"

She went on and on for days about this "fatal blow," and I sat there and tried to be sympathetic without getting her angrier. When she's this way, I'm like the sounding board in our piano, vibrating with every cry and accusation. Her anger is like waves breaking over me, and even though I know I am not to blame, I feel like crying. Now she seems resigned, and I'm happy she's here with me, even if we're just doing the laundry.

Later on, we bake a cake, using margarine instead of butter and water instead of milk because we don't have either today. It won't matter because we're making chocolate sauce to go with it. It's a special treat for Jonathan, who's studying hard for his exams as well as doing his tutoring job and practising for the Recital. He spends most of his time in the library and misses all the commotion.

When Mother goes to visit Daddy in the hospital, I am left with a page of math problems to figure out. I almost fall asleep. When I look at the sheet of paper, the numbers dance around and make designs in front of me. I make a guess at the answers and then go downstairs with my skipping rope.

Patricia is spread out on a lawn chair. She is wearing yet another dress with ankle socks and Mary Janes, and a gold bracelet gleams on her arm. It looks too expensive to wear out in the garden. She has sunglasses on and is reading a magazine. I stand looking at her for a moment. She knows I'm there, but she doesn't glance up.

"Do you want to skip rope with me?" I ask, desperate for company.

She shakes her head.

Her mother comes out and beats a rug vigorously against the wall. I move out of the way of the clouds of dust. She looks at me, then away, without saying a word. I don't say anything either.

"Keep your sweater on," she says to Patricia, and then she goes inside again.

I go over and sit on the grass.

"You shouldn't sit on the grass. It's damp," she says, looking at me.

I shrug. "It seems perfectly fine to me."

"Shows what you know." She opens the magazine again.

Now that I'm closer, I can see the bracelet she's wearing more clearly. It's gold, and dangling from it is a golden charm of a swan with a diamond eye. I stare at it, not believing what I see.

"What are you staring at?" she asks.

A thief, I say inside my head. Out loud I say, "Your bracelet. Where did you get it?"

"Mom gave it to me." She looks at it with pleasure.

I don't say anything. Is her mother the thief? But perhaps the box I saw down in the cellar belongs to the O'Malleys after all. Have I made a mistake? The feeling remains: the certainty that this is not hers, would not be something chosen by her mother, does not fit somehow. But there's nothing I can say without giving myself away.

"So what's it like being adopted?" Patricia asks, putting aside the magazine.

"It's like being special," I say, feeling a slight jolt. I think of the story Mother often tells me about the day she first saw me and knew I was the one. The special one.

Patricia laughs. "Your real mom didn't want you. What's so special about that?"

"At least she didn't leave me alone to roll into scalding water. I'm not the one scarred for life by *my* mother!"

She stares at me open-mouthed, colour staining her round face like dye spreading through water. I can't believe I just said these things. I should say I'm sorry, but I can't bring myself to say anything. I sit very quiet and watch as she hauls herself to her feet, gathers her magazine and sunglasses and hat, and turns away. As she gets near the back door, she begins to run.

I want to cry. I know I've been cruel. I don't know why I hated her so much at that moment, why I wanted to slash at her so hard. But now I'm scared. Her mother will rush out and scream at me, maybe. She might force Rona Layne to make us move away from the Music House. After all, she made us pay key money just to see the rooms we rent, even though the place was already promised to us. She might do anything. Mother says she is completely unpredictable.

I grab my skipping rope and run upstairs and hide in the Everything Room until I hear Mother coming up the hall. It seems like hours, but I know it isn't.

"What are you doing in here?" she says, looking at me keenly. "You look a bit peaked. Have you been inside all this time?"

"No. I was skipping for a while."

Mother changes into her cotton skirt and blouse. "Why don't you collect the small bits of soap from around the basin, put them in the soap jar, and bring it into the kitchen?"

"Are we going to make oatmeal soap?"

"That's right. And you can make animal shapes out of some of them. How's that sound?"

"Good," I say. "Salubrious."

Mother laughs. "Not exactly," she says, and tells me to go look the word up in the dictionary.

I feel happy and safe with Mother, standing beside her in the tiny kitchen a few minutes later while she cooks the soap and some other things in our largest pot. She cools it and adds the oatmeal at the end, and then I get to squish it in my fingers and squeeze it into shapes. This is the best part. I make teddy bears and dogs and some turtles mostly, but the bears are the easiest. Mother says she'll take my best teddy bear to Daddy tomorrow so he can have his very own soap and think of me when he washes his hands. Oatmeal is good for the skin. I like that idea.

We pour the sticky mess out on cookie sheets and take them into the living room to work on. Mother just makes hers into boring bars, but I like to be more fanciful.

"Don't waste any," Mother warns. "Gather up the fragments so that nothing is lost. When we're finished, I'll check your homework."

I decide to take as much time as possible with my soap shaping and am busy doing a teddy when there's a knock at the door. Mother looks startled. We rarely have unexpected visitors. She dusts her hands off with the small towel we use when we make soap and goes to the door.

"Yes?" she says, looking at the man in the brown hat who stands there. He carries a briefcase, but a small one, not like the Fuller Brush man's.

"How do you do. My name is Miles Runyon, and I'm the truant officer for this area. May I come in?"

"I don't think that's necessary," Mother says.

"Please, ma'am. We've had a complaint. I need to come in and discuss it."

Silently, Mother opens the door wider, and the man comes in. I can feel the electricity in the air, sudden and fearful. *Truant officer. School. Complaint.* I think of Patricia's red face, the tears welling in her eyes, and I know it's all my fault. Mrs. O'Malley has sent the truant officer because I have done things I ought not to have done and there is no health in me. *Selah*.

13. SCHOOL

MOTHER SENDS ME TO THE KITCHEN to make tea. Waiting for the kettle to boil, I put some soda crackers on a plate and cut up the end of the cheddar cheese into tiny cubes. We don't have biscuits or cake or other tea things, so I hope this will do. One part of me feels like bursting into tears, but some other part is excited, waiting to see what will happen, how this will change my life. I vow to throw away the prism. It has brought bad luck, not good. It was stolen after all, like Patricia's bracelet. But perhaps nothing will change. Mother has a letter from my eye doctor, so that will probably work. Or maybe the rheumatic fever I had two years ago will help. But do I want to stay here in the Music House forever? I shiver, afraid of what might happen, but excited in spite of myself. Brian is right. It's hard knowing what you want.

I arrange the six crackers we have left on Grandmother's Wedgewood plate, put the cozy over the teapot, and carry it all into the living room. Mother is looking tense. The truant officer has his briefcase open on the floor at his feet, and I almost stumble over it as I put the heavy tray on the table with a thump. Mother whispers, "Sugar," and I get the sugar bowl and rush off to the kitchen to fill it. Our family doesn't use sugar, and I always forget it for company. We ran out of milk yesterday, so I put evaporated milk from the can in the little blue willow pitcher and hope he doesn't notice.

Back in the living room, the truant officer is showing Mother an official-looking letter. Mother has pulled out a few letters of her own from the worn brown folder tied with faded red ribbons where she stores important papers, and is now pushing them at him.

"Yes, yes, but things have changed since you arrived here four years ago, Mrs. Dudley-Morris," he says, reaching absently for his tea. "This new sight-saving class is a godsend to our handicapped children."

I can feel Mother recoil. It is only her reaction that makes me realize he is talking about me. I take a cup of tea and sip it slowly, nibbling on a soda biscuit. Mother's hand trembles slightly as she pours her own cup.

"I am sure it helps many poor children, but Vanessa is doing well at home with the teachers I have for her, and as I already told you, I am a trained teacher myself. I am perfectly willing to have the department send someone to test her at whatever level you think right for her age. I have no doubt she will excel."

I look from Mother to Mr. Runyon as a sudden bolt of anxiety shoots through me. I do not share Mother's faith in my ability to pass a test, especially in math. Should I say something before it is too late? I clear my throat. Mother shoots me a warning look. I finish the biscuit too quickly, and now I have nothing to do with my hands. I clasp them on my lap and pull my fingers anxiously.

"This isn't negotiable, I'm afraid," Mr. Runyon goes on. "We did send a letter a while ago, which you ignored."

"Because it was about handicapped children! My daughter is not handicapped. She merely has eye problems."

"And that is exactly what this class is geared for: children with eye problems."

"I will fight this," Mother says, her whole body shaking as she rises to her feet. "I will not send my daughter to that ... that..."

"I'm afraid you have no choice, Mrs. Dudley-Morris. Your doctor should have explained this to you." He pulls his briefcase onto his lap, pushes the last paper inside, clicks it shut with finality, and stands up.

Mother is already at the door, her face red and eyes flashing in anger. "You haven't heard the last of this," she says. "I'll fight this tooth and nail!"

Mr. Runyon makes a peculiar little bow. "Next Monday at Jesse Ketchum School, Mrs. Dudley-Morris. Vanessa's name is already entered in the class." He smiles and goes out the door.

"What a pompous, smug, unimaginative little toad," Mother rages, pacing the floor. "How could he sit there and say those things, dismiss all we've done, just like that? Lump you in with the halt and the lame!"

"But it's a sight-saving class," I say. "Why would they be halt and lame?"

"Just you wait. You'll see!"

Lame ducks, I think. I'll be a lame duck.

She is still raging when Jonathan comes home for lunch twenty minutes later, but by now she is on the telephone. I follow Jonathan out to the kitchen where he opens a can of tomato soup and begins to make sandwiches.

"When did he get here?" he asks.

I tell him.

Jonathan sighs. "I warned her she couldn't just ignore those letters."

"Maybe it won't be so bad," I say tentatively, watching his face for a reaction.

He doesn't say anything for a minute. Then he hands the plate of sandwiches to me. "Cut those in quarters," he says. He pours the soup into three bowls. "You know, even if it is hard at first—a new routine, all those new people—it's June. School will be over in less than a month." He smiles. "You can do a month, right?"

"Right," I say, and we go back to the living room for lunch.

I don't know whether it is Jonathan who convinced Mother to stop fighting—or maybe it was Daddy, or her friend Dr. Hazel, or maybe the government man on the telephone—but two days later she announces I am going to school on Monday. We go down to Northways and buy two new blouses and two pairs of navy-blue knee socks.

On Monday morning, she takes me to Jesse Ketchum School, checks with the office to make sure I am registered, and leaves me there in the huge schoolyard, which is teeming with noise and motion.

"When the bell rings," she says, just before she leaves, "line up with the other girls and march into school. Your room is on the second floor—number 214. Your teacher's name is Miss Beaumont. Be brave. Jonathan will pick you up at four. Don't leave the schoolyard, whatever you do!"

I nod and watch her go. I don't know how I feel. Excited, nervous, a little afraid. But isn't this what I really wanted all along? To go to school like Janet? Like everyone else?

I stand alone, watching the others mill around me. I don't know how to approach anyone, what to say, who might be in my class. No one else is wearing a tunic like I am. The children are all sizes; some of them are really, really big. Grade eights, I guess. They make a great deal of noise, yelling at each other. Some boys are fighting on the ground, screaming and kicking. One has white hair. A small woman in a black cardigan marches over to them, leans over, and says something I can't hear. Their fists slow down, and they slowly get to their feet, looking sheepish. They are taller than she is, but they hang their heads. She scowls and reaches to grab hold of the ear of the dark-haired boy and leads him inside, his head twisted at an awkward angle. The white-haired boy laughs, his hands on his hips. His teeth are big and widely spaced. He winks at me, then ambles over.

"You new?"

I nod.

"Sight-saving class?"

"How did you know?"

"Those coke-bottle glasses kind of give it away." He laughs again, but it's not a nasty laugh, so I guess he's all right. "I'm in that class, too. It's not so bad. I'm Cedric."

"I'm Vanessa." I look at him more closely. He's not wearing glasses, but his eyes are pink and seem to be moist and sore-looking. And he's big, much older than me. "You tore your shirt," I say, looking at the rent on his sleeve.

He shrugs. "That Eddie's a mean one," he says. "Watch out for him."

The ringing of a bell pierces the playground noise and confusion, and at once the groups break up and reform into lines—girls on one side, boys on the other. I hesitate and look at Cedric.

"You go there," he says, pointing. "Wanda! Hey, here's the new girl." He gives me a little push in the direction of a thin girl with glasses and a bad squint. She wears a tired dress that was once red plaid but now looks like the life has been washed out of it. She pulls me into line beside her but doesn't say a word. I shake her fingers off my sleeve and turn my back on her. There's something peculiar about her that unsettles me. Already I want to go home; I want to get away from all these strange noisy children, the huge concrete playground, and the vast school looming over us—all those windows watching, waiting. I haven't even done anything yet, and I am already tired. This isn't like the schools I've read about.

At some unseen signal, the front lines lurch forward and wind untidily into the building, followed by the next one, and the next. Then it is our turn. I shuffle along with the others in my group, following them up the stairs to the second floor and turning into the third door on our right. I stop, looking around. The room is large and bright, filled with desks in orderly rows. At the front are chalkboards coloured green instead of black. Miss Beaumont's name is written with yellow chalk in perfect round script on the board, with my name underneath it. I stare at it. The letters up there surprise me, make me see myself as a different person, a person who goes to school with all these other children, some of whom are really big. I glance at Cedric. He is sprawled at his desk, punching the boy in front of him on the shoulder.

"Settle down, children, settle down." Miss Beaumont is tall, with little curls arranged on top of her head in pale rows, pink skin showing in between. She stoops forward as she talks, as if she is trying to shrink. She holds her arms in front of her, hands curled, reminding me of the pictures of a kangaroo in my animal book at home. Her bright-blue eyes blink out at us steadily. "This is Vanessa," she goes on, coming towards me. I tense, but she doesn't touch me; she just smiles down in a fake sort of way and then motions to an empty desk in front of Wanda. "This will be your desk, dear," she says. "I gather you haven't been to school before, so you'll have a lot of catching up to do. This is the section for grades one to three."

"But I'm ten," I say. "Shouldn't I be in the grade five row?" Mother told me this earlier so I'm pretty sure I'm right, but Miss Beaumont stares at me.

"You have a lot of catching up to do," she repeats and points at the same empty desk.

I sit down and take out the books I find on the little shelf underneath. I laugh. Everything gets quiet.

"Something funny, dear?"

I stand up and clear my throat. "Someone left these *Dick and Jane* books here," I say, handing them to her. "Could I have the proper ones for me, if you please?"

"Those are yours, dear," she says, her voice syrupy. The class titters.

I wave the books at her. "I need real ones," I say, but I can tell these aren't the right words.

"*Dick and Jane* are real books, aren't they, class?"

"Yes, Miss Beaumont." A ragged chorus.

"But they're too easy." I learned to read when I was four. "I read books like *Treasure Island* now. And *Ivanhoe*," I add, in case she doesn't know *Treasure Island*.

Everyone is staring at me, their eyes—behind the glasses most of them wear—looking large and bug-like. But I can tell Miss Beaumont is getting cross. I hear Mother's voice in my head: *No one likes a showoff.* I sit down and put the *Dick and Jane* books away and fold my hands on the desk, waiting to see what will happen next.

Miss Beaumont gives me a final scowl and goes back to the front of the class. Behind me, Wanda is whispering. I turn around, and she hisses at me, her tongue darting in and out like a snake's. Fascinated, I stare at her.

"Eyes front, Vanessa," says Miss Beaumont.

I turn around but swing back again when the classroom door crashes open and hits the wall with a thud and a rattle of the window panes. The class snickers. Everyone cranes around, watching as the boy who was fighting with Cedric in the playground ambles in with a grin on his grimy face. He looks like a fox, his hair red brown, the same colour as his squinty half-moon eyes. "Sorry, Miss Beaumont," he sings out and hands her a pink note.

"Take your seat, Eddie," she says, barely glancing at the note.

Eddie saunters over to the next row and slides into the seat right beside mine. He makes a face, crossing his eyes and rolling his lips back as if they're made of rubber. I look away quickly. Eyes front. Hands folded on my lap.

Every row in the classroom seems to represent a grade or group of grades, and every row works on something different. The last two rows, grades seven and eight, start by reciting the multiplication tables out loud, and the mind-numbing chant lulls me almost to sleep. My group is supposed to be doing silent reading of the silly *Dick and Jane* book. In my head, I try to translate *Dick and Jane* into Latin to make it more interesting, but to do it properly I need paper and pencil, and when I start to write it down, Miss Beaumont notices, comes over at once, and takes it away from me.

"What's this gibberish?" she says, looking at *Dickus et Jana in schola sunt. Spotus ex cella est, tamen procul fenestra....* "And why are you doing cursive? Only printing is allowed to begin with."

I stare at her, outraged. Words desert me entirely.

"She don't know no better, Miss," Cedric says. "She ain't been to school before, like you said."

"Hasn't been to school before," Miss Beaumont says absently. She crumples my translation in one hand and points at the book. "Read," she says, and walks away. Maybe she doesn't know any Latin.

Beside me, Eddie suddenly slumps over his desk. One arm shoots out straight, and his head jerks to one side. His whole body starts to shake. The others jump to their feet and move the desks away from him briskly, leaving a circle of free space as he flops to the floor and begins to convulse. Miss Beaumont slips over beside him, kneels down, and forces a thick piece of rubber she takes from her pocket between his teeth. Shocked, I just sit and stare at his jerking body.

School isn't at all like I thought it would be. I hear Mother's voice declaiming about the halt and the lame after the truant officer left. How did she know?

14. THE VIPERS

"How was it?" Jonathan inspects me as if expecting to find a few fingers or toes missing.

I think of Eddie convulsing on the floor, of Cedric's weeping pink eyes, of Wanda's tongue flicking in and out. "Fine."

"See? I told you."

We walk briskly out the gate and turn down Bay Street. It's dusty and cars honk irritably from time to time. A bus wheezes past. We always walk because it's healthy, Mother says. Really, it's to save money.

"School isn't the way I thought it would be."

"You've read too many British boarding-school stories," he says, "and most of them are Victorian."

I nod, but I don't really think that's it. How can I explain my day? I tell him about *Dick and Jane*, and he roars with laughter. "Wait till Mother hears about that! She'll fix them."

I feel uneasy, wondering if I should have mentioned it, if I might appear not to be trying hard enough to fit in. "Maybe you shouldn't say anything," I say.

"We'll see."

Everyone always says that.

We walk for a while in silence. I am beginning to relax when I sense he is working himself up to say something. "I'm thinking about inviting some people over on Sunday," he says. "It'll be a sort of musical soirée."

"Like a recital, you mean?"

"No, ninny, this is just for fun. Everyone playing and singing together. Helen plays the flute, and Geoffrey sings and plays the oboe, and maybe we'll invite Brian from upstairs. He plays the recorder, I think. You can sing, too."

I am stunned. I wonder why he is talking about this with me. "What does Mother say?"

"I'll ask her at dinner."

We walk along some more without speaking. I'm trying to contain my excitement, to rein it in, in case nothing happens. "Would they come for dinner? Where will they all sit?"

Jonathan shakes his head. "Dinner's too complicated. An afternoon affair will work better. We could serve tea afterwards. Perhaps some fancy sandwiches." He looks worried.

"Who's Helen?" I say. I know Geoffrey. He sings in the choir at church.

Jonathan jerks at my hand and begins to walk faster. "Stop asking questions and pick up the pace. Do you have any homework?"

I shake my head. "I don't think they do homework in that place," I say.

"That figures."

Mother is already home, humming in the kitchen as she slices the potatoes. She gives me a small block of rat-trap cheese to grate and asks about school.

"We're doing multiplication tables," I say, watching her face.

"Don't you know those already?" she asks, stirring something on the stove.

"Not very well, and not the nine times table." I demonstrate how much I have learned, falling into the sing-song rhythms of the grade sevens and eights in the sight-saving class.

Mother smiles. "Well, I guess that's something," she says and turns off the stove.

At dinner, Mother talks about her visit to Dr. Hazel. I'm not sure why she goes there so much, or if Dr. H. is a friend more than a real doctor, as Daddy says. When Mother comes home after one of these visits, she seems more lively and full of smiles. Daddy says she's going through the Change, something women do when they're older. We're supposed to be understanding when she gets snappish, but I'm not sure how to be since I have no idea what's going on. "Just be sympathetic," Daddy says. "She's having a hard time of it." I guess he means about losing all our money and my bad eyes and him being so sick all the time. But that's been going on for a long time now.

Tonight she doesn't need any sympathy. She tells us that Dr. Hazel understands her and it's so good to know someone who empathizes with what she's going through. When Jonathan mentions the musical soirée, she agrees at once. "As long as it's over before dinnertime."

"So it's not really a soirée," I say. "If it's in the afternoon, I mean."

Jonathan glares at me. Mother just laughs.

That night I want to lie awake for a while, thinking about the musical soirée-in-the-afternoon this coming Sunday, but I am so tired and full of the sounds and pictures in my head I fall asleep right away. When I wake up next morning, I don't even remember any dreams.

At school, I'm learning a lot of things. Now I know about Double Dutch skipping and can do it pretty well too. I'm learning all the rhymes that go with it. That's just for girls, though. When I asked one of the boys to join us, everyone laughed at me. But we all play Red Rover, Red Rover. It's pretty rough, but I don't care. I just want to be on someone's team. Cedric always picks me. Wanda's mad at me about this, but I don't like her anyway so I don't care. I like Rosemary. She's tall and gentle and speaks slowly in a soft voice. She can't play Red Rover because she has a steel brace on one leg from polio. She plays ball games and can juggle much better than I can. She says she's been in this class ever since it started. I didn't ask her how long ago that was. It seemed rude. At recess, she often stays inside even though we're not supposed to, and sometimes I stay too and we play pickup sticks or jacks and she talks about the books she reads, like *Nancy Drew* and *Cherry Ames*. And the *Bobbsey Twins*. I've never heard of any of these, and when I mention them to Mother, she turns her nose up at them and says they aren't well written and not to bother. I don't tell Rosemary.

Friday at recess, Cedric comes over to where I'm standing under the big advertising billboard at the edge of the schoolyard, waiting my turn to climb up to the shelf high above our heads. I haven't managed to make it to the top yet, but I am determined this time. Eddie is already up there, daring me to follow, his taunts infuriating. Cedric is with some other boys and a few girls I don't know.

"Want to join our club?" he asks, squinting in the bright light.

"'Nessa's got a boyfriend," sings Eddie from above.

"Shut your trap!" shouts Cedric.

"Make me!"

"Not now!" One of the boys tugs at his sleeve.

I move away, following Cedric to the schoolyard gates. "Is it a reading club?" I ask, that being the only kind I know about.

The short girl with the messy lipstick laughs, throwing her head back. Her name's Maisie and she's chewing gum. "Yeah, he's such a reader, eh?"

"How would I know?" I answer, flushing.

"No, no, it's nothing like that." Cedric shoves his hands in his pockets and smiles. He's wearing blue jeans that are turned up above the ankle. His teeth are stained. "We do things, exciting things that take guts. You've got guts, but you have to go through an initiation before you can be an official member."

I throw back my shoulders and think of Churchill. I look around at all the others who are not being invited into Cedric's group. "What's the name of your club?"

"The Vipers," he says, his voice so low I'm not sure I heard. "So you want to join?"

I nod. The name alone sends a pleasant chill down my back.
"Meet us here at lunch, and I'll give you your assignment."
"I do it and then I'm in? Just like that?"
"Just like that," he says and claps me on the back. I stumble, but his hand on my shoulder steadies me.

The rest of the morning crawls by. I have discovered the boy in front of me can't tell time. I teach him. Miss Beaumont doesn't seem to care that I'm not doing my map colouring. Maybe she noticed I did it yesterday.

At last the lunch bell goes. Chairs scrape back, everyone grabs lunch bags and metal lunch boxes and runs for the door, Miss Beaumont's raised voice nothing but a high droning accompaniment. In the hall, Eddie catches my wrist and gives me a Chinese burn. This is the third time this week. I kick him in the shins and run down the stairs. I forgot my lunch bag and now will have to eat lunch at second recess.

Cedric and the others are waiting, and we all slouch off quickly down the street. We're heading for the Five and Ten, its red-and-gold sign and crowded bright windows a promise of the delights inside. Everyone slows down as we get near.

"What you do," Cedric says quietly, "is just walk around for a while innocently, then pocket at least two things and leave the store, but not right away. Got it?"

"You mean steal them?"

He laughs. "You can take it back after, if you like. It's just a test. Everyone's done it."

I'm hot in my tunic and Oxfords, feeling them all staring at me accusingly as if I'm letting them down, letting Cedric down, the one who said I was tough. I start into the store. "Aren't you coming?"

"We'll wait here," Maisie says.

That almost stops me, but I keep going. Inside, the store looks bigger than I remember. I'm so nervous that at first all I see is a blurred jumble of colour and noise. I have no idea what anything is. I stop and force myself to focus on a display.

I realize I'm staring at a counter full of boys' underwear and feel the colour flood my face. I move on quickly.

In the next aisle, a group of women crowd around the notions section. One of them is buying grosgrain ribbon to trim a hat. I stand there quietly, looking at the pin cushions and rolls of bias tape; cards full of straight pins, snaps, and hook and eyes; lengths of elastic, some black, some white. Thimbles fill one compartment, and I reach out and take one, test its weight in my hands, slip it on a finger. It's too big. About to put it back, I slip it into my pocket instead. Nothing happens. I move on, away from the chattering women who have taken up the attention of the shop girl behind the counter, and into the hardware section. I think of Daddy, who always spends time looking at things like this, rarely buying. This part of the store smells different. I catch the scent of rubber, of oilcloth for tables, the kind Mother never uses. She says it's low class, but I like the bright colours and the shiny surface. There aren't many people here, but there are no small things here either, nothing I can easily slip into my pocket, except screws and nuts and bolts, but I don't think Cedric would count those. I need one more thing.

I slip back to the aisle where the group of women from notions are now exclaiming over some fake flower arrangements. Mother doesn't think much of fake flowers. Dust catchers, she says. I slide over beside one fat woman and finger a small paper rose. After a moment, I tuck it into my pocket with the thimble.

At once, prickles of perspiration break out under my arms, between my shoulder blades. I am positive the saleslady has seen me. I force myself to look at a bunch of improbably purple flowers, their poisonous blossoms stiff and smelling of dye and glue. I turn away and walk to the door. It's hard not to hurry.

As soon as the door closes behind me, I break into a run. The Vipers all let out a whoop and follow me, laughing and shouting. I feel as if I can run forever, wild and free and full of energy, but I am soon out of breath and have to stop around the corner. I can't see the store from here.

"What'd you git? What'd you git?" Maisie asks, reaching out her grubby hand. "Lemme see!"

"Let her get her breath." Cedric stands, legs apart, pushing his white hair out of his eyes. Beside him, Leon, his black legs under his baggy shorts pale with dust, imitates his stance. Leon looks tough, but I'm not afraid of him.

My heart slows down and doubt pours through me like cold water. The wonderful feeling seeps out of me, and I feel myself deflate like a balloon leaking air. I wish I was somewhere else. But I'm here, and everyone has gathered around me in a circle. I pull out the thimble, the rose.

"Jesus, Mary, and Joseph," Maisie says, disgusted. "What the hell kind of trophy is that?"

I push my glasses up on my nose, shocked by her swearing into defending myself. "Nobody said anything about a trophy. Just take two things, you said. There they are. One. Two." I throw them on the ground in front of Cedric.

"Shit," says a skinny boy whose name I don't know.

I try not to react, though tears prick behind my eyes.

Cedric bends down and picks them up. He squints at the thimble, holding it close to his weepy eyes. He hands it back to me, reaches over and puts the rose into Maisie's wild hair.

"You're both right," he says. "We didn't say what sort of thing to take, like we should have."

He hasn't finished talking, but I turn away, walking fast back to school.

"Hey!" Cedric's voice follows me, but I keep going. I don't care about their silly club anyway. The thimble in my pocket weighs me down as if it's a large stone, and my stomach lurches and growls. I want my lunch but am afraid I might throw up if I eat it.

Back at school, I hide out with Rosemary in the book corner of the classroom.

"What's the matter?" she asks, leaning forward, pushing her long hair to one side.

"Nothing. Just a stomach ache." I think of the word *viper*, what it means, how the real ones look. I don't want to be one. My stomach churns some more. Perhaps this is what evil feels like: what happens to people like me who keep too many secrets, people who are cruel and mean like I was to Patricia. People who steal. I lean over and give Rosemary the thimble. I don't even look at Cedric when he comes in for class.

15. THE SOIRÉE-IN-THE-AFTERNOON

"WILL DADDY BE HOME IN TIME for the soirée?" I ask at dinner that night. I'm still calling it that even though it's in the afternoon. It sounds very *bon ton*.

Mother shakes her head. "Maybe next weekend," she says. "Definitely in time for the Recital." She smiles across the table at Jonathan. He frowns.

I bow my head. My pleasure in the musical event is clouded by prickly memories of the Five and Ten, the sweaty anxiety, the incredible burst of pure excitement. And the sight of my rose leaving Cedric's hand, snuggling down in Maisie's birdnest hair. The only good thing was that Miss Beaumont made her take it off in class. "Not appropriate," she said crisply. I smile, remembering.

"What are you grinning about?" Jonathan asks, irritably.

"Nothing."

"You're being awfully quiet, dear." Mother gives me one of her searching looks.

For a few seconds, I'm afraid she can see what I did at lunch hour, will see a wretched thief sitting here at the table, someone who stole the prism even before meeting Cedric, someone who does not deserve to be a Dudley-Morris. I freeze. But when she asks if I'd like the last pancake, I breathe easy again and say yes.

"Don't give her that—she'll get fat," Jonathan says. "She already has a pot."

"I do not!"

"We should call her Pot. Maybe Potty for short." He grins.

"That's enough," Mother says, handing me my plate.

I feel him watching as I pour molasses over my hotcake and stop before I really want to. I try to think of a name to call him back, but my mind stumbles. "Blooberpuss," I mutter. I pull in my stomach.

Saturday afternoon, Janet is full of her school-closing activities. We are up on Mount Olympus, hidden by the great maple tree. I glance at the coach house, wishing I could tell Janet about my adventure up there, an adventure that has robbed Mount Olympus of its thrill. I wish I could tell her how Brian was my knight in shining armour that day, but it's a secret. Being secret gives it a special power. This part of Brian is all mine. And it's a happy secret, too, not like the Vipers. That's something I don't want to tell anyone about. Something shameful. Dark. Like a stain.

Normally we play games, sending messages by Hermes— usually Janet, who leaps from one roof to the next to deliver the missive to Zeus. I play Zeus and hurl a lot of thunderbolts to show my displeasure at whatever she says. But today she's too full of her own reality.

As she talks, describing the real play her class is staging, I think of the pathetic pageant the sight-saving class is practising ... or trying to. Between Eddie convulsing and Wanda muttering and spitting, not to mention yesterday when poor Rosemary fell off the platform, her steel leg clattering and knocking over the stool where Wise Owl is supposed to sit, we aren't getting very far. I'm Owl. Luckily I wasn't perched on the stool at the time. I was still waiting for my cue, which Maisie usually forgets. Pathetic.

"So what's your class doing?" Janet finally asks, hugging her scraped knees up under her chin. "Is it a play?"

"More like a commercial," I say. "You know on the radio when they sing those silly songs about 'You'll wonder where the yellow went, when you brush your teeth with Pepsodent' and 'Lucky Strike means fine tobacco?'"

"That one's not a song," Janet says.

"Yes, well, that one's more like what we're doing. Kids hold up cream Bristol board and chant about how this colour is easier on the eyes, oh yes. Someone points to the green chalkboard and says more or less the same thing. I perch on a stool wearing owl ears and recite drivel about saving our sight. It's embarrassing."

Janet laughs. "That's just because you've got really young kids there, too," she says. "They probably couldn't do a real play."

"You can say that again."

"Ca-a-all fo-or Phillip Morr-aise!" Janet shouts, dragging out the syllables the way they do on the radio and jumping to her feet.

I jump up too. "Ninety-nine and forty-four, one hundred percent pure. It floats!"

And we run around the roof, shouting radio commercials at each other.

I have a hard time not talking about the Sunday soirée to Janet, but Mother said we can't invite her without including her mother and father, too, because they invited us to Janet's party. Things are getting complicated. We have lots of people coming already, and everyone has to eat and drink. And there aren't enough chairs. Somehow the group has grown to include Brian's mother, Mrs. Pierce, and our neighbour, Mrs. Smyth, who is lending Jonathan several music scores. When it's all over, I can tell Janet they were all Jonathan's friends, which is true anyway. Still, I wish she was coming to hear me sing.

Sunday morning I stay home from church to help Mother clean the living room and bake in our tiny oven. Jonathan promises to bring home all the information about the Corpus Christi procession next week. It seems my note to Daddy worked! We bring all the pillows across the hall and put the special fancy covers on them so they look like cushions. You can't tell they are mostly just basted together and pinned in place with safety pins. Mother bought a piece of upholstery material to use as a cover for the daybed, with actual piping on the corners so it looks like a couch with all the pillows arranged across the back. Now people can lounge like Julius Caesar, though the only one I can imagine actually doing this is Brian. I stop dusting and think about this for a moment: Brian stretched out full length on our daybed, propped up by pillows, his golden curls bright like a halo around his head. He hands me a bunch of grapes, except we don't have any. But nonetheless, it's fun thinking about it, imagining how it could be, with me kneeling beside the couch, my hair bound up with gold ribbons and jewels while Brian lolls in his purple toga, dropping luscious sweetmeats in my mouth. I pat the cushions tenderly in place and smile.

Baggy Bones seems to have sensed something is going on and is on patrol. At one point, I'm afraid Mother is going to invite her, too. She says she feels sorry for her, but I guess she remembers the scant larder and restrains herself. After all, if we're inviting Lame Ducks, I think Miss David should come first. She's way nicer. And she brings candy.

"Poor soul," Mother says. "She has a son, apparently. I don't think he ever visits. How sad to be so bereft."

"When you're old, I'll visit you every day," I say. "So will Jonathan," I add, watching her face. Her eyes smile when I mention his name.

She gathers me to her and hugs hard, the powdery lavender smell so familiar, so secure. "You know what they say: A daughter's a daughter all your life; a son's a son till he takes a wife."

"Don't worry, no one will ever marry Jonathan," I say into her softness. I hug her back really hard till she gasps and pulls away, breathless.

The rain starts just after lunch. I hope it's not an Omen. I stand at the window and watch the slate-grey lines of water slice through the pewter air, hitting the square panes on an angle, driven by the wind. I hope people won't decide to go home instead of coming here.

I've cleaned my Oxfords using Daddy's shoe polish and brushes. They don't look as good as when he does them, but Mother says they sparkle. I wish I had patent leather Mary Janes like Janey Drew. I'm wearing white knee socks and my good dress, and I have ribbons on my pigtails, the bows big and stiff with newness. I flash on the notions counter at the Five and Ten: ribbons spilling everywhere; taffeta and velvet and satin; plaid, polka dots, even stripes. My stomach twists, and I go over to the table and rearrange the flowers. Some are from our window boxes and some from the bushes hanging over the fence of Rona Layne's Secret Garden. Mother picked them, so I guess it's all right.

Seth strikes the half hour.

They're here.

There's a burst of chatter, and damp air enters our living room as Jonathan comes in with Geoffrey and the girl who must be Helen. She shakes back her dark page-boy hair and laughs, flashing big teeth. She's wearing shiny silver barrettes. I put the umbrella on the porch, taking some time to tie the handle to the door of the icebox in case the wind takes it away, sending it flying over the rooftops like Mary Poppins, only by itself without the nanny attached. When I come back in, Baggy Bones is in the hall, standing lopsided outside our living room door, looking as if she's about to fall over. She has forgotten to bring her brown paper bag, the usual excuse for the trip. When she sees me, she startles, doesn't even try to go to the garbage can. She turns around and scuttles back to her lair. Brian and his mother pass her on their way to our place, nodding politely.

"Hello, Vanessa," says Mrs. Pierce.

"How do you do?" I hold out my hand. My other hand goes to the door to open it, and for a moment I'm confused as to which I should do first. Then Mother opens the door from the other side, and suddenly everyone is talking at once. The living room looks different with all these people in it, feels different. Light bounces off things oddly. Sounds wash over me like waves, not making much sense. Mrs. Smyth is here, too. She must have come while I was on the porch tethering the umbrella. She holds one hand clasped in the other. A lace hankie is stuffed inside the cuff of her mauve silk blouse. The few times I've seen her, she's been wearing the same one. It has tiny pleats down the front. I wonder if she'll tell her husband in his urn about our party when she goes home.

Mother worked out the seating plan with us in advance, and I watch as Mother and Jonathan subtly manoeuvre people into their appointed places. I drop to my spot on the piano bench, waiting for the music part to start. Helen talks a lot, her voice strong like her teeth. She's wearing a white blouse and pearls, navy-blue pleated skirt, grown-up nylons, and red shoes. I love red shoes. I asked for some for my birthday. Mother said I'm too young, but I think they just cost too much.

Geoffrey is talking to Helen a lot. I'm used to seeing him in his choir outfit, so he looks really different in a regular shirt and grey pants. I imagine a whiff of incense still attached to his clothes, trapped under his robes all morning, now finally able to escape.

Brian is talking to Mother, but I can't really follow what they're saying from here. He's holding his recorder in his hands. It's a long one, and his fingers run restlessly up and down the length of the instrument. It must be a tenor. Helen has two recorders in an open case on the daybed beside her: a soprano and a treble. Jonathan has told me all about recorders, but I've never seen them except in the museum. Brian's face, his golden hair, his hands, the way he holds himself—it all looks like a painting. Helen spoils the picture.

I can feel that Mother is nervous. Her fingers move too, but not obviously like Brian's. Probably no one else would notice, but I know where to look, what to look for. This electric energy sparks directly from her to me, running along my nerves, winding me tight as a spring. I glance at Jonathan and wonder if he feels it, too. My throat begins to close under the pressure, and I make quick clearing noises. The talk suddenly dies down. Everyone looks at me.

"Are you all right, dear?" Mother says.

I feel my face hot with embarrassment. I nod mutely.

"Clearing the frogs out of your throat?" Geoffrey asks. "I often do that before I sing." He demonstrates. Everyone laughs.

I wish they would all just ignore me. I wish Daddy were here. Things are usually less tense when he's around.

"Did you find out about Corpus Christi?" I ask Jonathan. I meant to whisper, but my words drop into a pocket of silence, and everyone looks at me again.

"There's a rehearsal on Thursday," Jonathan says in his normal voice, "but I can't take you because I'm tutoring that night."

I look at Mother, moistening my dry lips with the tip of my tongue. I see myself in a long white veil, processing solemnly through the incense over the deep-red carpet of the church, turning every few steps to cast rose petals in front of the monstrance, while the choir's chant soars around me.

Mother sighs. "I guess it won't work out this time, dear. I have to go to a late appointment that day. It's the only time Dr. Hazel can fit me in." She reaches over and pats my knee.

It's over.

I blink, praying I can keep the tears away.

"I wish I could help," Geoffrey says. "I have to be there anyway. Choir practice night, you know. But I wouldn't have time to come all the way over here after school and then get back to the church on time."

"I can take her." Brian says.

Mrs. Pierce looks startled, and for a moment I think she may protest. She opens and closes her mouth like a fish running out of air.

Mother looks at Brian uncertainly. "Are you sure, dear? It's not an imposition?"

"Not at all. It'll be fun, won't it, Vanessa?"

I nod mutely, afraid to speak, afraid that words from me will shatter the dream.

"Besides," he goes on, "I've always wanted to meet Dr. Willan."

"I'll introduce you," Geoffrey says.

"It's settled then." Mother pats my knee again. "Thank you very much." She turns to Helen. "And what are your plans after school is over, dear? Are you pursuing your music studies, too?"

"I've been accepted at the university here, but also at a music school in the States. I haven't made up my mind, yet."

"I don't know why everyone thinks they have to go to the States," Mrs. Pierce exclaims, startling everyone. "We have perfectly good teachers here, don't we, Mrs. Smyth?"

"Unless it's the Juilliard," Mrs. Smyth murmurs. "She'd be a fool to turn them down."

"Oh, the holy Juilliard is not to be gainsaid!"

Brian has turned a bright pink. He shifts farther away from his mother and looks at Geoffrey, then down at the floor.

"It's not the Juilliard," Helen says. She looks as if she's going to cry.

"Well then, why bother?" Mrs. Pierce says. "You're going to get married anyway, aren't you?"

"I haven't decided about that either," Helen says, looking right at Mrs. Pierce, her eyes very bright and fierce. I sit up straighter.

Mother laughs, but it comes out too high. "In any case, dear, I'm sure there's a brilliant future ahead of you." She stands up. "Just look at all the young talent in this room! All these bright futures! Why not give us a sample now? Then we'll have tea."

Jonathan jumps to his feet and dumps me unceremoniously off the piano bench. The music he wants is all arranged inside. I know because I watched him do it. But now it looks as if he's just taking out some pieces and choosing them on the spur of the moment. I wonder why he's doing this, but I don't say anything. The others are gathering around, holding recorders, talking about the pieces. I hope they don't do *Orpheus*. It's too hard for me, holding those long notes. My voice begins to warble and shake. To my relief, the *Orpheus* isn't in the chosen group. Instead, Geoffrey starts off with another Handel, "Oh, Had I Jubal's Lyre," singing in a light sprightly tenor, even though I think it should be alto. Everyone has changed the key to accommodate him, I guess. I'm lost, but luckily I don't have to sing this one.

Just as I'm beginning to think Jonathan has forgotten his promise, he chooses "Barbara Allen." As I sing, the recorders twist around the tune, echoing my notes, enhancing the melody. I feel so full of the music I think I may burst. When we go on to "Sheep May Safely Graze," Geoffrey joins me. I've never sung with anyone else before, except in church, of course, and for a moment I hear my voice waver, then gain strength, rising to shine beside his. I can see it sliding up, up in the air, a bright wire of sound, taut and true. It is wonderful. I have never been so happy. I close my eyes to concentrate, to revel in the pure sounds of the music.

When I finish and open my eyes, Mother and Mrs. Smyth clap. My face is hot with excitement. Mrs. Pierce is looking at one of our books, flipping through the pages as if bored. She closes it with a little snap and gives Brian a tight smile. "Don't you think the recorder is a little childish for someone at your level, dear?" she says, dusting her hands together as if our books are dirty.

"It's hard to play the recorder well," Geoffrey says. "You handle it beautifully," he adds, turning towards Brian.

"You must all be thirsty after that wonderful performance," says Mother, standing up, her hands clasped in front of her. "Let's have tea." She throws her bright smile at everyone in the room.

Once they all leave, Mother plunks down on the wing chair in an exaggerated collapse, arms and legs splayed like a rag doll. She reaches out and catches me and pulls me in with her.

"You sang like an angel," she says, giving me a quick squeeze.

Jonathan makes a sputtering noise. "You must mean Lucifer, the fallen angel."

"Don't be rude," I say.

Jonathan begins to collect the cups and saucers, serviettes, and plates, piling them carefully on our one tray.

Mother stands up and gathers the crumbs from the table in her hand, throwing them into the fireplace. "I think that went quite well, don't you?" she asks, seriously this time.

Jonathan agrees.

"And Helen is a lovely girl, very talented. It's clear she's smitten with you, dear."

Jonathan blushes. "She's just a friend," he says.

"She talked most to Geoffrey," I point out.

"Ah, but she had eyes only for Jonathan," Mother says, and winks.

"Really, Mother!" Jonathan says, shaking his head. His face is flushed.

Mother begins fluffing the pillows. "It did go well," she says thoughtfully, almost to herself. "In spite of that rather inebriated Mrs. Pierce. Now there's a woman whom life has disappointed."

"How do you know?" I ask.

Mother pauses, a pillow clasped to her chest. "Oh, I know," she says, staring out the window. "I'm an expert."

16. CORPUS CHRISTI

AT SCHOOL, I TRY TO STAY AWAY from Cedric, but it's hard. I try to stay with Rosemary inside during recess, and mostly it seems to work. Rosemary tells me Cedric is my guardian, but I don't believe it. On the other hand, Eddie doesn't try to give me Chinese burns anymore, so maybe she's right. It makes me nervous, the way Cedric watches me, turns up beside me, brings me little presents. I wonder if the lollipops are stolen, if the red ribbons he gives me on Wednesday were taken from the Five and Ten. I give them to Rosemary, who is really pleased. But Cedric isn't.

"That's supposed to be *your* present," he says to me at lunch, standing on the bottom step in front of the school, towering over me. He has the ribbons in his hands.

I don't say anything. I'm holding the hem of my tunic between two fingers, twitching the cloth back and forth. My mouth is dry. I look around but don't see anyone I know except Maisie, standing with one hand on her hip, watching. She's not a friend.

I look back at Cedric, still at a loss for words.

"You think I stole it, don'cha?" he says, leaning closer. "You'd be wrong. I bought them ribbons with the money from my paper route. So there. What do ya say now?"

"I can't accept gifts," I say. "My mother doesn't allow me to take gifts from people she doesn't know." I watch Cedric's face relax, the redness fade from his cheeks.

"Well, that's just plain dumb, ain't it?" he says, but he's

smiling, the gap between his front teeth plainly visible.

"Told you she's stupid," Maisie says.

"Lay off." Cedric scowls at her. She steps back. "So, guess I better get to know your Mum, eh?"

I have a brief vision of Cedric meeting Mother, the strained exchange of pleasantries, Mother's gentle laugher afterwards. I clear my throat. "Usually these days, it's my big brother who picks me up," I say.

He shrugs and walks away.

"How come you always wear the same stupid dress?" Maisie asks, pushing up her glasses.

"It's a tunic," I say.

"You're a dummy." Maisie flounces away.

I watch her follow Cedric across the playground. I wish I'd stayed inside. I look up and see One-Eyed Jack, the janitor, standing on a ladder just outside the main doors, fiddling with the bracket that holds the doors open. He really has two eyes, but one is all puckered shut into a permanent squint. I want to go back inside, to join Rosemary in the safety of our classroom, but I can't risk walking past One-Eyed Jack. He makes me feel as if ants are crawling over my skin. He sees me looking at him and stops fiddling to stare.

I whirl around and start running. "Cedric! Wait up!"

When I reach his side, he thrusts the ribbons into my hands.

"Thank you," I say. I glance over my shoulder. One-Eyed Jack is gone.

I have a clean blouse on under my school tunic as I get on the Carlton streetcar ahead of Brian. We sit in the front and I can see Eaton's College store. The big Recital will be held in the auditorium upstairs.

"Are you excited about the Recital?" I ask as we rumble past.

Brian has been quiet all the way down Jarvis Street. All my efforts to make conversation the way Mother does haven't worked out very well. This doesn't seem to be working out either.

Brian sighs and looks at me sadly. "It'll be a memorable night, all right," he says and turns away to look out the window again.

I give up my efforts at social discourse. After all, I can't be expected to do all the work. For a moment, I wonder what he would say if I told him about One-Eyed Jack and Cedric and the Vipers. Probably that the man was just an unfortunate with a limp and a terrible squint, maybe even a brave serviceman; in short, he would explain it all away just as Mother would. What can I say anyway? There is no way I can talk about the Vipers or what I did to Patricia. Our dance on the roof seems like a long time ago, that day when I told him the truth, what I really wanted.

By now we're getting into Little Italy. There is a sign in Italian outside our church, telling everyone that it's not a Roman Catholic church. I guess it's hard to tell because we do so much of the service in Latin and use all that incense. When I told Janet about the sign, she was impressed. I think she sees me differently now—not just any old Protestant, but almost like her, only without the Pope.

Brian seems to cheer up as we walk along Manning Avenue to Euclid. The houses on either side are painted bright improbable colours, giving an exotic air to the place. I know the front gardens later on will be alive with vegetables: vines climbing up thin sticks and creeping over wire arbours, tomatoes peering out from their wrappings of twine, and dusty grapes hanging in luscious bunches. But for now, all this is only a possibility.

Inside, the memory of incense hangs heavy in the air. Music floats from above as the choir tries out a new anthem. I smile, knowing Helen and Geoffrey are up there. Brian seems to have woken up.

"Do you know where to go?" he asks.

I nod and start towards the front of the church, heading for St. Joseph's altar, which is beside the door leading downstairs to the rabbit warren of bilious green rooms where the Sunday school meets.

"When you're finished, wait here by the front door," he calls after me. Now he sounds like Jonathan, and not my friend who shares secrets.

I nod and keep going. Downstairs, a group of girls about my age is clustered around Sister Mary Michael while she hands out white veils and demonstrates how to put them on. It does not take a giant brain to figure this out, but Sister goes on and on about it. I tie mine under my braids, choose an empty basket from the pile on the table, and wait, trying to be patient.

After little Susie Willis goes to the bathroom one more time, we troop noisily up the stairs. Sister puts a finger to her lips before she opens the door to the church and looks at us sternly. Susie catches her breath.

We file into the church. Everything is quiet. We hear a man's voice from somewhere, but I can't make out what he's saying. Then laughter. Sister rings a small bell she produces from her habit, and we fall into a line behind her, two by two, holding our baskets in our left hands as instructed. We genuflect at the main altar, then turn around, facing the back of the church and the gallery where the main choir is. I don't see Brian anywhere. I thought he would be watching.

I wasn't in the procession last year, but I begged to take part this time, and Mother finally gave in after Daddy intervened. She found a white dress on sale at Northways. She says she can dye it later for summer. I know she probably gave up another piece of silverware to do this, and I feel a rush of love so strong I touch the pew next to me to keep my balance. Because of her, I will be part of this ancient rite. On Sunday, the thurifer will swing the censer, the incense will rise in clouds, the choir will sway along the main aisle in their lace and long gowns. One of them looks just like a Velázquez painting, with his black hair longer than most, intense dark eyes, and pale skin. The white ruff suits him. I always watch him, especially during the processional.

Sister rings the bell again, longer this time. It must have been a signal to Dr. Willan because the organ peals forth and we start to walk: five steps, pause, turn, bend the knee, cast petals, turn, walk. I can hear the girl behind me counting under her breath. Then Susie loses her balance and falls over, spoiling the effect. I have the urge to kick her but restrain myself as the line lurches to a halt. Sister helps her up, pats her on the head, and we start off again.

On Sunday, everyone will wear white dresses. I see it now: the church full, the monstrance moving along behind us, carried by altar boys in lace-trimmed robes. It isn't kept in the church for some complicated reason involving the Archbishop, so we only see it once a year, but I remember it from last time, so it's easy to imagine now. I hear the murmurs from the congregation, the shuffling of feet, the clearing of throats. I see the smiling faces as we move past: girls in white dresses and veils, rose petals cast on the red runner, incense rising like prayers, and the music lifting us all.

Someone ahead of me trips and everyone stumbles to a halt, spoiling the moment once more. Sister doesn't say a thing. I feel like crying.

The choir has finished practising by the time we get our veils off and return the baskets and get our final instructions from Sister Mary Michael. A couple of the girls live nearby, but most are being met by mothers or other family members.

I rush upstairs to the front door and look around, but there's no sign of Brian. I wait and wait. It's shadowy in the vestibule, and odd noises creak around me in the emptiness. The choir has gone. I look inside the church. The dim, vaulted space feels empty without the music, the people, the voices. Flickering candles throw a blood-red glow at the feet of the Virgin. I turn away.

Maybe everyone left by another door. Maybe Brian did, too, forgetting all about me. What will I do if he has? How can I get home?

"Sorry," he says, suddenly appearing. His face is pink and his eyes seem darker than usual. "I met a friend. We lost track of time."

I am shivering with nerves. I was right. He did forget. I decide to punish him by not talking, but he doesn't seem to notice. He chatters on about the music and Dr. Willan and what a great choir it is. He walks to the streetcar very fast, and by the time we get on, I am out of breath.

He turns to me suddenly and smiles. He looks so happy. I guess the music has cheered him up a lot. "I saw you in the procession," he says. "You didn't make any mistakes."

"I didn't see you."

"I was in the gallery." He smiles, tells me about some of the singers, mentions Helen.

"And Geoffrey," I say. I know it's rude to interrupt, but Helen is Jonathan's friend. "He was there, too?"

"Yes," says Brian, turning away. "I suppose he was."

It is getting dark by the time we get home. Brian walks me to our living room door, bows with a flourish, and kisses my hand. I lose the power of speech. For an instant I feel the closeness of our rooftop dance, but then from the other side of the door, Mother's voice rises suddenly to a pitch I recognize. Something bad has happened. I swallow, and Brian raises his eyebrows and backs away with a conspiratorial grin. I open the door.

"As if a child of mine would stoop to anything so low!" Mother shouts. "My Vanessa is not a thief!"

Mrs. O'Malley is standing in front of the fireplace, hands on hips, glaring at Mother. "My Patty does not lie!"

Mother sees me and scoops me up, holding me close to her side. I can feel her trembling. I have one hand in my tunic pocket, holding the prism I stole. How do they know? I feel as if I'm about to throw up.

"Miss Layne won't stand for thieves in the house," Mrs. O'Malley goes on.

"Vanessa, this woman says you stole a gold bracelet and gave it to Patricia," Mother says. Her face is red, her eyes glassy with tension.

"Why would I give Patricia anything?" I say, more honestly than is polite, I realize too late.

Mother smiles and nods her head emphatically at Mrs. O.

"We'll just see how long you last once Miss Layne hears about this!"

"Between the two of us, I'm sure Rona Layne will know whom to believe," Mother says to her departing back.

Mrs. O'Malley slams the door, and we hear her stomping down the hall.

"God the Father, God the Son, and God the Holy Ghost!" Mother shouts to the ceiling. "How long, O Lord? When will it end?" She paces back and forth between the dinner table and the window, wringing her hands. "No matter what I do, how hard I try...."

She falters and collapses onto the floor as if in slow motion. I watch, but she doesn't move.

"Mummy?" I feel the tears running down my cheeks. "I'm sorry, Mummy." I crawl across the rug and touch her face.

Please, God, make her be all right! I'll throw away the prism! I'll never steal anything again!

Her eyes flicker open. "I'm fine," she whispers.

"Shall I make tea?" I'm whispering too.

"Just let me lie here for a moment."

Her fur coat has been thrown on the daybed. I snuggle close to her, reach up, and pull it over us. "We can play Park Bench," I whisper. It's a game Mother and I play when she wants a nap. We lie down on the bed, covered by the fur coat, and pretend we are on a park bench and it is our cozy place, and Mother starts the story about how we can make a home anywhere, even here. Usually we both fall asleep before she can finish the story. This time I don't think I will.

I try not to cry so she won't feel my sobs. The prism is digging into me as I lie on my side, but I don't care. I think about Patricia, getting back at me for being mean to her. I deserve the pain.

17. ONE-EYED JACK

MOTHER IS WRITING POETRY AGAIN. She writes the stanzas by hand and then types them up on our big Remington typewriter that sits grandly on the oak desk by the window. Then she pastes them in her notebook with the swallows on the front. She calls it her *Testament to Loneliness*, and all the poems are sad. Sometimes she says she has nothing. Other times, she hugs me hard and says she has everything, as long as she has me and Jonathan. We are her life.

Even though Mother assures me she knows there is nothing to the accusation, she is worried. We all know deep down that Mrs. O'Malley called the truant officer. "That woman is capable of anything!" Mother says. "She is like a snake, coiled, ready to strike."

I think of a cobra, of vipers, of Cedric, of the real stealing I have done, and wonder at this accusation which is false. She could have picked something real.

Mother is especially worried that this O'Malley threat is erupting just before the big Recital. She wants things to be calm for my brother, for herself, for Rona Layne. This will be a big event for Jonathan—a turning point, says Mother—his first appearance on the professional stage. The Kiwanis doesn't count because it's for amateurs, although he won a few years ago, before that boy Glenn Gould came along. That year, Jonathan came second. Anyway, this time his big competition is Brian, and Jonathan thinks they have quite different styles, so he isn't really worried. Except now he's worried about all this. Mother is going to talk to Mrs. Dunn this morning about Mrs. O'Malley's threat to get us thrown out. She's gathering support for us in the Music House, Jonathan says, just in case. He's the only one who asks me if I did it, if I stole the bracelet. When I deny this with righteous indignation, he gives me a long look. "What did you do to Patricia?" he says.

I stare at him. "Nothing." I can hear the quaver in my own voice.

"Something, I think." He gives me another long look. "She can't play your kind of games, can she?"

I shake my head. His grey eyes bore into me.

"She was mean first," I burst out. "Anyway, I already apologized."

He nods his head. "Patricia is sly," he says. "Keep away from her."

He doesn't have to tell me that. I don't want to ever see her again. I tell Jonathan, and he smiles.

At school, I find it hard to let myself drift the way I usually do, now that I've given up trying to learn anything here. I keep seeing Mother lying on the floor last night; seeing Mrs. O'Malley's angry, hate-filled face shouting; hearing Mother shouting back. She never shouts like that. At least, only when she's alone, and she shouts at God now and then. The Music House, our refuge, seems to have turned against us. We've only been here six months. If we have to move again, it won't be the piano's fault this time. It'll be mine.

Eddie is having a fit again. I'm sort of used to it now, but it's still upsetting, seeing him like that, helpless and jerking. I try not to watch, but I can't help it. Something draws us all, keeps us all watching, as Miss Beaumont kneels and stuffs the rubber thing between his teeth, motions us all back in a circle around him. How he must hate knowing we all stare at him when he's like this. Maybe he doesn't know. Maybe he doesn't remember. He never, ever, acknowledges it. Afterwards, he seems to be sleepy, and Miss Beaumont helps him off to the nurse's office for a nap.

When Eddie comes back again and begins shooting spitballs at Maisie, I put up my hand to go to the washroom. Usually Miss Beaumont sends two girls at once, but today she seems rattled and I slip out alone. The girls' washroom on our floor is closed with some plumbing problem, and the closest one is downstairs. I begin to skip down the steps, feeling suddenly free and light. Then I see One-Eyed Jack standing at the bottom with his mop and pail, swabbing the floor. He grins at me. I stop skipping and wonder if I can turn around and go back to class, but I can't. That would be rude. Besides, although I didn't really have to go when I started, I do now. I move over to the opposite side of the steps and keep going down. Slowly.

"Hiya," he says, grinning.

I nod my head.

"So, girly, how come you always wear the same thing every day, eh?"

I clear my throat. "It's my school clothes."

"Whatcha got on underneath? School panties?"

I stare at him. Should I answer? Maybe he won't know about bloomers. Maybe he'll want to see them.

"Cat got your tongue?"

I'm at the bottom now and start to run. I'm so rattled I almost miss the door to the girls' washroom.

I hear him behind me—"Gotta gotta go, gotta gotta, go"—like a steam engine puffing out of the station. "Hey, I'm only funnin' with ya, kid!"

I slam through the swinging door and rush into one of the stalls. I stay there for a long time. By the time I come out and peer around the door into the hall, he is gone. I run to the stairs but slip on the damp floor, hitting my knee on the sharp corner of the step. The pain is sudden, but not too bad really. I think briefly of just walking out the door, of walking down Bay Street, along Bloor, down Jarvis to home. But then I remember Mother will be there, writing her sad poems. I don't want to make her sadder. So instead, I go to my classroom and let Miss Beaumont tend to my wound in her exaggerated way, talking to me as if I'm a three-year-old idiot, dabbing at my knee with such a light touch I grit my teeth in irritation. I think of one of Mother's favourite quotes, the poem about the king who has a maxim true and wise engraved on his ring: *Solemn words, and these are they: Even this shall pass away.*

"Does it hurt a whole lot, dear?" Miss Beaumont asks in her whispery voice. She ties a length of bandage around my leg which makes it look as if I've been in major accident.

I pause for a moment, thinking of all the different ways I could answer. In the end, I smile bravely and say, "No, Miss Beaumont. Thank you for fixing it up."

When Jonathan comes to walk me home, he asks about the bandage. By now it looks much more dramatic, with a little blood leaking through.

"God almighty, don't let Mother see that," he says. "As soon as we get home, go into the washroom, clean it up, and put a Band-Aid on it. Even if you need more than one, it'll look better than that thing."

"I just fell on the stairs," I say.

My knee's a bit sore, but he doesn't walk any slower, and I know he's thinking about everything that's going on.

"Are you worried about the Recital?"

"Oh, for God's sake, don't you start," he says.

I wince and pull my hand away from his. Everybody seems to be swearing a lot lately. It makes me nervous.

He stops, sighs, looks down at me. "I'm sorry. Now give me your hand."

He doesn't sound really sorry, but at least he has performed the appropriate ritual so I have no excuse to pull away. I give him my hand, and we walk the rest of the way without a word. By the time we get home, my knee hurts more and I'm feeling as upset as Jonathan appears.

We meet Mother coming out of Mrs. Smyth's door. She's smiling her company smile, but that soon disappears once we're in our own living room.

"I wish your father was here," she says, beginning to pace. "I think everything will be all right, though. Mrs. Dunn seems to think Mrs. O. is all bluster. A bully. She gets her jollies this way. Mrs. Tyndall thinks so, too. She suspects Mrs. O. is jealous of Vanessa. She wanted her daughter to take lessons from Rona Layne, apparently, and she wouldn't take her on, and yet she suggested taking on Vanessa here. I guess this got back to her somehow." Mother smiles down at me and notices the bandage. "What happened to you?" She kneels down and begins to untie the dirty cloth, her hands sure and caring.

"I fell in the basement when One-Eyed Jack was … I mean…"

"Who?"

"I mean the janitor. I don't know his real name."

"What did he do?"

I see alarm in her eyes and feel panic. I look at Jonathan for help, but he just shrugs and walks away. "He was there when I went down to the basement," I say.

"The *basement*? Alone?" Mother jumps up at once, forgetting my knee and begins to pace again. "That's the last straw!" she says, throwing out her arms, as if to a big crowd of people. "You are not going back to that place again."

"Mother, there's only one more week of school left anyway," Jonathan says.

But it's too late. Mother has made up her mind. She takes me to our little washroom, cleans my knee, puts on a large Band-Aid, talking all the time, her gestures quick and jerky.

"Maybe the truant officer will come again," I say when she pauses for breath.

"Let him," Mother says, getting to her feet. "We'll fight them to the highest court in the land!"

"We'll fight them on the beaches," I murmur.

"Exactly," Mother says, and kisses my forehead. "That man

should not be around children." She goes right to the telephone and calls the school.

Now that I no longer have to go, I wonder if I will miss the sight-saving class: the lulling chant of multiplication tables, the sad spectacle of Eddie's fits, the dangerous attentions of Cedric, the quiet times with Rosemary. I wonder who will say Wise Owl's lines in the Closing Day Pageant, who will jump in to help Maisie when she forgets her cue. And I know that in a strange way I will miss it all.

On Saturday, I tell Mother I want to keep away from Patricia and she takes me over to Janet's house for the morning. While we're there, she talks to Mrs. Sullivan, tells her about the threat. Janet and I linger in the hall, listening.

"That woman!" exclaims Mrs. Sullivan. "She goes to our church, but she might as well be a heathen. No wonder that poor Patricia doesn't know right from wrong. You know how she got to go home to Ireland last year, don't you?" Mother must have shaken her head, so Mrs. S. goes on. "She flung herself in front of a truck, then sued the company for damages and used that money for her trip. She bragged about it to the ladies of the altar guild."

"Really!" Mother says.

"I wouldn't worry about her threats. What power does she have? She's only the caretaker for the building—the janitor, that's all."

I wonder if Mother will tell Mrs. Sullivan how she thinks Rona Layne is lazy for having a housekeeper for their own apartment, or that she lets that housekeeper, whose name is Miss Jones, make all the important decisions that have nothing to do with music. I wonder if she'll tell her Mrs. O'Malley and Miss Jones are friends, that I've often seen them chatting together in the hall, Mrs. O. leaning on her mop handle, the housekeeper leaning against the wall, arms crossed. I wonder if Mrs. Sullivan will have to go to confession because she was relaying gossip about someone else in her church. We have confession in our church too, but I don't think we're very serious about it. Nobody in our family ever goes. Perhaps I should.

"Come on," Janet whispers, punching my arm lightly. She turns and runs up the stairs and along the hall to her room. I run after her. The room is like a narrow slice cut out of the second floor, with a long narrow window, but it's hers and it has a bed, a dresser, and even a wardrobe which has been shoved into the tight space at the foot of the bed.

"She goes to my school, you know," Janet says, closing the door.

"Patricia?" I wonder why this hasn't come up before.

"She's in my sister Magda's class. Nobody likes her much." Janet combs her hair with her fingers for a moment. "So tell me what Brian's been doing lately," she says, and then she smiles and licks her lips.

I'd been hoarding the story of the Corpus Christi rehearsal and him keeping me waiting, but now it seems flat. I have to make an effort to tell her.

"Maybe he wasn't visiting Helen," she says, sitting on the edge of the bed, leaning forward a little. She has her concentrated look—a slight frown between her eyes—and she's fiddling with a ringlet.

I sit cross-legged at the foot of her bed, leaning against the footboard. "The only other person he knows in the choir is Geoffrey," I say.

"As far as you know," she says and tilts her head as she looks at me. "Maybe there's a Mystery Woman."

"I don't care," I say. "It was rude to keep me waiting so long." But I suddenly remember the shadowy figures in the Secret Garden that night I couldn't sleep and looked over the railing in the middle of the moonlit night.

"I wouldn't mind how long he kept me waiting." Janet hugs herself. "He's so dreamy."

Dreamy. I think of the tapestry in our long hall, the boy who looks so much like Brian, the way he gazes out at me every day as I pass by. The way his face changes, his hand beckons. The gleam of gold in his hair.

"That Patricia is full of lies, you know," Janet says. She flops back down on the bed. Above her head, a large palm frond is stuck behind the picture of Jesus with his bloody heart open in his chest, shooting out rays. I look away.

"Mother will fix it," I say. "She would never believe I could steal." Except it's not *all* lies. I can't tell her that.

18. THROUGH THE GLASS DOOR

THE WORLD IS CRYING OUTSIDE our living room, trailing tears of rain on the windowpanes. Fog shifts and rolls, hiding the city outside, reminding me of mornings in our family's small summer house on the Bay of Fundy, with the tide coming in hard against the pebbled beach, noisy and invisible in the swirling greyness. But there you can be pretty sure the fog will burn off soon and the sun will burst through, dancing on the waves and making the sea sparkle. Here, one never knows.

The dampness has set off the pains in my legs. This morning I woke up early to the familiar ache, as if someone were twisting the bones inside my leg, like wringing out a bed sheet, making the hurt throb and shimmer up and down, bringing tears to my eyes. I crawl out of bed, trying not to disturb Mother, and wrap my leg in the ghastly afghan Aunt Dottie sent us for Christmas. She uses whatever wool she has lying around, leftovers from various other projects, and sometimes the results are jarring. But it's warm, which is the point after all, and the heat helps my pain almost as much as if Mother was rubbing it, as she used to do so often. But I am too old for that, I tell myself. She needs her sleep. I will do it myself.

By two o'clock in the afternoon, the fog still lingers but my pains are gone. Mother is visiting Daddy at Sunnybrook Hospital. She doesn't want to worry him about Mrs. O., but she says she has to talk to someone. It seems to me she has already talked to just about everyone we know, even Dr. Hazel whom she called on the telephone, but I guess she means someone who really counts in our world. I'm supposed to stay put and memorize "Kubla Khan." I know most of it already. I wonder if a pleasure dome would be anything like our living room, only with lots of colourful cushions and a rounded ceiling. And more stately, of course.

I am feeling all rainy inside, full of dark clouds. Mother will be gone a long time. Jonathan is out with some people he met when he was tutoring. They are taking him to lunch. No one ever takes me to lunch. Well, to be honest, Mother and I go to the Honey Dew on Bloor Street sometimes for a special treat, and Jonathan sometimes takes me to Eaton's Annex down in the basement and we get a chocolate malted ice cream cone—but that's not lunch. Janet loves chocolate malted cones too, and we promise each other that someday we'll go together, just the two of us, and buy one each, and I won't have to share it with anyone.

I wander around the living room, study the tiles around the fireplace, dust a few books. I find the tin box with a Dickensian scene painted on the cover, which used to have English toffee in it once. Now it holds a collection of keys, some for locks we have, others for doors long forgotten. The keys fascinate me, and I make up stories as to what they might someday open—some wonderful door I might find and because we had this box of magic keys, I could get inside. And I remember the frosted glass door on the landing of the Music House, the door we pass almost every day. The door I have tried over and over, but it's never open.

Holding the box, I walk down the long hall to the bathroom. There is no sound from Baggy Bones's room today. Her door is tightly shut. This makes the hall feel different. I pause and look at the page boy in the tapestry. He seems to look older, his golden hair dimmed by dust. It must be raining everywhere.

There is no one in sight, no creak of footsteps on the stairs, no murmur of Mrs. Smyth talking to her dead husband on her mantel. I keep going, turn right at the steps, run down to the landing. I know the lock is not a Yale lock. A few days ago, I saw Mrs. O'Malley cleaning around the frosted glass door, and she used a long thin key to unlock it. She carried the key on a big ring in her apron pocket. Daddy calls this kind a skeleton key. There are four in our box. The third one works. My hand trembles as I open the glass door and slide into a world of fog.

Everything is grey; a warm cocoon-like grey that slips around me, hiding details. I close the door behind me and put the box down on the floor. The greyness stretches out in front of me; it's dense on one side, but on the other it dissolves enough for me to see the pillars of the porch and the ghostly shapes of the overgrown bushes in the Secret Garden. Of course, I know the rest of it must be down there, but looming like this through the fog, the nebulous shapes make me shiver, even though the air is warm.

The porch floor is painted what Daddy calls battleship grey, another reason everything seems all of a piece here today. As I stand there, a breeze comes up and the mist twirls away in long wisps. It's like the second act of *Giselle*, I think, when the Willis swoop out of the gloom and whisk about. I start to dance, hearing the music in my head. The long balcony runs the length of Rona Layne's studio, and there's lots of room to leap and twirl and run, pretending I'm *en pointe*. The tall white pillars between the railings make it like the space on stage, open on one side, where the adoring audience watches my every move. "Wonderful," one says. "She's like Pavlova come back to life," another whispers.

At last I pause to catch my breath, give several ballerina curtsies to the invisible audience. And then I notice the floor. It's obvious that it's been a long time since anyone was actually out here, and the swoops and slides of my feet are clearly imprinted there for anyone to see. *God the Father*. I guess Mrs. O. only cleans the windows when she comes here. When I look more closely, I can see that there are scuff marks all along that section by the windowsills. I shrug. There's nothing I can do about it now.

I lean on the wide balcony railing, not minding the dampness. I can see parts of the Secret Garden emerging from its shroud as the fog begins to lift. And then I hear a series of clicks, a creak of hinges, and voices floating into the garden air. Rona Layne and her housekeeper, opening the French doors of her studio, talking together.

"...And all I ever wanted was to be shut of the man." That was Libby Jones, her housekeeper.

"Well, you've got your wish. Few people can say that. Would you open the other doors, it's stuffy in here."

More creaking. Mr. O'Malley really should oil those hinges, but he has a bad back. He tells everyone he meets about it. I lean over, trying to see them, but they still are too far inside. Then I see the top of Rona Layne's head as she moves onto the red brick path. You can always tell it's her because she has her hair done up a lot like Queen Victoria. Janet says it's like cootie garages on both sides of her head. I pull back quickly in case she looks up.

"I always meant to hire a gardener and bring this place back to its former glory," she says, gesturing vaguely with one hand.

"You've got enough on your plate."

Rona Layne sighs. "These tenants are more trouble than I expected," she says. "And now this child—what's her name?"

"Vanessa."

"Yes, Jonathan's sister. I can't really believe this nonsense. Stealing things in the basement? Surely not."

"The O'Malley girl may not be the brightest, but her mother swears she doesn't lie."

"What mother wouldn't swear that?" says Rona.

"Here, let me wipe that off for you."

I hear the scrape of iron furniture against the brick. She must be pulling one of the chairs into position, sitting down, making herself more comfortable. There is the clink of china.

Perhaps they are drinking tea? I know there's a table out there; it's iron, like the chairs.

"Vanessa seems very bright, but I sometimes wonder if she actually is, or if she simply knows how to use the little facility she has."

"She's just a parrot. And she's sneaky," Miss Jones says. "That's what I think."

There's a pause. I hold my breath, afraid to breathe in case I start to cry.

Then Miss Jones says, "It's not easy finding a couple with the skills to look after a big place like this."

"Well, I don't really care who is to blame, Libby. Just make it go away, will you?"

"I don't know, Rona. This could get ugly. There's a lot of stuff stored in that basement, including some of your things."

Miss Layne sighs again. "Maybe we should bring our things upstairs and store them at the end of the studio. There's lots of room."

"That's hardly the point. You don't want tenants up in arms, and you don't want to lose the O'Malleys."

"I hardly think the old dears who live here are going to man the barricades and start tossing paving stones at us, Libby." She laughs. "And I like Mrs. Dudley-Morris. I'd hate to have to throw her out."

"I don't know. O'Malley is really exercised about all this."

"Oh, for heaven's sake, Libby, just take care of it! I've got this recital coming up next week and I need all my energy for my charges. Angelica has the flu and may not be able to perform, and Freddy Ascher is getting cold feet. He's never too stable at the best of times, you know. Not to mention Brian Pierce, who seems strangely jumpy lately. He was the last one I was worried about. I'd swear he has more experience than he's letting on, but I can't prove it. Strange how he just appeared like that, with no real history. Not that it matters in the end, I suppose. He's good, and they pay their bills."

"They'll all come through for you," Miss Jones says. "They always do."

"It'll all come out in the wash, as my mother used to say," says Miss Layne. Her voice is getting fainter, so I gather she's moving back inside.

The sun is breaking through the last remnants of the fog now, sparkling on the damp foliage. I feel hollow inside. My leg is beginning to ache again. I shouldn't have stayed out here so long. I wish I had never heard this conversation.

I creep back to the glass door, open it, and take care to lock it again behind me. Downstairs, I hear Miss Layne's voice in the hall, and I begin to run. By the time I get back, with the living room door safely closed, I am in tears. I wrap myself in the afghan and curl up in a ball on the floor in the corner behind the wing chair.

A knock on the door a few minutes later throws me into a panic. Did they find out I was up on the balcony? Do they think I was spying? I rub my eyes and crawl out of the afghan and walk to the door. Brian stands there, smiling, his golden hair damp and the smell of the outdoors on his clothes.

"Is Jonathan home?"

I shake my head. "He's out."

"He promised he'd lend me some sheet music. Would it be all right if I came in to look for it?"

"I suppose so." I back away, letting him into the room, letting his presence soak up all the air.

He comes in and closes the door behind him.

I gasp, my mouth opening in a large O like a fish out of water.

"What's the matter?" He looks at me searchingly.

"Nothing." But the word comes out too explosive. No one would believe that.

"I thought we were friends," he says, sitting down on the piano bench. "You help me; I help you."

"My leg hurts," I say, hoping that will be enough. I can't confess what I just overheard. Even a parrot wouldn't do that.

"Well, that's easy to fix. Did you take any Aspirin?"

When I shake my head, he gets up and shoves his hand into his pants pocket. Bringing out a small metal box, he pinches it on one side and it pops open, revealing some pills. "I have lots of headaches," he says. "I always carry these with me. Here. Take two."

I take the pills and go across the hall for a glass of water. Sometimes Mother gives me pills, but mostly she just rubs my legs. When I get back, Brian is checking through the music in the piano bench.

He shows me a Bach concerto. "I'll bring it back in a few days. Are you okay? You want me to stay for a while?"

I do, but I'm afraid he'd want to talk, and then what would I say? I might blurt out something, expose myself as a sly parrot accused of thievery. My eyes fill with tears.

"I have a sister, you know," he says, looking over my shoulder towards the window. "She's a little older than you, though. Should be just finishing her first year of high school."

"Where is she?"

"Back home in Vancouver. Tell you what. I'll just give this concerto a try here on your piano and then I'll go. Would that be all right?"

"Oh yes." I drop down on the daybed and wrap my leg in the afghan again while he sits on the piano bench and opens the music.

I've heard Jonathan play this piece many times, but when Brian touches the keys with his long slender fingers, it's completely different in some way I can't figure out. I know it's to do with touch and phrasing, but I can't analyze it. As I listen, I forget my throbbing leg, the nasty words I just heard, the fear of possible eviction. I watch the gentle sway of his body, the sunlight on his hair. The pure sound of joy coming from the piano wraps around me. My friend. I feel warm all over.

When he stops playing, all I can say is thank you. Then I feel like an idiot.

He turns around and smiles, and then he thanks me for listening. I expect him to get up now and go, but he leans forward, his elbows on his knees, and looks at the floor between his feet. His hair hangs over his forehead, longer than anyone else I know.

"I have a favour to ask," he says, looking up briefly. He flashes that sunbeam smile again. "Can you keep a secret?"

"Oh yes." I nod vigorously but instantly wonder how I can keep from telling Janet. Things become more real when I talk to her. And she always asks about Brian.

"I'd like you to take a message to someone in your church choir on Sunday. You'll be doing your procession thing then, right?"

I nod, watching him closely.

"Just give it to Helen."

"You want me to take a secret message to Helen?" This makes me feel uncomfortable.

"It's not *for* her," he says, with a quick laugh. "It's for someone else."

"Why don't you send it to that person directly?" I ask.

"It's ... complicated. Helen knows who to give it to."

"Oh," I say, understanding blossoming. "You can count on me." I want to say *friends forever*, the way Janet and I do, but it seems childish with him so I just nod my head decisively.

"I knew I could," he says, and he hands me a small envelope he had in his pants pocket. It's warm from his body. Once he has gone, I slide it into my prayer book.

Janet is right! There is a Mystery Woman!

19. THE MISSIVE

DADDY IS COMING HOME for the Recital. Isn't that grand? Mother says he should be here in a few days, so that's worth celebrating. Also, Mother has a new job looking after a pair of troublesome twins while their mother is in the hospital having another baby. It's only for a week, but that's worth celebrating, too. I have had to swear to behave and stay inside our rooms unless I'm at Janet's, and then Jonathan has to take me there and bring me back. But Daddy will be home by then anyway, so he will probably release me from this cruel and unusual punishment.

The other news is that Mother has heard of an eye doctor who has all sorts of new theories about bad eyes like mine. Mother heard about him from the twins' parents. Their friends' son went to him and now leads a normal life, going to a regular school and even playing sports. Not that I want to do anything sporty. Mother, her face bright with hope, keeps looking at me across the dinner table as she tells us, willing me to explode with happiness. The thing is, I don't want to get too excited. I've been to so many eye doctors, each one gloomier than the last, it seems. But hope springs eternal, as they say, so I admit to a bubble of excitement about it, in spite of past experience. His name is Dr. Bachmann, and we have an appointment on Tuesday morning at the Medical Arts Building on the corner of St. George and Bloor. The really good thing about all this is that it takes everyone's mind off the recent unpleasantness over Patricia's lie. I squirm whenever I think of it. Sometimes I wish I could shut off my brain so no more thoughts would come in, especially about Patricia, but on the other hand, that would be like sitting in a white room all day long with no music. Or like being in a padded cell like that old childhood friend of Mother's who went mad when Mother got married and moved out west. I wonder if Janet would go mad if I got married and moved away. Or perhaps it would be the other way around.

"Is a padded cell really padded?" I ask Jonathan.

He looks at me crossly. "If you keep up the way you're going lately, you'll probably find out," he says, and goes back to packing up his school books to sell to next year's students.

The thing I'm most excited about is the Secret Missive. I wonder what Jonathan would think if he knew about that! I keep looking at my prayer book, feeling the small envelope slipping between the tissue-paper-thin gilt pages. It's a struggle not to keep picking it up and checking to make sure it's safe, but that would be really obvious. One must be careful when keeping secrets. Loyalty is of prime importance. *Semper fidelis.*

On Sunday morning Mother and Jonathan talk a blue streak on the way to church. He's explaining something about the music that Dr. Willan has chosen, or maybe written, for the Corpus Christi mass. Usually I listen to this sort of thing, but today my mind is busy with my own plans: how to find Helen, how to pass along the Missive, how to let her know who it's from and what she's to do with it. There are many questions it occurs to me that I should have asked Brian, but it's too late now. We are already on the Wellesley Street bus, rocking along Harbord Street to Manning Avenue.

By this time, no doubt, Brian will be at St. Paul's on Bloor Street with his mother. It's quite Low Church so no incense or candles and such, but Dr. Peaker is the organist there and Jonathan has taken some organ lessons from him, so

I've met him, too. He seems a jolly sort of man, who makes jokes and draws picture on a chalkboard down in the choir room where we met him. Mother and I go to that church to hear the free concerts he gives sometimes—Bach, Buxtehude, Handel. It's always thrilling when he makes the organ thunder and shudder, sigh and whisper and sing high up in the Gothic ceiling above our heads. It's a grand Casavant organ, Jonathan says, and when Dr. Peaker lets it loose, it's as if the whole huge building shakes, the sound reverberating inside my body, filling me up, becoming a part of me. One time Jonathan took me to visit the organ way up in the choir, with its four different keyboards and numberless stops and all the long wooden peddles you have to dance on to get the effects that make the mighty organ thunder from different parts of the church. When this happens, sometimes the sound from the back takes a few seconds to catch up, and so there's this wonderful delayed sound, a kind of musical echo in the vast space that makes me shiver. Our church organ is smaller, but so is the building, so maybe we would really shake apart if we had such a mighty instrument, and anyway, Jonathan says it's a fine organ already.

I am wearing my new white dress, with pie-shaped pieces so the skirt swirls out like a dancer's. The sash is eyelet embroidery, like Mother's good summer dress. It fits me perfectly, and I love it. I feel as special as Mother says I am as we walk along Manning Avenue.

It's hot and all the gardens are bursting with bloom. Some of them are shimmering with new greenery, as vines begin their journey up the string ladders and long narrow sticks laid out for them to climb. There are grape arbours with runner beans and peas and tiny tomato plants crowded together in the small garden plots outside each colourful house. And the flowers! I don't even know half their names! Maybe these flower people are counting on the generosity of their neighbours to give them the overflow when their vegetables finally mature.

As it turns out, when we reach the church, it is easy to find Helen. I have to go downstairs to get ready for the procession, and for a moment I am afraid Mother will insist on coming to help. Jonathan saves me. Sometimes he comes in handy and does the right thing, usually without meaning to. Of course, the choir is down there getting their robes on. When they are ready, we are all in the same room, milling about, waiting to line up. I see the man who looks like a happy frog, the tall one Mother calls the Streak of Misery, the man who looks like a Velázquez painting, the large lady with the feet like sausages. I can feel my heart beating hard up in my throat as I spot Helen and go up to her. I smile and almost stumble, and say "hell" under my breath.

"Oh dear," Helen says, trying not to laugh.

I feel my face burning as I thrust the envelope into her hand. "It's from Brian," I whisper.

"What?" She looks down at the note in confusion. "For me?"

"No!" I clear my throat. The man next to us is staring at me. "He said you'd know who to give it to," I whisper.

"Oh. Right." She shoves it carelessly in a pocket under her robe. Then she laughs. "It's like a Sabatini novel, isn't it?"

"A potboiler," I say, and she looks confused again. "An adventure," I amend, and this time she nods and moves away to take her place.

Sister Mary Michael is flitting about like a friendly crow, trying to get us into an orderly line, adjusting veils, straightening hair ribbons. Another sister is handing out the baskets, this time with real rose petals in them, saying the same thing to each one of us: "Waste not, want not." It seems an odd thing to say, and one girl obviously thinks so too.

"But we *are* wasting them," she says. "We're throwing them on the floor!"

"Yes, but to the greater glory of God," Sister says firmly. "And don't spill any. They need to last for the whole procession."

"A handful is a handful," another girl says.

"A *small* handful," Sister says, and peers at the girl fiercely. This time the whole experience is different. The church is full, and by the time we get there, incense is rising like prayers. Music wraps around me, and several times I almost lose count and turn too soon, but catch myself at the last moment. I try not to look at people as I walk by because it's too distracting, but I know everyone is watching us. Afterwards, I don't really remember the service.

Helen comes in while I'm taking off my veil downstairs and slips another note into my hand.

"The answer," she says. "Isn't this fun?"

I just stand there. It never occurred to me there would be an answer. Brian should have said something, should have warned me.

Helen winks and then goes over to talk to Jonathan who is standing by the door, waiting for me. I swallow. Did he see the note pass from her hand to mine? Will he demand to see it? Or maybe give it to Mother? I turn my back on him and stuff the note into the sash of my new dress.

On the way home on the street car, Mother sits with one arm around me, talking about the service, her chat with Father Wayne, the other people she talked to afterwards. Nobody mentions the note. All the way home, I can feel it bent in two, pressing against my waist. My secret. Something I share only with Brian. The next problem will be figuring out how to get it to him.

I hang my new dress up carefully in our cardboard wardrobe. It's really for moving, but it works well for us all the time, shoved back in a corner of our Everything Room. My old dress from last year used to have bright flowers on a mauve background, but it's been more of a washed-out pale blue ever since Mother made a mistake and added Javex to the wrong washtub. But it has pockets, which give me a place to keep the Missive in case I come across Brian somewhere, and it's cool enough for a hot day, so I put it on. I take off my new hair ribbons and roll them up to keep them un-creased, the way Mother showed me.

We have Kraft Dinner for lunch. *Make a meal for four in nine minutes*, it says on the box, and it's true. Mother has the new spoon this time. It's her turn, and she'll use it for the pudding she has made. Caramel sponge.

"When this job with the twins is over, we'll have enough to complete one more silver setting," she says.

Regaining what was lost is very important to Mother. If I lost something important, I would want to replace it too. At the moment, I can't think of anything I would miss that much except books, like the *Princess and the Goblin* and *Lorna Doone* and *Robinson Crusoe*. And my family. And Janet. I would certainly not want to replace Patricia in my life if she were lost. The thought of her makes me almost lose my appetite for the pudding, but one sniff of that warm sweet caramel is enough to make my mouth water. I would not want to give this up!

I help Mother wash and dry the dishes and put everything away because Jonathan is practising for the Recital. He is playing the same thing that Brian played the other day, but it sounds so different. Brian's touch was delicate and sprightly. Jonathan's is powerful and making a statement, demanding to be listened to. It's about interpretation, Rona Layne said before one of her in-studio recitals last year. I don't really understand this, and maybe this is why I will never be a great artist even if we could afford lessons for me.

He stops playing and jumps up, searching through the piano bench for something. "Did you take anything from here?" he asks, looking at me accusingly.

"No! Why would—?" I stop, remembering Brian borrowing the music. "Oh," I say, trying to sound calm and collected, "Brian borrowed the Bach thing. Is that the one?"

"Brian? When?"

"I'll go get it," I say quickly.

"Hurry up. I need it." He sits down again and starts playing some exercises.

I glance at Mother, who's sitting by the window darning socks. She doesn't seem to be paying any attention, but she nods at me so I know it's all right.

I almost run down the hall to the stairs, relieved to have a reason to see Brian, not even looking at the tapestry. The stairs creak as I go up. When I emerge on the third floor, I am out of breath from the excitement.

There is laughter coming from behind the door to number 8. When I knock, it stops abruptly. Brian opens the door, and for a moment I can't say anything. He has no shirt on and his pale skin gleams with a sheen of sweat. His legs look longer in the baggy shorts that look more like underwear. Golden hair gleams against his skin.

"Yes?" he says, as if he doesn't recognize me.

My tongue feels like flannel. I pull out the note and hand it to him. "And besides," I say, as if continuing a conversation, "Jonathan needs the music back."

"Oh," he says too loud, and shoves the note into his waistband. "The music. Sure." He turns to go to the window where the harpsichord is, and I see Mrs. Pierce reclining on an unmade bed in a satin and lace negligee the colour of ripe peaches, the kind I have seen in magazines like *Vogue*. I can almost see through the plunging lace inserts; I probably could if I had better eyesight. She's smoking, her lipstick leaving a bright red stain around the end, and she stares at me as if she hates me.

"What is it, darling?" she says, watching Brian rifling through the music on the windowsill. "What does she want?"

"Just some music I borrowed. Won't take a minute."

"Well, get rid of her." She takes a drink from a glass half filled with amber liquid. She is whining like a spoiled child. Mother would not approve.

Brian grabs the music and comes back to the door. Thrusts it at me. "Thanks," he says softly, and I'm not sure if he's thanking me for the Missive or the music. Or both.

He closes the door suddenly and I hear Mrs. Pierce cry out, "Finally!" and then a thread of laughter spirals up and stops abruptly. All is quiet.

"What took you so long?" Jonathan says when I get back.

"He had to look for it." I hand over the music. And I see Brian's bare back gleaming in the heat and Mrs. Pierce's white limbs tangled in the crumpled sheets.

20. ANGELICA

JONATHAN IS PRACTICING MOST OF THE DAY now that his school exams are over and the Recital is so close. We all have tickets to go and sit in the special section for family. Janet and her mother are coming too, so I'll have company. Isn't that grand? I haven't seen Janet often lately because of her exams and all the end of school events she seems to be involved in.

"When I went to school during the First World War, we actually did real school work right up to the very last day," Mother says. "Then in the afternoon, we sang songs and the certificates were awarded."

"What kind of songs did you sing?"

Mother looks out the window, furrowing her brow. "All I can recall are the patriotic songs we sang every morning at the top of our voices. We'd sing songs like 'The Maple Leaf Forever' and 'Rule Britannia' and that hymn 'Jerusalem' that goes: '*And did those feet, in ancient times,*' etcetera. Do you know that one?"

"I always cry when I hear it."

"Everybody does. They used to sing it in London at the Prom concerts during the Blitz in the Second War, Aunt Dottie says. The bombs could fall, but everyone went to the Proms."

"And they'd sleep in the tube stations afterwards," I finished.

"Well, not every time." She laughed and went on with her dusting.

I think about Mother being at school during the Great War, wearing a middy blouse and a huge ribbon in her long blonde hair. She was singing fierce, heart-swelling songs while Daddy slogged through the trenches, giving orders that meant that men would die. He rarely talks about it now, but he has mentioned the screaming hell of noise during the bombardments; people going mad from the relentless pounding noise; and the mud, thick and oozing and everywhere. I imagine it like molasses on a cool day, only smelly, like old socks. Most of the time, he refuses to talk about it at all, but I sometimes play with the little shovel he still has, snapped into its khaki case in pieces you have to fit together. I imagine I can still see bits of Flanders Fields mud on it. But it doesn't smell anymore.

Aunt Dottie's vivid stories of the Second World War on the home front in London seem almost jolly in comparison, although I'm sure it was no fun at the time either. She was in charge of the children's wing of a big London hospital, so she was so busy she didn't have time to be scared, I guess. We have a picture of her in our photo album, standing outside the hospital in her crisp uniform and the regulation navy blue cape with the red lining, not that you can tell it's red. She showed it to me one time. She keeps it in a trunk, just the way Daddy keeps his 48th Highlanders kilt packed away. Sometimes Mother says we should make a blanket out of it—there is so much warm material there—but she's afraid Daddy would be upset, not that he'd say anything. I think it's a bad idea because just seeing it there, even as a blanket, might make him remember things he's trying to forget.

It's not easy to forget, I'm finding. Much as I'd like to consign Patricia, her mother, and my life of crime to oblivion, they are always there in my head, lurking, like a bad smell in a closed room. Mother is so busy washing and ironing her things, getting ready for the twins job, and talking about the new doctor, it seems she has completely forgotten the O'Malley threat, but I know she has not. Sometimes I catch her unawares, looking off into space, and her face has lost all vitality. Lines of anxiety you'd never notice before are plain, etched deep from years of worry: the outward and visible signs of a troubled life. And then she sees me watching and she smiles and it all melts away, or goes into the poetry she writes in her *Testament to Loneliness*.

One of the things that's making her secretly sad, I think, is Miss David. She came by last night to get Mother to help with some more papers, and when Mother found out what they were, I saw her face suddenly fall. For an instant, I thought she might cry, but the pleased expression was back almost instantly. I looked over at Jonathan, and I'm sure he saw it too.

Miss David and her brother have bought a house.

Afterwards, Jonathan called it "Lame Duck Lodge" and laughed about it, describing what it probably looks like, how dilapidated and tiny it must be, with mice gnawing on the floorboards and ivy pulling down the chimney. But Mother shushed him and said maybe Daddy could help them fix it up. If anyone knows how to fix up a house, it's Daddy, who actually built an entire house once many years ago next door to my grandfather's—this was where he met Mother. He tells the story about going to Mother's front door to ask for water, and Mother opening the door and him thinking, I'm going to marry that girl. I just wish he was fixing up a house for Mother right now. I'm pretty sure she wrote a sad poem later about Miss David's news.

I am going to wear my new Corpus Christi dress to the Recital. Mother has dyed it a pale blue, and I have new hair ribbons to match. I wish I could wear my hair loose, but it looks horrible like that, I have to admit. Janet's mother offered to show us how to put my hair up in rags so I could have ringlets like Janet, but when she tried, she said my hair is too short to make it work, so pigtails it is.

Yesterday, Mother went down the hall and tried to talk to Rona Layne for the third time, but Miss Jones said she was not to be disturbed. We know Miss Layne has sick headaches, and before a big recital is probably a good time to get one. But Mother says it's also a good excuse. It's a great ploy, she says, since one would seem excessively boorish to keep on insisting on an audience after being told this. So she'll wait until after the Recital and then try again. Having decided this, she seems to have put the problem aside.

I don't tell her that I saw Miss Jones and Mrs. O'Malley chatting together on the landing earlier that day when I went to check for the early mail—Mrs. O.'s hands clasped on her mop handle, Miss Jones leaning one shoulder against the wall. They were talking in low voices and laughing. When they saw me coming, they stopped talking and watched me as I went by. In embarrassment, my face flushed hot and sweat sprang out under my armpits. I couldn't get by them fast enough, but once downstairs, I was almost shaking. I am sure they were talking about us. I could feel it.

We are in the Everything Room when Mother asks me to go downstairs to check for the second mail. She's expecting letters from Grandmother and Uncle Charlie, the artist, who's not really a relative but an old friend of Mother's. As I pass the tapestry, a current of air causes it to ripple. The trees move. I pause as goosebumps break out on my arms. For a moment, the air quivers, and I see Mrs. Pierce lolling in her tangled sheets, Brian's sweaty body, Patricia's fat face red with anger. I hear Baggy Bones's voice droning on behind her half-open door. "Now Marie, I don't badmouth anyone, you know that, but there's something off about that Mrs. Pierce, if that's really her name."

Something snaps back into place, and I hurry downstairs. There's someone standing by the griffin's bench. One of Rona Layne's Special People, no doubt. She has long hair running down her back like dark water. She turns around and smiles at me. Her face is pale, black bangs low over her black brows, dimples on her cheeks. Her red silky dress hangs just below the knees and looks very grown up, but her mischievous expression is that of a child. As I get closer, I see she's wearing a gold bracelet with what looks like a swan charm hanging from it.

"Where did you get that bracelet?" The moment the words are out, I am appalled at my bad manners.

"You like it?"

"It's lovely," I say. "Unique."

She smiles and holds out her wrist so I can see it better.

I touch the gold charm. I know how it feels on her wrist, the weight of it, the way the swan moves as her wrist turns.

"My father gave it to me just before my first big recital," she goes on. "I thought I'd lost it a few weeks ago, but someone just returned it." She holds her arm out straight in front of her and looks at the bracelet lovingly. "I'm waiting for him to pick me up. He'll be so pleased."

"Did Mrs. O'Malley find it?"

She shrugged. "I don't know. Some cleaning woman, I guess. She found it in Miss Layne's studio. I'm so glad to get it back before the recital. It's my good luck charm, you know. I was actually thinking of pulling out until I got it back."

"My brother Jonathan is playing in the Recital, too," I say.

"I'm glad Janey Drew isn't. I don't want to share the stage with her."

"You don't like Janey?"

She puts two fingers to her nose and pinches her nostrils closed as if there was a bad smell in the hall. "Have you met her?" I nod. "And do *you* like her?"

"Well, I only met her once."

"That's enough, believe me. But Dad says it's not all her fault. Her mom is a real backstage mama, you know? Really pushy. And she keeps her dressed like a kid. But you want to know something?" She moved close and whispered into my ear behind her hand. "She's almost two years older than she lets on, so she's really older than me!"

"How do you know?"

"My sister's best friend, Carla, goes to the same school as

her, and you know what? Janey can't keep that game up for much longer. Soon she'll have to start binding her boobies." She laughs gleefully and presses both hands over her mouth.

"Angelica?"

"Dad!" She turns and runs to the front door where a tall man with silver-grey hair is waiting. She hugs him and shows him the bracelet, then waves at me as they leave.

I wonder if what she says is true. Janey certainly acts young. I look at the griffins guarding each end of the oak bench. They look smaller than they used to.

Finally I look at the credenza by the staircase where Mrs. O'Malley leaves the mail, sorted according to name. The second delivery has come, but there is nothing for us, so I look through everyone else's. Mrs. Smyth has a bill from Eaton's and something from the school where she used to teach. Mrs. Dunn has a telephone bill and two letters, one of them from England, written on a pale-blue single-sheet airmail form. She always has mail. Mrs. Pierce and Brian never have anything. Strange. Even Baggy Bones gets mail now and then. I glance at Mrs. Tyndall's postcard from Boston and see that her first name is Marie. She must be Baggy Bones's friend! Amazing. And I have never seen her going either in or out. She's better at being invisible than I am.

I know Mrs. O'Malley is out because I saw her leave, and Mr. O'Malley is at his day job so I know he won't be there when I knock. Patricia opens the door and stares out at me. She looks rumpled, as if she was sleeping. She seems to do that a lot.

"What do you want?" she says, squinting at me.

I put my hands on my hips like Mrs. O'Malley. "Your mother decided to give the bracelet back to the real owner, I see."

"I don't know what you're talking about. Go away." She starts to close the door.

I think of Cedric and Eddie. They wouldn't back down. I put my foot in the way, and for once I am glad I am wearing Oxfords.

"You didn't steal the bracelet, did you?" I say, suddenly seeing the whole thing.
"I told you I didn't, Four-Eyes."
"Well, I know that's true now."
"So is this your apology?"
"It was your mother who stole it."
"Liar!" she shouts.
"It's true."
"Oh yeah? Prove it."
I pull my foot away, and she slams the door in my face. I can't prove it. She knows that. I run back upstairs and tell Mother about Angelica and the bracelet and how I saw it in the basement.
"Mrs. O. is like a magpie," she says thoughtfully, "picking up shiny things, feathering her nest. I wonder..." She looks at the eiderdown she bought from Mrs. O. in the winter, and I can see her thoughts as plainly as if she has spoken. Who really owned that duvet before we bought it?
"Possession is nine-tenths of the law," I say, and she laughs and hugs me and tells me I should study law someday. "I must say that this whole story doesn't say much for Mrs. O.'s housekeeping abilities. She gave the bracelet back today and tells them she found it cleaning the studio? But the bracelet was lost weeks ago, which means either she's lying or she doesn't clean the studio very often."
I hadn't thought of that.
"Not that it matters," Mother goes on. "I suspect that Rona Layne will take the path of least resistance if we don't persuade her otherwise. But after the recital. And Vanessa, don't ever go down to the basement again, no matter the circumstances. Promise me?"
"I promise." I feel much lighter now that I have told at least a version of the saga of the bracelet. Mother makes tea and we go out to the porch and sit surrounded by the cascading flowers from the window boxes she takes such care of: nas-

turtiums and petunias, even a pot of lavender to add scent to the air, along with the peppery geraniums that Mrs. Dunn has donated from her windowsill collection.

"Angelica says Janey Drew is older than she lets on," I say, dipping my big Dad's cookie in my tea.

Mother looks off into the distance, stirring her tea absently. "Sometimes we need a comforting story to tell ourselves about the competition," she says. "And sometimes we need a façade to hide behind. Either way, it doesn't take away from her talent."

It's not the response I anticipated, and I don't know how to react, what she expects from me now. I munch on my cookie, trying to make it last. Tomorrow Daddy is coming home. Maybe things will return to normal then. Maybe the little worm of disquiet will stop gnawing on my entrails, like the raven picking at Prometheus's liver when he was chained to the rock. Maybe one more cookie will make it go away.

21. OYEZ, OYEZ

WE ARE IN THE MEDICAL ARTS BUILDING at the corner of St. George and Bloor, waiting for Dr. Bachman, the new eye specialist. Mother is clasping and unclasping her hands, reaching over to pat my arm, picking up a magazine, putting it down again. I swing my legs, but Mother lays a hand on my knee to stop me. I try not to think about the possibilities a new doctor might open up. It's always this way. And it always turns out the same. We even went down to Florida one time to see this doctor Mother had heard about who had theories about eye exercises. We went on the Greyhound bus, and Jonathan came, too. On the way home, we didn't have enough money for him to get farther than Buffalo, so he had to sit in the bus station until we got home to Toronto and Mother could wire him more money. Daddy was in the hospital and *hors de combat* at the time. There was no joy in the eye exercises, but I got to swim in the Gulf of Mexico and Mother met a large lady on the beach named Mrs. Laughingwell who taught me how to do the Australian crawl.

In spite of myself and all my previous experiences and disappointments, my stomach flutters with hope.

There are a lot of people in the office. Two little boys play on the floor with big plastic blocks. They are both wearing glasses almost as thick as mine. One shrieks suddenly and throws one of the blocks at his brother. Mother reaches over and catches it, lays a hand on the little boy's shoulder, and smiles at him.

He is so surprised he just sits there and stares at her.

"Look," she says. "If you put the block here, you will have built a doorway. What can go through that doorway without making it fall down? Can you show me?"

The little boys pull some small wooden cars out of a cloth bag on the floor beside them and begin to push them carefully through the gateway. One of them is concentrating so hard his tongue is sticking out. A woman sitting opposite us knitting a baby sweater smiles at Mother gratefully.

We go in next and finally meet the new doctor. He is slim and neat and has kind eyes, dark as chocolate. It doesn't take him long to realize I have memorized the eye chart, and he begins to use other charts: shapes, pictures, random letters. I begin to relax, but Mother watches anxiously from her perch in the corner. She is on edge. I can hear her thoughts swirling and racing, the questions waiting to burst out, sharp and never-ending.

At last he leaves me, giving me time for my eyes to recover from the drops. I can hear him talking to Mother in the other room, their voices going up and down. Mother sounds excited and keeps asking what sounds like the same questions over and over. I lay my head back on the soft leather chair and close my tired eyes. The next thing I know, Mother is waking me up. Her face is full of joy.

"You can go to school," Dr. Bachman says. "Eyes like yours should be exercised. The diagnoses you have received are very old fashioned. Thinking has changed, and our research has found new ways to understand severe astigmatism like yours."

He says a lot more, but I can't hear him. I am still hearing those words: You can go to school.

"Do you mean I can go to a *real* school?" I say, for once not caring that I am interrupting an adult. Even Mother doesn't chide me.

"Yes, a real school," Dr. Bachman says.

Mother talks a blue streak on the way home, but I am living inside my head and don't really follow her. I am hugging around me the idea of school. Real school. No Eddie convulsing on the floor, no Dick and Jane, no gang of Vipers. We take a short detour up Walmer Road and walk past St. Mildred's College, and we stop and look at it. "You will go to a school like that," Mother says.

As we stand there, a group of girls come out the door, running down the steps. They are wearing tunics similar to mine, but theirs have a crest in the middle.

"Hope goes to school here," I say, remembering a girl from church.

"And so will you," Mother says, firmly. "So will you."

We have a picnic on the grass in Queen's Park: peanut butter sandwiches and an apple cut up in slices with lemon juice and a hint of cinnamon sprinkled on it. I am so excited I can barely taste anything.

Then Mother says, "How would you like to go to a movie?" She says it casually as if we do this all the time.

I stare at her. She is shaking off the crumbs, then folding up the waxed paper and putting it in her handbag. Her eyes are sparkling. "*The Secret Garden* is playing at Loews."

I am almost afraid to speak. I don't know what to expect. As we walk to the cinema, I wonder how a book I see in my head will look up on a screen—if the characters will look the same, if the walled garden will be the way it is in my mind.

When we get to the theatre, Mother buys two tickets and we go inside. It is very grand, with red plush everywhere and brass railings on the swooping balcony. But Mother ushers us right up to the front, and we sit down in the middle. I cross my legs on the seat and look up at the giant red and gold curtains covering the screen. Mother pats my arm.

For the next hour and a half, I am in another world. Everything is amazing: the purring sound the curtains make as they draw away to reveal the screen, the newsreel, the snippets of other movies coming to the theatre later on. And then the main attraction. I don't know if there is anyone else there, and I don't care. I am transfixed by the colour. It's just like the illustrations. And the beautiful old house is even grander than I imagined. There's Dickon up on the screen, just like in the drawing in my book. There's that nasty Colin with his skinny legs and his temper tantrums. There's Mary, being sensible and cheerful in spite of everything. And there's the garden. I think of Miss Layne's garden, enclosed by its iron fence, hidden behind the tall bushes. It needs some loving attention too.

When it's all over, I feel a little stiff and realize I haven't moved all the time I was watching. I walk out into the sunshine in a daze.

"Did you like it?" Mother asks, taking my hand.

"It was perfect," I say. "Just grand."

Daddy comes home at noon the next day. Mother makes his favourite things: beans on toast for lunch and finnan haddie with potatoes is planned for dinner. Daddy looks better, his skin glowing and his blue eyes brighter than ever, especially after he hears about the new eye doctor. When I show him the wood Jonathan and I rescued for him, he smiles even more.

"Your mother's birthday is coming up. We can make something special for her."

We sit out on the balcony talking about what would be best—what would fit best with the grain of the wood and what Mother might like. We decide on a small chest. Daddy thinks he can get some cedar to line it with so Mother will have a place to store woollies and keep them from reeking of mothballs. He puts a finger to his lips. "It's a secret now," he says. "Not a word."

We smile, sharing this moment.

But it's not all good news. "Do you know about Lame Duck Lodge?" I ask.

"Your mother told me," he says, and I can see there's a part of him that's sad, too. "I telephoned Miss David from the hospital and offered to help show them how to fix it up."

We don't say anything else for a few moments, just enjoying being together. Then I say, "Do you know all about what's been going on in the Music House?"

He sighs and nods and looks off into the distance. I wonder how long he will look rested and well, now that he's back.

"Jealousy is a terrible thing," he says at last. He gets up and goes into the living room to talk to Mother.

I climb up the ladder and peer over the edge of the roof. No one is there. I wonder what Daddy would say if I told him about Mrs. Pierce in her negligée on a Sunday afternoon. Probably that it was none of my business. I climb the rest of the way and walk over to the Pierces' window. I can see the harpsichord, gleaming with polish. Music is open on the stand. The window is up a few inches, but there is no sound coming from within. I move over to the other side; from here I can see the alcove where the bed is. I wonder if the couch pulls out for Brian like the one in Janet's house. The room is surprisingly big.

Their door opens and Brian appears. He flings himself on the couch and puts his head in his hands. "Shit," he says loudly. I back away, but not quickly enough.

"Hey!" He is at the window, motioning to me to come closer. "Wait a minute, will you? I'm coming out."

I sit down with my back against the wall. The pebbles of the roof feel rough against my bare legs. It takes a while for him to come out, and when he does, he sits down beside me. We don't say anything for a moment.

"I wasn't spying," I say.

"Who cares?" he says and grins.

I laugh, a loud explosive sound that doesn't sound at all ladylike.

"Could you take another message to Helen for me?" he asks. He picks up a pebble and throws it into the Secret Garden.

"Why don't you just mail it?" I ask.

"It wouldn't get there in time." He throws another pebble, this one with such force I can hear his wrist snap.

Something is wrong. I can feel it in the tension in his body, in the tightness of his voice. I don't know what to do, but I don't want to take any more messages to Helen. But what excuse do I have? If I say we aren't going to church tomorrow, he will know it's a lie.

"We're still friends, aren't we?" he asks.

I nod.

"It's just tickets for the recital," he says softly. "Please. Just take it."

"Helen has tickets," I say. "She's coming anyway."

"I helped you off the roof," he says. "Why won't you help me?"

There's no answer to that. "Okay."

He hands me a sealed envelope. I can feel a ticket inside, as well as paper. The message. To the Mystery Woman whose name he will not tell me? Surely a friend would tell me her name. I stuff it in the pocket of my shorts, get up, and dust off my hands. Without another word, I climb down to the porch, feeling the worm in my stomach shift and gnaw. *Why didn't I just say no?* But right away, I know the answer. Loyalty. It is even part of the family crest. I may not be a blood relative, but I can keep the faith. I can be as loyal as d'Artagnan!

Mother puts the beeswax candles Jonathan gave her for Christmas in the silver candelabra we brought back from Grandmother's house last summer. She lights them, and it begins to smell a little like church. "We'll have some of the wine I was saving for after the recital," she says. Daddy has the complete silver place setting. I have the one that's almost complete. Soon, Mother says, everyone will have a complete set.

We are halfway through dinner when Jonathan drops a bomb.

"I've been thinking," he begins, and I can tell he is nervous. I have felt it from the time he came in and helped set the table.

"I've waited till everyone is here to tell you what I have decided."

Mother smiles. "What's that, dear?"

"Remember how you used to talk about not having just one string to your bow?" he says, looking intently at Mother. I watch her smile waver. "I've decided that what I want to do is go to university next year, instead of continuing to prepare for a concert career. I want to study comparative literature. Maybe teach afterwards."

Everyone looks at Mother.

"But your whole life is music, dear," she says. "How can you leave? After all this work! After all we have sacrificed!"

"And thanks to you, I will always have music," he says. "I appreciate everything you've done, believe me, but it's time to assess my chances of success in this field, and after careful consideration, I've decided they are slim."

"Nonsense! You are very talented."

Mother is holding the edge of the table in one hand. I can feel her tension like a wound-up spring. Even Daddy is looking worried. He is not eating his favourite meal. I wish Jonathan would stop talking and the last few minutes could be erased.

"There are thousands of people out there more talented than I am, Mother. Just off the top of my head, there are the three others on the program with me. There's Janey Drew. There's Glenn Gould. And Patsy Parr. All of them have more than I do. I am not that exceptional."

"What utter nonsense!" Mother says, her voice rising. "Everyone says you have a special talent."

"Now, Lil, let the boy have his say," Daddy says. But I don't think Mother even hears him.

"It's too big a gamble," Jonathan goes on. He has obviously rehearsed this with someone. I wonder who it is. *Helen?* "We don't have the money to finance the Carnegie Hall thing, you know that, and besides, it's not fair to Vanessa. If you choose St. Mildred's as her school—and I think it's a great choice—there are fees to pay. Besides, she has talent too. What about her?"

Amazed, I turn and look at Mother, interested to hear what she'll have to say to counter this unexpected gambit.

"Let me worry about Vanessa," she says. "She'll be fine. It's you I'm concerned about. And speaking of money, how do you plan on financing university?"

"I have a scholarship."

Silence descends. We all stare at Jonathan.

"You've certainly thought this through," Mother says, "and for quite a long time too." She gets up, collects the plates, goes to the kitchen. We hear her scraping and rinsing.

"You do what you think is best for you," Daddy says. He gets up and follows Mother.

Jonathan and I look at each other. I feel full up. He said I have talent.

"That wasn't so bad," he says.

"So far," I say.

He nods thoughtfully.

"Janey Drew is really almost two years older than she says," I whisper.

"How do you know?"

"Angelica told me."

"Showbiz," he says disgustedly. "Most of them aren't like that, though."

When Mother and Daddy come back, they bring the dessert. No one mentions music or school again.

I wake up late that night and realize Mother is not beside me. Daddy is snoring lightly on his side of the bed, the way he always does: a few gentle puffs and then a long sniffling snort. I wonder if this is what has wakened me. He has been in the hospital so long this time that perhaps I have become unaccustomed to his sleeping noises. Maybe Mother has, too. But I know inside that this is not really the cause of her sleeplessness. I am so finely attuned to her that I am surprised I didn't wake exactly when she did. I have done that before.

Carefully I climb over the foot of the bed so as not to disturb Daddy. It was probably not the homecoming he was expecting. I am disappointed that my good news has been so completely overshadowed by Jonathan's startling decision, by the lingering guilty sadness of Miss David's acquisition of Lame Duck Lodge. I am wearing an old T-shirt of Jonathan's over underpants. It's so big and stretched it's almost like a dress. I go out into the hall and listen at the living room door. Nothing. I peek inside, but Jonathan is asleep in the daybed as usual, so I close the door again and go down the hall to the bathroom. No one there, either. The porch is the only place left. I tiptoe back up the hall and open the back door. I find Mother crouched in the corner where the window boxes are. She is filling a pot with soil and sniffling.

"Go back to bed," she says, looking up. Her face is damp with tears.

Shocked, I back up and hunker down, waiting. I never know what I am waiting for at times like this. I just know that I have to be here so that I will know when she feels a little better or exhausts herself. It's scary, but I have to be here to send out my loyalty and love. She feels it. I know she does. Eventually.

She gives the pot a vigorous shove, and dirt spills all over the floor. I move closer, begin to sweep the soil into the pot again with my hand. Mother sits down on the floor and blows her nose.

"Shit!" she says. "Bugger. Blast. Hell."

"Holy Willy," I say. It's Daddy's favourite curse.

She smiles and wipes her eyes. "Oh, Nessa," she says and opens her arms. I crawl in and snuggle close, not caring about the dirt. "You'll never leave me, will you?" she whispers.

"No, Mummy," I whisper into her softness. "Never."

My eyes fill with tears.

22. LOYALTY

ON SATURDAY I TELL JANET all about Dr. Bachman and the movie and going to school next year. I have been looking forward to telling her this news for days. I have tried to imagine her expression, her face, her eyes, her bright laughter when she hears how my life will change.

She hugs me and grabs my hands and swings me around, hooting with joy. Luckily we are outside in her mud-packed yard, and so not liable to knock over crockery and such in the kitchen. I look up and see the trees spinning. When she lets me go, I stagger and grab hold of the fence.

"That's so wonderful!" She shouts out loud, and her mother comes to the kitchen window and knocks on the glass, a stern look on her face.

I pull the excitement around me, driving out the darkness from the Music House, the black news from Jonathan, the accusation of thievery that may mean we lose our new home, our haven, but the happy moment bursts even as I try to hold it fast. Janet pulls me inside and is telling her mother my news before I even get a chance to open my mouth, the words spilling out of her, stumbling over each other. I feel a stab of disappointment that I didn't get to tell her myself, but soon I am filling her in on everything about St. Mildred's and Jonathan's news. I don't say anything about the bracelet. By now, Mother seems to think me going to St. Mildred's is almost a *fait accompli*. "Of course, they'll take you," she says. "Your godmother is a nun." I wonder if Mother will tell them my godmother was thrown out of her order and started her own shortly afterwards. But maybe a rebel nun is better than none at all, I think, and grin at the unexpected play on words.

"I wish you could come to my school," Janet says.

So do I, but one part of me thinks Roman Catholic nuns might be scarier than the Anglican variety.

Janet's mother keeps coming back to Jonathan's decision about dropping his music. She asks a lot of questions about it as if it's more important than my news.

When we go upstairs to Janet's room, she asks an unexpected question. "What does Brian think of Jonathan's decision?"

I kick at the baseboard. "Who cares?"

"Well, it cuts down the competition, doesn't it?" she says.

That hadn't occurred to me. Janet is better at this sort of thinking. "I guess he should be pleased then," I say.

"Maybe Brian talked him into it." Janet leans forward, her grey eyes bright.

"Why would Jonathan listen to him?"

Janet shrugs. "What does Rona Layne say?"

It's my turn to shrug. "I don't think she knows yet. He says he'll tell her after the Recital."

"If it was me, I'd not bother doing the Recital," she says.

"Oh! Mother would just die!"

Somehow we can't seem to get into any game today and just drift around, each in our own world. We wander down the street to the 48th Highlanders' building at the end of Cawthra Square. I don't know what they do here. Daddy never comes, so I can't ask him.

"Brian gave me another message to take to Helen to give to the Mystery Woman," I say, kicking a pebble.

Janet sits down under a tree and frowns. "Why is he still going through Helen?" she asks. "He knows the Mystery Woman's name now. So why not tell you?"

I sit down beside her and shrug.

"Unless she's married!" Janet grins wickedly.

"How do you come up with these things?" I ask. I feel the thrill of the forbidden.

"It's either that or the Mystery Woman is Helen herself, and that's not fair because she's Jonathan's girlfriend, isn't she?"

"I guess so." I ponder this new idea. Jonathan always says she's just a friend, but maybe boys always say this. Mother seems convinced Helen is special. "In either case, perhaps I shouldn't deliver it at all."

"An ethical dilemma," Janet says thoughtfully.

"But I promised I'd do it," I say. "How can I break a promise?"

"But there's the question of loyalty," Janet says, pulling up some grass with one hand. "What would d'Artagnan do?"

"Support his comrades," I say at once. "But which one is my comrade? Brian or Jonathan?"

"The only person one could break a promise for is family, wouldn't you say?"

"What if I just ask Helen if the note is for her?"

"What if she lies? Or what if it's really for the mysterious married woman?"

"You're not being much help!" I get up and stomp back up Cawthra Square to Janet's house to find out what time it is. For the first time ever, I am going home alone. I'm supposed to go at three o'clock. This new freedom is overshadowed by the weighty question of what to do about Brian's note. The easiest thing would be to deliver it, I decide, and I do owe him for saving me when I was stuck on the roof. But if I do deliver it, what about the consequences? What if Jonathan loses his girlfriend? What if Brian is lured down the path to perdition by a married woman? Thou shalt not covet thy neighbor's wife. *Selah*.

At dinner I have a headache and have lost my appetite. Mother sends me to bed and puts Vicks on my temples. The smell is comforting, and I soon drift off, wrapped in blankets even though it's a warm night. Somewhere after midnight, I throw up, and Mother and Daddy have to clean everything up, change the sheets, throw the smelly ones out on the porch to deal with later. My whole body is heavy. It's an effort to move.

The next thing I know, the radio is playing softly and Mother is buttering toast and cutting it into quarters, trying to tempt me to eat. I shake my head. Talking seems to take too much energy. I fall asleep again.

This time when I wake up, I feel better. I get up and go to the bathroom, come back, and wash my face and hands. I go across to the living room.

"Where is everybody?"

"Church. How are you feeling now?"

"But I have to go to church," I say, panic rising.

Mother motions to Seth sitting atop the mantel. Just as I look at the clock's face, he strikes half past eleven.

"Oh no!"

"It's all right to miss the occasional Sunday, dear," Mother says, smiling. "God will not smite you dead."

"It's not that. It's just ... I promised!"

"You couldn't help being sick, dear. That's a perfect excuse for everything. God will understand."

Perhaps, but would Brian? He would be at St. Paul's with his mother by now, thinking Helen had passed on his message.

Mother goes to the kitchen and brings back a bowl of cream of wheat smothered in brown sugar, just the way I like it. Even this treat doesn't make me feel better about Brian.

Just as I'm finishing the cereal, Mother comes back and stands looking at me. I freeze. She is holding Brian's envelope, and it's open.

"That's private!"

"There was no name on it," she says. "I need to know who is writing to my young daughter. Only it's not yours, is it?"

I shake my head miserably. How could she have opened a private letter?

"Who is the 'B' who signed the note?"

I close my mouth in a tight line.

"Who?" she repeats. "Look at me!" She reaches over and takes my chin in her hand, tilting my face to hers.

Her grey eyes are wide and scary. They pierce right inside like searchlights. I'm surprised she can't read the name in my thoughts. "Brian," I whisper, my eyes watering.

"Brian *Pierce*?"

I nod.

"Good God!" She sits back and stares at the note. I can't imagine why she looks so stunned.

I take a deep breath and actually feel a little better, having unburdened myself in a way that makes me not to blame. Getting sick made everything fall apart. Surely he'll understand. Now he'll have to find another way to contact the Mystery Woman.

"Stay away from that boy," Mother says.

"But I have to explain—"

"I'll talk to his mother."

"Oh no! I mean, I don't think he wants her to know.... I mean..."

"I'm sure he doesn't." Mother stands up and puts the note away in her pocket. She has that fierce closed-in look that means that no amount of talking will change her mind. I'll never get to see what the note says now. Mother sends me back to bed.

In spite of worrying about Brian, I fall asleep again, and this time I sleep till I hear Daddy and Jonathan coming back from church. Something about Mother's voice as she greets them at the door sets the worms of anxiety crawling in my stomach. She's telling them about the note. I glance at the alarm clock on the table and realize Brian and his mother may be back from church too. Unless they went out to lunch. He told me they do that often. Going out to lunch is something we rarely do, except for when Mother and I go to the Honey Dew on Bloor Street as a special treat. I love that orangey drink and the cone-like waxy bottle it comes in if you want to take some home. Somehow I don't think Mrs. Pierce would like the Honey Dew much.

I get up and wash my face and pull on my faded dress with the pockets. I am just putting on my shoes when I hear the living room door open.

"...And we passed Brian going out when we came in," Jonathan is saying.

"You should stay out of it, dear." That's Daddy. "It's not our business."

"She's his mother. She should know," Mother says firmly. "If it was me, I would want to know."

"If it was you, you *would* know," Daddy says.

"That note's ambiguous anyway," Jonathan says, but Mother has apparently decided to ignore them. I hear her heels on the thin carpet as she marches down the hall to the doorway where the stairs lead to the third floor.

"It's none of our business," Jonathan calls after her. He slams the door.

But it is as if Brian is stealing Helen out from under Jonathan's nose!

I wait a few moments, then slip into the hall in time to see Baggy Bones withdrawing her head into her own room. What will she tell Marie about this? I go out to the porch and climb up the iron ladder to the third floor. The roof is in shadow now, the sun just beginning to inch across the open space as I slip quickly into the embrasure beside the bow window. I can't see anything from here, but the window is open and I can already hear Mother's voice at the door with Mrs. Pierce, exchanging strained pleasantries.

"Do come in," Mrs. Pierce says. Her voice doesn't sound very inviting.

"This is a lovely room," Mother says. "And what a beautiful instrument." She is right by the window now. She must be looking at the harpsichord. I hear a faint tinkle and picture her fingers caressing the black keys.

"It gets out of tune very easily," Mrs. Pierce says, and I hear a quiet *thunk* as the lid closes over the keys.

I shift in my seat, inching further out from the wall on my bottom. From here I can just see them, both still standing, looking warily at each other.

"Is there something I can do for you?" Mrs. Pierce asks.

"I'm sorry to disturb your Sunday," Mother says. "I see you're busy with correspondence. But I'm concerned about your son."

"Brian?" Her voice slides up in surprise, and her body stiffens.

"There's no delicate way to put this. I'll just give you this note and you can see for yourself." I hold my breath as she hands over Brian's note. "I found this in my daughter's pocket and I thought you should know."

"I should know what?" Mrs. Pierce glances at the letter, then at Mother.

"If *my* son were writing that kind of a letter, I would want to know," Mother says, her voice slow, emphatic, as if she's weighing every word.

"Why, whatever are you implying?"

Mother clears her throat. "It's unhealthy, for one thing. *And illegal!*" she added. "Of course, I'm sure it's only a phase he's going through, but in any case I don't want him involving my daughter in this subterfuge."

Mrs. Pierce laughs.

"Read the letter," Mother says, "and you'll see."

I watch Brian's mother scan the note, her red lips pursed. She lifts a long white hand to her perfect hair, tangling her fingers in her curls. Her eyes flash fire as she looks at Mother and laughs in her face. "You fool," she says. "You think you know Brian? Me? What's best for us? You are a meddling fool! He has me! He doesn't need anyone else! Now get out of my house!"

"Mrs. Pierce, I'm sorry to be the bringer of bad news—"

"This? This is nothing. It means less than nothing! It does not even exist!" She throws the letter up in the air and laughs again, her voice high and shaky.

"Perhaps I'd better go," Mother says, edging towards the door.

"What a bloody good idea!" Mrs. Pierce shouts. She slams the door behind Mother, then turns and leans against it for a moment without moving. Her face is whiter than ever, a high spot of colour on each cheek.

When at last she moves, she swoops down on the letter where it has fallen on the carpet near the bed. She drops it in the large overflowing ashtray and lights a match. She stands for a long moment as the match burns ever closer to her fingers, then touches the flame to the paper. She watches the note burn, the corners curling inward, dropping into ash.

"He has me," she growls. "He doesn't need anyone else."

I scoot backwards along the roof and slide onto the iron ladder. My heart is beating hard in my throat, and it's difficult to swallow. I feel as if something dark and scary is inching under my skin. As I climb down to the porch, I hear Mother calling my name. I lean over the closest window box, wipe a tear away, and study the flowers.

"Out here," I call. My voice sounds small and timid. I'm glad when Mother comes out and sits down in our Muskoka chair and draws me onto her lap. I know I'm too old for this, but right now I want it. I want to feel close and warm and safe. I want the dark itching to go away.

23. THE RECITAL

FOR THE NEXT FEW DAYS, Mother doesn't let me out of her sight. I am desperate to talk to Brian, to tell him it wasn't my fault, that I was sick, that I didn't betray him. But I did betray him, in spite of everything I tell myself. Whatever he was trying to keep secret, now my mother knows. His mother knows. Only I don't know. I feel stupid and slow.

The next few days pass in a whirl of unusual activity. There are my new glasses to get and appointments with St. Mildred's. Mother takes me with her everywhere, even to visit the twins to make the final arrangements for her to take care of them next month. By Wednesday night, I am filled to the top with so many conflicting feelings that the excitement is almost making me sick. Jonathan hasn't mentioned university again, and Mother seems to have forgotten about it. I know she hasn't, though. I suspect she thinks he will change his mind, but I have heard him make a few telephone calls that prove he intends to go through with it. He will have a new life next year. I keep quiet and think about my own new life.

We get to Eaton Auditorium early and go backstage. I see Brian for the first time since being sick. He looks tense, but that's not surprising. His mother is here, of course, talking animatedly to some man in formal wear. I see Angelica too, and she waves. She's wearing her good luck bracelet. She's the only girl on the program. The fourth person is Frederick Ascher. Jonathan said he's the oldest, but he doesn't look it.

He's slouching on a straight chair and chewing his fingernails, and he doesn't even glance up when someone speaks to him. Rona Layne walks in wearing an emerald-green velvet gown with black trim. She has a jewel in her hair. On her tiny feet are matching beaded slippers like the ones I found in the trunk in the basement of the Music House. I look away.

By the time we sit down, the Sullivans are here, and Janet and I whisper together. I tell her about being sick and the fiasco with the note.

"What did it say?" Janet asks.

"I don't know, but Mother was really cross. She went upstairs to talk to Mrs. Pierce, and it was terrible. Mrs. Pierce slammed the door on her."

"In her face?"

"No, on her way out."

"But what did they say? What was in the note?"

"Something illegal," I whisper.

Even Janet has no comeback to this. "Maybe he's a smuggler," she says at last, and I think of the artwork at Ryan's Art Gallery next door to us and wonder how easy it would be to slice a canvas out of its frame and slip it into his music case.

"Well, he can't be very good at it," I say, "or they'd have more money, wouldn't they?"

We stop talking as the lights go down. Around us I see some of the men have taken out small pads to make notes in. They must be the critics and important people Mother has been talking about. These are the men she is counting on to change Jonathan's mind by raving about his performance. They have a lot of influence in the music world, she says. Surely that's why he is going through with it. Maybe it's like my Fate Game, where I decide the future by telling myself that if I see a robin in the next two minutes or if I hear Taffy Layne bark, something I want really badly will happen. Maybe Jonathan is doing this with the reviews; if they are good, his new life will be in the music world after all, just as Mother wants it to be.

Jonathan is first on the program. I don't know if this is bad or good for him, but I'm sure *I* would be glad to get it over with. He is not wearing his glasses, and it makes him look different. I wonder if this was Mother's idea or Miss Layne's. While he plays, I glance at Mother. She looks supremely happy. Daddy is holding her hand.

The nail-biter is next. He has bad acne and has tried to hide it with some skin-coloured pasty stuff that doesn't quite match the rest of his face. His hair is plastered to his skull, parted in the middle like some man in a Victorian portrait. He sits for a moment, staring ahead, then shrugs his shoulders a few times and flexes his fingers. He is skinny, but when he finally touches the keys, there is real power. It's surprising. I look at the man in front, and he is scribbling frantically in his notebook. I hope he had something good to say about Jonathan.

Mother is relaxed now that Jonathan has finished, and she reaches over and squeezes my hand. Janet is fidgeting. I stare at the folds in the curtain closest to us. I wonder if it makes a noise when it closes, how you get the dust out for spring cleaning. The longer I stare, the more a faint pattern emerges, like ripples in the deep velvet. Like the tide coming in.

When Angelica comes on stage, Janet nudges me. I know she's looking at the bracelet too. Angelica looks smaller up there, standing next to the shiny black hulk of the concert grand. She's wearing a red taffeta dress that goes right to the floor, and she obviously isn't binding *her* boobies. Janet looks at me and grins, reading my thoughts. Angelica sits down, tosses back her long glorious hair, and puts her palms together as if in prayer before touching the keys. She has decided to go for the playful approach in the music she chose. Or perhaps Miss Layne chose it. With Jonathan, it seemed to be a discussion between the two of them. Angelica is playing something modern that I don't recognize, but it holds my attention. Mother shakes her head as if she doesn't like it.

By the time we get to Brian, the evening seems long. I am

looking forward to the reception. Jonathan said closing the evening is a strong position, but I'm not so sure. Brian walks on quickly, bows, and sits down, pausing briefly to adjust the bench. In contrast to Frederick, the nail-biter, his colour is high. His cheeks are flushed, and his green eyes sparkle. The stage lights dance in the gold in his hair. He attacks the piano with gusto, waking up the woman behind me who makes a harrumphing noise. Mother grins. Janet sticks her elbow in my ribs. I cover my mouth so as not to snort. Brian crashes on, triumphant. It is Mrs. Pierce's turn to be filled with joy.

Afterwards, all four of them come out on stage along with Rona Layne, and a young man in a red cummerbund presents everyone with flowers. It seems odd to give flowers to boys, but they seem happy so I guess it's all right.

The applause goes on for a while, but it is writ large in the program that there will be no encores. I'm glad of this because I'm hungry. I've never been to such a big recital before and am hoping for grand things at the reception.

Although I was a bit sleepy earlier, I am wide awake now as we make our way through the crowd to the room where the reception is. It feels special to be going to an invitation-only event, but it looks as if no one is actually checking invitations. Still, one does have to know about it, I guess, so that's special enough.

As soon as we get through the wide door, I see Brian and slip over to talk to him while Mother is busy looking for Jonathan.

"You were wonderful," I say, and I mean it. "I'm sorry I was sick and couldn't deliver your message." I whisper this last part, and he leans closer to hear.

"Never mind. It doesn't matter anymore." He looks over my shoulder, scanning the room as if looking for someone more interesting to talk to.

"I'm really sorry Mother found the note," I go on. "She shouldn't have read it. And no one wanted her to show your mother, honestly, but—"

"What?" His full attention snaps back to me. "What?" he repeats.

I step back. "I couldn't help it. I was sick!"

"Oh, God," he says. "Well, that explains a few things." He lets out a bark of laughter, takes a silver flask from his inside pocket, and drinks from it. "That's life." He turns away suddenly, pushing through the crowd.

Stunned, I just stand there, looking after him.

"You should have introduced me," Janet hisses, at my side. "That was rude."

"The time was not propitious." I take her hand, and we weave our way to the food table.

"He really is dreamy, isn't he?" She's gazing after him as if he's the Messiah.

I poke her in the ribs. "Don't stare."

"How come he's mad at you?" she says. "You were sick. You couldn't help it."

"He's not," I say, but I'm not sure.

"Maybe the Mystery Woman is here anyway." Janet looks around, although how she would possibly recognize the Mystery Woman is beyond me.

I shrug. I don't want to talk about this anymore. I pile my plate high with different kinds of pinwheel sandwiches as well as two finger-sized slices of pound cake. We are guests here so I can eat all I like. Eating will make me feel better.

A man in some sort of uniform fills a glass cup with sparkling punch from a huge bowl and then makes a shooing motion with his hand. That's just rude. He wouldn't do that if Mother was beside me. I want to tell him that I'm an invited guest, that my brother was one of the performers, but instead I turn my back on him and move away from the table, head held high.

"Who does he think he is?" Janet mutters. "A high mucky muck?"

"Too big for his boots." I cram a whole sandwich into my mouth and make appreciative noises.

Janet does the same.

We look at each other and grin.

Soon after that, her mother comes to collect her, and I watch them disappear in the direction of the big double doors. Around me the room shimmers with the noise of conversations. Light sparkles on the chandeliers. Perfumes mingle in the warm air, adding another layer to the pungent odours of food, sweat, and aftershave. Faces are getting red and shiny in the heat. Everyone looks happy, even Frederick who is shaking hands with some man with a bowtie. I wonder where his parents are.

I find Mother and Daddy talking to Rona Layne.

"This has been such a wonderful night," Mother is saying as she shakes Miss Layne's hand.

"It's the first major step in what I am sure will be a great career for Jonathan," Miss Layne says, covering Mother's hand with her own.

I look at Mother, waiting for her to break the news that Jonathan is not going on with his music, but she is beaming with pride and only nods in agreement. Rona Layne smiles and smiles before moving on to Angelica's father.

I pull at Mother's sleeve. "Why didn't you tell her what Jonathan said?" I whisper.

"That was just nerves talking," Mother says. "You'll see. He'll change his mind, now that everything went so well."

I look around, trying to spot the men with the notebooks, but they have gone. I guess they have to write their reviews. Jonathan says sometimes they write them in a taxi on the way to the newspaper office.

Jonathan is in a group by the podium, talking to Helen. Brian is with them. I see him pull the silver flask from his pocket and take another drink. He begins talking animatedly to a man who looks vaguely familiar. As I stare across the room, I realize it's the man who sings in our church choir, the dark-haired one who looks like a Velázquez painting. As I watch, Brian takes yet another drink. I guess he's still angry with me. It's not my fault about the note, I want to shout, but of course I don't.

Mrs. Pierce seems giddy with joy. She smiles at Mother and laughs, that tinkling false laugh of hers that grates on my ears. "Brian is so talented," she says. "Sometimes I can't even believe he's mine. Closing the program too. Such a good choice."

Brian is close enough to hear this and scowls at his mother. "I am not yours," he says loudly.

Mrs. Pierce laughs again. "You know what I mean, dear," she says.

"I certainly do," says Brian, and turns his back on her.

Mother takes my hand and turns away. "There's no excuse for bad manners," she mutters to Daddy, who shrugs and suggests we go home.

Before we get a chance to discuss it, a young man steps up to the podium and flicks the microphone with his fingers, making it whine. "Ladies and gentlemen, may I present Miss Rona Layne." She steps up on the little platform, folds her hands in front of her, and begins to thank us all for coming. She thanks the pianists for all their hard work, and then she talks about this being the first big step along the path to Carnegie Hall and a successful musical career.

Everybody cheers and claps. We are still clapping when Brian suddenly leaps up on the podium and grabs the microphone before the man turns it off.

"I want to give a special thank you to Miss Layne for taking me on when I arrived from the west coast out of the blue and for pushing me like a slave driver all these months since."

Everybody laughs, especially her students.

"She is right. I will keep going along this path, but next weekend I leave for New York City with a friend to study there. I wanted to take this opportunity to thank everyone who has helped me, and to say goodbye in case I don't get the chance later on. See you all in Carnegie Hall!"

We look at each other.

"How very theatrical," Mother says.

Mrs. Pierce makes a small strangling noise and crumples, senseless, at Mother's feet.

"Holy Willy," says Daddy, kneeling down and feeling for a pulse.

I look over and see Brian and the man who looks like a Velázquez painting with their arms around each other's shoulders. They are laughing.

As it turns out, Mrs. Pierce has only fainted.

"It must be the heat," everyone is saying, fanning themselves with their programs.

We leave shortly afterwards, and I am glad because I am suddenly very tired. We take a taxi home, something almost unheard of. Streetlights are a blur as we drive along Carlton Street.

The car smells like stale smoke, but we don't care. Everyone is still happy from the concert, even Jonathan. Mother is carrying Jonathan's flowers cradled in her arms like a baby. Their exotic scent gradually fills the back seat.

"Isn't it wonderful?" she says. "The first of many wonderful concerts, just as Miss Layne told us."

"Miss Layne told everyone exactly the same thing," Jonathan says, but nothing makes any difference to Mother's great happiness.

"I almost felt sorry for Mrs. Pierce," Mother goes on. "Her son making a spectacle of himself like that."

"Maybe it was the only way he could get up the nerve to tell her he's going," Jonathan says.

"He was drunk." Daddy makes a disgusted noise as the taxi swings into our driveway.

They send me to bed right away, which is fine with me because I am so tired. Strangely, once I am undressed and cuddled under the covers, I seem to wake up again, reliving everything that happened at the Recital. Images whirl about in my mind, a kaleidoscope of photographs in technicolour: Angelica in her grown-up dress, Miss Layne's beaded green slippers, Brian drinking from his silver flask, Mrs. Pierce crumpling to the floor in front of us.

I must have dozed off because I wake up again as Mother and Daddy come in and get ready for bed, whispering together. Mother gets in first and spoons against me. Daddy has just gone into the small washing room when there is a knock at the door. Mother jumps up and pulls on her old paisley dressing gown. It still looks good in the dim light.

She opens the door a crack. "Yes? Is there something the matter?"

"Sorry to wake youse up." It's Baggy Bones. "There's a terrible racket upstairs. The Pierces are going at it something fierce, and I can't get a lick of sleep in all the commotion."

"What can we do?"

"I thought your mister could go up there and speak to them," she says. "I don't want to call the police, but I will if I have to. I need my sleep!"

By this time Daddy has put on his suit again, and he opens the door wider, edging Mother aside. "I'll go up and speak to them," he says. "Just go back to bed, everyone."

I'm wide awake, sitting up when Mother closes the door. Things like this are not supposed to happen in the Music House. I wonder if the Pierces are fighting about Brian's Mystery Woman, if she really was at the Recital as Janet suggested, if my undelivered note has anything to do with it.

"That poor woman," Mother says. "I may not like her, but I can sympathize. It's obvious she had no idea of what he was going to do. Poor soul. She loves him more than life itself and has sacrificed a lot to get him where he is today, I'm sure. I can certainly understand that sense of betrayal she must feel."

She slides back into bed, dropping one arm around me protectively. "As if she doesn't have enough to deal with," she mutters.

I lie staring at the damp spot on the ceiling that's shaped like South America, and finally I understand—Brian is going to New York City with the Mystery Woman! That is just so romantic. I can hardly wait to tell Janet.

Mother starts to get out of bed to find out what's going on, just as Daddy finally walks in the door.

"Go back to bed," he says. He looks really tired now, his face grey and drawn. "It's over."

"What happened?" Mother asks.

"Everyone just got over-emotional—fueled by alcohol, no doubt. Neither one of them was being very... rational. Some of the things they said...." He shakes his head. "Anyway, they've promised to go to bed and get some sleep. And I want to do the same."

"That poor woman," Mother murmurs, slipping her arms around me again.

I settle against Mother, waiting for the bed for dip under Daddy's weight, for sleep to come, for the images to stop rolling through my mind. The last image I remember is Mrs. Pierce slipping to the ground while Brian laughs with the man who looks like a painting.

24. WEIGHED IN THE BALANCE...

THE NEXT DAY EVERYONE IS TENSE, waiting. Jonathan goes down to the corner to get the papers as they come out, checking the reviews. First comes the *Globe and Mail*, then the early editions of the *Star* and the *Telegram*. The headlines all say more or less the same things: *Angelica: Teenage Version of Janey Drew*, *Angelica Dazzles with Technique*, *Angelica: Rival for Patsy Parr?* Then they get around to everyone else: *Jonathan Dudley-Harris delivers a balanced rendition of Bach cantata*; *Frederick Ascher leaves his heart on the stage*; *Brian Pierce plays with a fierce intensity and the sort of control usually seen in older performers. The recital opened with caution and ended with assured passion.* But it's mostly about Angelica.

Mother flings the papers aside. "Men!" she says. "Thinking below the belt, as usual."

"It's true," Jonathan says. "It shows I've made the right decision."

"Nonsense." Mother picks up the papers and folds them roughly. "You need more experience, that's all."

"A 'balanced rendition' is not enough to build a career on." Jonathan shakes his head. "It's over," he says. "I have to go out and pick up a few things I need."

Mother watches him go then sits down in the desk chair and puts her head in her hands.

It's as if all the wind has dropped suddenly and the kite we were flying on has crashed on the hard ground. Everyone seems depressed. It's the "let down" effect, Daddy says. We have been looking forward to this event for a long time, and now that it's over, there's nothing left to look forward to.

Except me going to a real school. I feel hurt that no one seems to think of this as such a big thing, but it doesn't really change anything, I guess. I hug this to me, but still feel somewhat desolate. I wonder what Brian must be feeling? At least they said some good things about him. "Assured passion" sounds really good.

We are outside on the balcony now. Mother tries to find out what was going on upstairs last night, but Daddy is never good at relaying what he considers gossip. He just shakes his head.

"They were both nearly hysterical," he says. "People say things when they're tired and upset and have had too much to drink. They always regret it the next day."

"But what did they say?" Mother wants to know.

"Nothing that needs to be repeated."

"Oh, Ned, you're hopeless," she says. "I feel for the poor woman. I just want to know so I can figure out the best way to approach her. To show some comfort."

"The best thing you can do for that woman is leave her alone," Daddy says, and he goes back to sanding rust off the old tin trunk he is giving to Jonathan to take to his summer job up north.

Mother makes a disgusted noise and goes back inside.

I can hear Patricia downstairs bouncing a ball against the wall. I don't want to see her. I would like to climb up to the roof and see what's happening up there, but I know Daddy won't let me, so I hang over the railing and gaze at the neglected yard behind Mount Olympus. The grass is long and green and bent over, covering secrets with a pattern pretty to the eye. I wonder if anyone will ever find the prism I threw there. I hear the screen door slam downstairs, Patricia going inside, and decide to risk a trip to the garden. Daddy waves as I head down the steps.

I haven't been over the fence by myself since Brian rescued me from the coach house roof that rainy day long ago. I slide behind the bushes and find the footholds he used, and soon I am in the green waving grass, hidden from sight among the overgrown bushes. Crickets sing, the sun beats down, and bees circle lazily among the wild flowers in one corner of the neglected yard. The dusty windows of the old building gaze down, sightless and dead. Sometimes I find it almost hard to breathe in the Music House, and lately it is less and less like the haven it seemed in January. Here I can relax. No one expects anything of someone who is invisible. I push my way into the middle of a thicket of bushes. There is a circle of long grass here—a fairy ring—and I kneel down, running my hands close to the ground looking for treasures. I find only a short section of pipe and what looks like a bed spring.

Then I feel what Daddy describes as "a call of nature," but I don't want to leave yet. I look up and around, seeing nothing from here but sky and the arching branches of the bushes. No windows overlook this secret place. I ease down my underpants, squat, and let loose the hot stream into the grass. It feels good. Afterwards, I crouch there, then move sideways, crab-like, and sit down on the ground. The grass feels oddly exciting against my bare bottom. I rock back and forth, enjoying the strange fluttering feeling shuddering through me. This is wicked, I think. And I smile. I wonder if Janet has ever done anything like this. If she has ever felt the wildness of this mounting excitement. But after a few minutes, I hastily pull up my pants, vaguely ashamed, and decide to look for the prism. I want it back. In a sudden premonition, I think we might not be much longer at the Music House and I want to take the prism with me, a tangible memory of this place. I look for a long time, crawling through the grass, scraping my knees, getting stains on my shorts, but I can't find it. Perhaps it was bad luck anyway.

When I climb back over the fence a while later, I find Patricia standing there, her fat arms crossed over her chest.

"That's trespassing," she says smugly.

"If a tree falls in the forest," I say. I'm not sure what this means. It just pops into my head, and it's enough to confuse Patricia.

She frowns. "We'll see what Miss Layne has to say," she says at last, and smiles in triumph.

"You're just jealous because you can't get over the fence," I say. "You're too fat."

She shrugs. "Why would I want to?"

"Perhaps to get a little exercise," I say. I turn my back and walk away. I hear Patricia's running feet, the slam of the screen door. I hear her voice calling her mother.

I feel ashamed. And afraid of what she might do, what her mother might say to Rona Layne. "I'm sorry!" I call after her. I run over to the back door and pull it open. "Hey, Patricia, I said I was sorry."

"Get out of my house," Patricia screams. The kitchen door bangs shut.

"It's my house too." But she is gone.

I run down into the cool darkness of the basement and make my way through to the stairs that come up just outside Rona Layne's studio. There is no sound in the dimness, so I cautiously appear and make my way to the front hall. Baggy Bones is on the staircase, struggling with two paper bags clasped to her chest. One is slipping, and I run up and catch it just before it falls. She looks startled and peers at me for a moment as if trying to figure out who I am, where I came from.

"Let me help," I say. I wish I knew her real name. It seems rude not to address her properly.

"Oh, yes. The girl from up the hall," she says almost to herself. She doesn't know my name either. Maybe she has a mean name to call me when she talks to her friend Marie.

Now she can hold onto the railing and uses it to pull herself up. I follow along behind. Her bag holds a small bottle of milk, baking soda, Ovaltine, and chocolate fingers, the kind I like. She probably bought them for her friend, for tea. I suddenly remember that Mother says she has a son, but he never comes to visit so the biscuits wouldn't be for him. There's cat food in the bag too. That surprises me.

When we get to her door, she fumbles with her key, opens the door, and pushes inside. She hesitates, then opens it wider for me to come in. I glance up the hall, but no one is in sight so I slide into the room I have never seen. Inside, it smells stale, like old clothes. Maybe she doesn't know Mother's rule: it only takes ten minutes with the window wide open to air out a large room.

She motions for me to put the bag down on the small table by the window and unpacks everything quickly, then slips the milk and the block of cheese outside onto the windowsill in the shade cast by the ivy.

"Do you have a cat?" I ask, handing her the tins of cat food.

"No, no," she says. "We're not allowed to have pets here." She looks at me, her gimlet eyes sharp.

"But it's all right if it's a stray, surely," I say. "That would be like Saint Francis of Assisi helping the animals. It would be a good deed."

Her winkled face collapses into a smile. "Would you like a chocolate biscuit? I usually have a cup of tea when I come in from shopping."

She plugs in the kettle and pulls out two cups and saucers from behind a limp chintz curtain strung up under the sink in the corner. Her room is crowded, and she has a lot of plants, all green and healthy looking, unlike any potted plants we have ever had in our house. Shiny vines climb up strings surrounding her broad window, making a frame of green. It's like an extension of the Secret Garden down below. The sun casts dimpled shadows through the leaves. She has a lot of framed photographs scattered in amongst the bric-a-brac: old people in formal poses; younger people looking as if they'd rather be somewhere else; a young man standing in front of a car with no top, looking serious. Her son?

"That's me," she says, pointing to a round portrait of a smiling plump baby in the lacy dress and bonnet of a bygone age.

"You look like Queen Victoria," I say.

She laughs. It is the first time I have heard her laugh … ever.

I sit down in a small slipper chair, leaving the armchair for her. It's obviously where she spends most of her time. It looks like a nest, with magazines and newspapers piled up on the floor on one side and a basket of knitting balanced on a stool within reach. She probably knitted socks for soldiers during the war. Mother used to do that when she was young. She always says she pitied the poor soldier who got her socks.

Baggy Bones puts sugar and milk in the tea before handing it to me, but I drink it anyway. And eat one biscuit. She leans over and pulls a crocheted tea cozy, its hideous colours clashing violently with the flowered wallpaper, over the pot. Upstairs, someone drags a piece of heavy furniture across the floor. I look at the old woman, and she shakes her head.

"She'll sup sorrow with a spoon of grief, that one," she says, and she rolls her eyes up, indicating the third floor. We are right under the Pierces' room.

I freeze, waiting for her to go on.

"If anyone should be leaving this house, it's them two," she goes on. It seems she's forgotten me as she stirs more sugar into her tea, looking over at the window. "Shameful. The things I've heard…." She shakes her head again. "But you know I'm not one to gossip."

I pick up my cup and take a careful sip.

"The first time I clapped eyes on them two, I knew something was off. I told Marie. I told her."

She pauses and takes a noisy drink.

"Brian wants to go to New York City," I say into the silence.

"You don't say." She looks at me directly. "Just him? Not her?"

I tell her about the Recital, how he announced it to the whole place. About how she fainted.

Her face seems to gather more colour as I talk. She passes the biscuits. I tell her about Brian's note.

"Well, I never," says Baggy Bones. "I always thought that boy had lying eyes."

"But he doesn't lie," I say, quick to defend my friend, whose name isn't really Pierce, who has a secret girlfriend he won't tell me about, who didn't talk to me about going to New York before announcing it to the world. "I don't think he lies," I amend.

"Are you sure?" She leans forward, her eyes bright, tiny pinpricks of light. "He's bad news," she says. "Mark my words."

We shake hands after that, and I leave. I walk up the hall to my door, past the tapestry. I pause to look at it, but the figures are flat today. There are no moving shadows in the woods. No glint in the golden hair of the young men. No faint sound of music. The horses are still. The page boy doesn't really look like Brian, I think, and I turn away, wondering what has changed.

25. MOTHER'S BIRTHDAY

TODAY IS MOTHER'S BIRTHDAY, and Daddy has finished her present. This afternoon, he and I are going over to Hunt's Bakery to pick up the special cake he ordered and a bottle of ginger ale. Before we even get ready, there is a knock at the door, and Mrs. O'Malley shoves her red face into the living room.

"You people are on borrowed time here," she sputters when Mother asks politely what she wants.

"I have no idea what you mean," Mother says.

"You think you can lord it over everyone, treat people like dirt, and get away with it, but let me tell you something: no one gets away with insulting an O'Malley."

"And they shouldn't," says Mother, still politely smiling.

Mrs. O. glares at me. "You'll rue the day, young missy." She turns on her heel and clumps off down the hall.

"Rue the day?" Jonathan says, smirking. "What did you do, piglet?"

"Nothing."

"You don't 'rue the day' over nothing." He looks at me closely, but Mother shushes him and bursts out laughing.

"That poor woman. I don't think she's quite right in the head, do you?"

But Jonathan is still scrutinizing me. He knows. He must know how mean I've been to Patricia, but he doesn't say another word.

Daddy and I walk over to Church Street to pick up the birthday cake. Usually Mother bakes the special-day cakes for our family, but Daddy has insisted this time. "One should not have to bake one's own cake," he says to me. "Your mother is a special person. She deserves something really special." And it is. It's round and high, with a cluster of pink roses along one side and yellow scalloped icing all around the edge. There's even a spray of green leaves nestled in the candied flowers, and her name is written in looping red writing in the middle: *Happy Birthday Mother*. I remember when we used to celebrate Jonathan's birthday on the same day as Mother's. She says he was her birthday present. She brought him home from the orphanage that day, so what she was celebrating was how long he had been part of our family. But that stopped years ago, and now he has his own cake in August on the date he was actually born. I guess he wanted a day just for him.

There are no guests at Mother's party this year. She says she wants it that way. Mrs. Dunn has gone to visit her daughter in Montreal, so she couldn't come anyway, and she's the only one Mother visits in the Music House. For a while, she was thinking of inviting Miss David, whom Daddy is helping fix up Lame Duck Lodge, but she changed her mind, so it's only us. It seems a pity we have this lovely cake and no visitors to share it with, but in another way I'm happy knowing I can have seconds and maybe even thirds. I don't say anything about this, of course.

I give Mother the booklet of illustrated sayings I have been working on for a long time, and she loves it. Daddy gives her the cedar-lined chest he made, and she exclaims in delight and pretends she didn't find it hidden under the table in the Everything Room last week. Jonathan gives her a book, a first edition of Walter de la Mare's *Memoirs of a Midget*. She loves this author, so this is a really good present and a genuine surprise too. She doesn't mention Mrs. O'Malley once.

In the days that follow, it's as if everyone is holding their breath. Smothered emotions swirl in the air. I can feel them, and it makes me nervous, makes everything uncertain and a little shaky. Nobody talks about the Threat, and it's almost as if the Recital never happened. Or as if we are just ignoring what happened there, what Jonathan said at dinner that night, what Brian said at the reception. Things have changed in some nebulous way. One thing I'm sure of: I am staying well away from Patricia.

Janet has gone to stay for a month in the country with some relatives. They have a farm, she says, and she gets to help with milking and making cheese and feeding the pigs. There's a big vegetable garden too, and she'll be doing a lot of weeding, I expect. Even our window boxes need weeding. I try to visualize Janet and her sister Magda in the country, wearing yellow boots like Christopher Robin, and in overalls too. She showed me the overalls the last time I was at her house. They have a bib attached and metal loops that fit over the buttons, sort of like the garters on my garter belt. I told her she would look like Tom Sawyer, and she liked that idea. I miss her. I want to talk to someone about going to school and maybe about seeing a movie together. *Fantasia* is playing now. Jonathan said he would take me, but I think he's forgotten in all the excitement of getting ready for college and the summer job he'll be going to soon. Anyway, I'd rather go with a friend like other girls do. That would be grand.

Late one afternoon when Jonathan is out, Mother is with Dr. Hazel, and Daddy is helping at Lame Duck Lodge, I wander onto the porch and stand for a while, staring down at Rona Layne's secret garden. No one is caring for it, and it is getting a bit parched looking for want of watering. Someone has tidied up the red brick paths, though, so maybe help is coming and it will be resurrected, like the one in the book. But somehow I don't care about this the way I did. I climb up into the crow's nest and peer about, one hand shading my eyes, but the sun is hot and saps the magic out of everything. I wonder if Brian is up on the roof, reading in the shade near his window. Or maybe he is packing for New York City.

Maybe he needs help.

I swing around to the front of the ladder, climb up the rest of the way, and crawl onto the roof. No one is there. I inch my way over to the window and peek in. I'm glad they always leave the curtains open. Mrs. Dunn has this theory that it is cooler with the curtains closed, but that makes everything dim and gloomy in her place. Mother doesn't like it this way either, and the last time she visited Mrs. Dunn, she told us at dinner it was like visiting a house of mourning.

Inside the Pierces' large room, I can hear murmuring voices. A suitcase and Brian's brown leather music bag stand near the door. I guess he must be leaving soon. I have been making a goodbye present for him and it's almost ready, so I'm relieved he's still here. Mrs. Pierce is mixing tall drinks that look like sparkling water, but they have slices of lime in them so I guess it's G and T. There is ice in the drinks, and I wonder if she has been chipping ice from our icebox again. She has tears on her cheeks, and her face looks polished like marble. Brian looks very tired. His eyes are sad and bruised-looking.

"Indulge me," she says, handing him one of the drinks. "You'll be gone soon enough. You'll never have to see me again."

Brian sighs, takes the drink, and moistens his dry lips. "Don't talk like that," he says. He takes a long drink from the glass and grimaces a little as if it's unexpectedly bitter.

"Perhaps I shouldn't talk at all," she says. She reaches over and strokes his arm. He shakes her off. "I love you."

"I know, and I'm sorry things got … out of hand," he says. "I never meant for that to happen."

"It's all right. I know you never meant it. It's just that I've sacrificed everything for you."

Brian stood up abruptly and slammed down his glass. "Not that broken record again!"

"You don't want to hear this, I know, but it's true. I can't go back. Surely you realize that? I've burned all my bridges."

"I can't stay." He walks out of sight, and I can't hear what he says next. I see Mrs. Pierce wince as if he hit her.

She wipes her eyes and takes a deep breath. "Come and sit down," she says softly. "Finish your drink. I won't say another harsh word."

Brian reappears and sinks back into the armchair. "I've sold the harpsichord," he says. "They'll pick it up on Monday at three o'clock. Is that all right?"

"Perfect," she says. She leans forward and watches his face intently as he takes another long drink from the glass.

"Refreshing, isn't it?" she says. "Want another?"

"Why not? Easy on the bitters this time."

Mrs. Pierce walks across the room to the table, which is shoved up against the opposite wall. There are no decanters there with little necklaces with the names on them like the one we have, just several bottles standing along the back and a small glass for measuring. She pours gin into the glass without bothering to measure, adds another slice of lime. She opens a small bottle and shakes something else into it. Bitters?

I hear voices from the Secret Garden so I crawl over and lie on my stomach so I can see who is down there. Miss Jones is talking to a man in overalls, leaning on a spade. They're going to bring the garden back to life! They really are! It's almost as if they have heard my thoughts. Maybe Rona Layne saw the movie too, and got inspired. I watch for a long time, but mostly he just walks around, making notes in a small notebook. He's estimating how much he has to do, I think, like Daddy estimating a building job for a bridge, the work he used to do in the old days before the Great War. When the man goes inside, I inch back to the window to see what the Pierces are doing.

Mrs. Pierce is helping Brian across the room to the bed in the alcove. He seems very tired now and not able to stand up properly. Maybe he's drunk. I remember him sipping from his silver flask during the reception, his cheeks getting red, his voice loud. Now he just seems worn out. Mrs. Pierce lowers him to the bed, smooths his hair on the pillow. She lies down beside him and slides one arm around his shoulders, cradling him like a baby.

"Oh, Brian," she says softly. "Oh, my dear, dear boy."

He murmurs something I can't hear. Butterflies flutter unpleasantly in my stomach as I watch her stoke his hair with her long fingers. I wish she would stop. After a moment, she gets up and comes to the window. I crouch out of sight as she closes the sash. Curtain rings rattle as the drapes close, too. I crawl away to the ladder, my heart beating painfully hard in my chest.

As I step down on the porch, I hear Daddy in the Everything Room, back from Lame Duck Lodge. He opens the window. "Don't go up on the roof," he says. "Leave the Pierces alone."

"All right," I say. "I'm just going to read for a while."

I go inside and find my copy of *The Water Babies*. I'm too old for it, but it's comforting, like an old friend. But I'm too restless to read for long. My skin feels prickly, but not with heat.

Last week I had friends: Janet to play with and to call now and then on the telephone, and Brian to talk to sometimes on the roof. I loved the feeling that he trusted me, valued me. And now I am bereft. Janet has already gone, and by tomorrow, Jonathan will be gone too. Brian is about to leave, and he hasn't even said a proper goodbye yet. I see the canvas suitcase at the door, the shabby brown leather music bag leaning against it—two old friends. Maybe he plans to say goodbye just before he goes. That would make sense. And he'll send me postcards from New York, brightly coloured shiny postcards of big city streets and famous buildings—one of Washington Square, perhaps. I close my eyes and imagine his handwriting. He has written a message just to me. *Studying music at the Juilliard.* I'm sure it will be the Juilliard. *Having a great time. Wish you were here. Love, Brian.*

I get out the bookmark I have made for him as a farewell gift and set about adding a few final elegant curlicues. This will make the motto really stand out: *Ars longa, vita brevis.* Tomorrow I'll run upstairs and slip it under Brian's door. He'll take it with him to New York, and this way, part of me will go along too.

26. THE SWORD OF DAMOCLES

UNION STATION IS GRAND, full of echoing noise and crowds of people. We are all here to say goodbye to Jonathan. Helen is with us for a while too, and she gives him a book to read on the train as a going-away present. Mother thinks they are more than just friends, but Daddy shakes his head and smiles and says nothing. Mother looks annoyed. I think of Brian and when I can give him my going away present. I haven't had a chance to slip it under the door yet.

We stand in the line-up for a long time with all these people waiting to get on the train going up north. Some sit on bulging suitcases. A baby somewhere down the line is crying monotonously. Children run about shouting. Mother purses her lips. I know she is thinking that they ought to be taught how to behave in a public place. I stand quietly, showing how it should be done, this waiting. In front of us, an Italian family is having a sort of picnic, sitting on their suitcases tied in the middle with belts made of webbing and passing around food wrapped in wax paper. My mouth waters. Eating in public is something I am not allowed to do. But it smells so good, and I envy them.

Finally a man's voice begins to call out the stations where Jonathan's train will stop. It's a long list, and most of the names are muddied by the echo. We try to guess what they are until the disembodied voice concludes with "Now boarding," and the line inches forward.

Finally we get to the front where stairs go up to the train track, and we all hug and say goodbye over and over.

"Write!" Mother says. "Write to me!"

"Yes, yes, of course."

Jonathan looks embarrassed and finally pushes his way up the stairs. Mother stands looking up into the crowd jostling their way up to the platform until long after we can't see Jonathan anymore.

Daddy takes Mother's hand and squeezes it as he steers her back to the street. The garbled announcements from the loudspeaker echo above us. I can still smell the enticing odours of onion and garlic and salami from the Italian family's picnic. We never have those things in our house. Mother says there's no food value in salami. I sometimes wonder if Mother says there's no food value in things she doesn't like.

As we ride the streetcar up Yonge Street, rocking gently from side to side on the wooden seats, I wonder if Brian has already left. I see the image of his suitcase by the door, try to remember when he said he was going. I hope I haven't missed him. I haven't had a chance to drop off my present yet.

We get off at Wellesley and walk back home to the Music House. No one is talking. I can feel Mother beside me, stiff and wound up tight. Every now and then she squeezes my hand hard. I hope she doesn't start to cry. I hope she writes some sad poetry in her *Testament* instead.

Outside our living room door, Mother leans down to pick up a square white envelope. I catch my breath. Maybe it's a goodbye note from Brian. But it's addressed to Mother, and she opens it as we walk into the living room and I take off my good shoes.

Mother throws the note on the table and sinks into a chair. "My cup overflows!" She flings out her hands dramatically. Her cheeks are pink. "What in God's green earth have I done to offend Him so utterly?"

"What now?" Daddy picks up the letter, adjusts his glasses,

reads it slowly. "It's not even signed," he says. "Just ignore it."

"Ignore it? Ignore it?! It says Rona Layne right there at the bottom." Mother lunges over and points to the bottom of letter, her finger trembling with rage. "So your suggestion is we ignore it and just get evicted? Have what's left of our goods and chattels flung out the window?"

"They won't do that," Daddy says. His face is getting pink too, and that's not good for him. I take a deep breath, but there is nothing I can do. I see Mrs. O'Malley's fat face glaring at Mother on her birthday. Turning to glare to me. *No one gets away with threatening an O'Malley.* Did I do that? Am I to blame? I move closer to Mother's chair, but she suddenly pushes it back hard, hitting me on the arm. She doesn't notice. She begins to pace back and forth between the table and the cupola windows.

"That bitch!" Mother says. "That petty little tyrant, Rona Layne, is getting back at us because Jonathan decided not to continue studying with her."

"Lil, that is ridiculous."

"Oh, you think so, do you? You think she's a shitty little saint about to be beatified by the bloody Pope and this note is all an illusion? Some feat of *léger de main*? You imbecile!"

I back away, making myself small as I hunker down against the cool tiles of the fireplace. I hate it when Mother lashes out like this, her words turning sharp like razor blades, tearing at the air. A fist tightens in my stomach. Mother's face stretches into odd angles like a hideous mask. Daddy is red-faced, too, but on him it looks less scary. As I watch, he loosens his regimental tie and sinks into a chair. The high colour drains from his face, and I wonder if he will faint. He clears his throat.

"Lil, that's enough," he says.

"Have you forgotten how hard it is to find a place to live in this hellhole?" Mother rages. "Someplace above the level of a rat hole that we can afford? That will take children? And the piano? It was the merest stroke of luck we heard about this place!"

"Hard, yes, but not impossible."

"That woman cannot be allowed to disrupt people's lives like this for no other reason than spite."

"You're assuming that Rona Layne actually wrote this thing," Daddy says. He scratches absently at his wrist.

"She just forgot to sign it. Or do you mean that Jones woman wrote it?"

"It's typed, and without a signature we don't know who wrote it, do we? And Miss Layne is an educated woman. Does this sound like the writing of an educated person to you?"

For the first time, Mother stops moving. Her fierce silver-grey eyes focus on the note, still lying on the table where she had flung it. "There's only one way to find out."

"Ignore it," Daddy says. His voice is tired now, sounding hoarse.

"I will not be caught unawares again," she shouts. "One eviction is enough in one lifetime. I will not be a naïve victim again!" Mother tosses her head and grabs the note. She pauses, straightens her shoulders, and checks her face in the mirror over the fireplace. Then she puts on more lipstick and marches out the door.

"God almighty," Daddy says and closes his eyes.

I jump up and rush to the door.

"No."

I draw my hand away from the doorknob as if it's scalding hot. I ache to know what is happening, what Rona Layne is saying, whether Miss Jones even lets Mother in to see her.

"We'll know soon enough," Daddy says. He leans against the high back of the chair.

A few minutes later, Daddy rouses himself and goes into the Everything Room to change out of his good suit. I take a quick look down the hall, but Rona Layne's door is closed and Mother is nowhere to be seen.

Twenty minutes later, Mother comes back, looking more like her old self. She slides the letter back into the envelope and drops it on the table.

Daddy says nothing; he just sits there, watching her face as he pours her a cup of the tea we made while she was gone.

Mother shakes her head. "What a strange place we have landed in this time," she says in a conversational tone, as if she's about to tell one of her amusing family stories. "They didn't even offer tea."

I stifle a nervous giggle.

"Sometimes I think that apart from her music, that woman is a complete imbecile, or maybe an idiot savant, and it's really Miss Jones who runs the rest of her life."

"Did Miss Jones write the letter?" Daddy hands her the teacup.

"Miss Jones was out, which was probably the only reason I got into their apartment, and Miss Layne seemed almost confused, as if she couldn't follow what I was saying. She was like a child, Ned. And then Miss Jones came in with some shopping, and she seemed quite upset that I was there, though she couldn't really say much in front of me. After that, Miss Layne kept glancing at her, as if looking for approval every time she said something."

"So which one of them wrote the letter?" Daddy asks.

"Neither, apparently. Although no one came right out and said this, I suspect they both think Mrs. O'Malley wrote it."

"And tried to make us think it was Rona Layne. That's fraud."

"I doubt it, since she didn't forge Layne's signature."

"So the letter means nothing?"

"Not exactly. The O'Malleys are important to the running of this house, even though Mr. O'Malley is more of a shadow figure around here, as far as I can see. That came through very clearly. I think we're all right, but I get the feeling we're on thin ice and I can't figure out why. Miss Layne is impossible to pin down, and Miss Jones is forever answering one question with another, like a politician."

Daddy gets to his feet, lays a hand on her arm, and pats her. "I need a rest."

Mother waits until he is out of the room. "Oh, God! My God, why have You forsaken me?" She covers her face with her hands and begins to cry.

I push hard against the tiles of the fireplace. I wish I could disappear. But in a strange way, I need to be here too. To let her know she is not alone. I'm afraid to move. If I were not here, would she come out of this Slough of Despond?

After a moment, she opens her eyes and looks right at me. "Oh, Vanessa," she says, opening her arms, "you're my one comfort now!"

I run into her arms and sink into the safety of her body. I don't want to think about how I may have caused this whole problem. I have done those things I ought not to have done. What will happen to me now?

We are eating lunch—tomato soup and cheese sandwiches—when someone scratches at the door. Mother straightens her shoulders and nods to me, and I open it. Baggy Bones is standing there, wringing her claw-like hands. Her mouth is working as if she's chewing something with not enough teeth.

"Sorry to interrupt," she says, stretching her neck into the room and looking at Mother and Daddy.

Daddy stands up politely and wipes his moustache with the linen serviette. "Is there something we can help you with, Mrs. Slinger?"

How does he know her name? I look at Mother who is also standing, reaching for another cup and saucer from the glass-doored cabinet. "Would you like to join us?" she asks.

"No, no." Baggy Bones looks shocked at the very idea. "It's them Pierces again," she says. "I'm real sorry to bother youse about this, but there's someone up there banging and shouting and carrying on outside their door. I don't want the cops coming 'round. This used to be a respectable house."

Mother and Daddy exchange glances. Daddy takes a breath. "Would you like me to see what it's about?"

"Oh, thank you! I just want some peace and quiet, and them Pierces are always causing a hullaballoo. If you could speak to them..."

"Certainly." Daddy lays down his serviette and slips on his second-best suit jacket from the back of the chair. He's still wearing his house slippers and hesitates. "I'll just get my shoes," he says, sliding past her to cross the hall into the Everything Room.

Baggy Bones's impatience fills the doorway as she waits. She makes no response to Mother's efforts at polite conversation and refuses to move into the living room.

When Daddy returns, Mother follows them and everyone troops down the hall. Now we can hear the noise upstairs. Mother is still talking to Baggy Bones, but I don't catch what she's saying. She shepherds the old woman through her door with a comforting arm around her shoulders, and I quietly follow Daddy up the stairs to the third floor, where a man is banging on the door of number 8, shouting Brian's name.

"Stop that at once!" Daddy says.

This must be his army voice, the one he used to order his men over the top in the trenches. I've never heard it before.

The shouting stops. I peer around Daddy and see the man from our church choir who looks like a Velázquez painting, one fist raised to strike the door.

"There's something wrong," the man says. His face is flushed, his eyes shiny like tears. "I was supposed to meet Brian at the bus station at ten o'clock, and he never showed up. I waited an hour, but when the New York bus finally pulled out, I came here to find out what happened. I've been practically pounding on the door but there's no answer."

"Maybe no one's in," I say, pointing out the obvious.

Daddy turns around, startled, and tells me to go home.

Why can't they see this fact? I wonder, as I trot back down

the stairs. If someone were there, they would open the door. It's simple. Mother is still with Baggy Bones, so I keep going out the back way, determined to prove I'm right, and climb the ladder to the roof. But when I get to the big bay window, the curtains are drawn again. Perhaps Mrs. Dunn has convinced Mrs. Pierce of the wisdom of her shadowed-room-equals-a-cooler-room theory. I peer through the gap, but I can only see a thin slice of the place: the top of the harpsichord, the end of a table, part of the door.

As I am shifting about, trying to see more, the door bursts open and Daddy appears, balancing himself in the doorframe. At once his hand shoots out, stopping Brian's noisy friend from rushing in. Daddy shouts something I can't hear, and I fall back out of sight, frightened by the look on his face. Why does he have one hand covering his nose and mouth like that? The last thing I see before I scuttle away is the suitcase on the floor and Brian's scuffed music case leaning against it.

A few minutes later I am sitting on the porch, sucking on an old Scotch peppermint I found in the pocket of my shorts. It was a bit fuzzy at first, but now it's smooth and sharp like a new candy. In the distance, I hear sirens: first one, then another, then one more. They wail together, answering each other, rising and falling, coming nearer and nearer till they suddenly stop, so close now they sound as if they are in our driveway. Prickles of apprehension crawl along my spine. I run down the back stairs in time to see two police cars pull up under the *porte-cochère*, lights flashing, gravel spraying under their tires. A couple of uniformed policemen jump out. Over the crackle of the car radios, I hear Mother's voice frantically calling my name.

We are being evicted. Mrs. O'Malley has called the police.

I turn around, feeling cold, wanting Mother to tell me everything's all right, but her face is tense, telegraphing her anxiety. She scoops me close with one arm.

"Come," she says. "Inside."

The air crackles with strange energy. Do we have to leave right away? Leave everything behind? Our records? My books? Mother rushes me up the stairs, telling me we are going to Mrs. Sullivan's for tea. What? I haven't heard about this before, but now is not the time for questions. I go inside and get changed. Maybe this is Part the First of Eviction: getting dressed and out of the way, making it easy for everyone to throw us out. Being polite. Another form of *noblesse oblige*, perhaps.

Strangely, when we are both dressed up, we go out the back way. We never do that. The police cars are still there, but no police officers have come to our door so far. That's a good sign, surely. Mother holds my hand very tightly as we hurry by.

Perhaps Mrs. Sullivan will let something drop about what is going on. I will just have to listen extra hard.

27. EXEUNT OMNES

July 1, Dominion Day, and we're moving. Again. But we're *not* being evicted.

Everything happened very fast. I don't know exactly how, or even why, except it probably has something to do with Mrs. O'Malley. No one mentions this, but what else could it be? Except maybe something to do with the policemen....

I didn't find out anything when we were at Mrs. Sullivan's. The whole outing was very odd. For one thing, no one had mentioned this invitation before. We didn't even take a hostess gift. And it was strange being there without Janet, sitting in their dim dining room eating, with no one to exchange glances with, feeling really alone even though Mother, Janet's oldest sister, and Mrs. Sullivan were sitting right there. I guess it was more like a peculiar high tea because we ate little sandwiches, some strange potato-and-egg salad, ladyfingers, cookies with jelly in the middle, some pound cake, and even some cheese and grapes. And everything was on the table at the same time, so it couldn't have been dinner, really, could it? Mother didn't mind me taking more than one of everything, which was a good thing because eating eases the butterflies in my stomach.

Everyone talked in a stilted way about what Janet was doing on the farm and about Mother's hopes for a new job with that private kindergarten in the fall in spite of having lost her certificate, and Mrs. Sullivan talked about the trip to Montreal that Mr. Sullivan was taking for business and how the first time she was there she went up all the steps of St. Joseph's Oratory on her knees. I wonder what state her stockings would have been in at the top. There are a lot of steps. I've seen pictures.

Then we went into the living room, and Mrs. Sullivan brought some of Janet's old school books from grade six and gave them to me. "It'll be like summer school for you," she said, laughing in that sparkly false way adults have with children sometimes. She doesn't usually do this, so it grates. It will be fun using Janet's books, though, seeing her handwriting here and there in cryptic comments, looking at her occasional doodles, knowing she read exactly what I was reading. While I looked through the books, Mrs. Sullivan and Mother talked in low voices as they cleared the dishes in the dining room, something I would usually have been expected to help them do. Now and then, I caught snippets when Mother got carried away and raised her voice: housing shortage, nothing in the paper, no one wants children, that madwoman. I had heard all this before, though perhaps not about the madwoman. Later on, Mother made several calls on the telephone in the hall, one of them to Daddy, I think. We were there so long I fell asleep in the window seat. It was almost dark when we finally came home. There were no police cars to be seen.

So now it's only five days later, and we are moving to Lame Duck Lodge. "How appropriate," Mother says bitterly, and then reminds us we mustn't call it that anymore, not even in jest. We're to have the first floor of Miss David's new house, which Daddy will finish fixing up for her so we can live for free for a while. And I will have my own bedroom! It's just a sleeping porch really, Daddy says, but it leads out to the garden, so maybe I can feed some stray kitties and have secret pets like Baggy Bones does. Better still, a stray dog. Or maybe the five cats Mother says live with Miss David will come for a visit sometimes. All this should be very exciting, especially the part about me having my own room, but I feel numb. Mother says this is a bitter pill to swallow, but Daddy is happy. He's the one who "sealed the deal," as he says. Strange how the Music House was supposed to be our haven but now we can't get out fast enough. Everything is happening at top speed and I can't figure out why, so sometimes I don't know whether to be happy or sad. It's almost dizzying.

When I am gathering old newspapers for packing from the discarded pile on the porch, I find stories about Mrs. Pierce and Brian splattered all over the front pages. *Scandal in Jarvis Mansion*, says one. *Murder–Suicide in Musician's House. Older Woman, Youth, Pose as Mother and Son. Woman Poisons Teenaged Lover*, screams yet another. The words make my heart race, my stomach flutter strangely. Most are newspapers I've never seen before. A few moments later, Daddy finds me reading one of the articles and takes them all away.

"Trash," he says, and flings them in the fireplace and lights the fire, even though it's a hot day. "You can't believe anything they print in those rags. Pack the books."

After a few minutes, I raise my head and look at Daddy hard until he looks back. "Brian didn't go to New York, did he?" I know the answer, but I have to hear it from him to make it real.

"He's gone, dear. That I can tell you. Here. Don't forget Jonathan's music books."

"But it said in the paper Brian's dead," I say, trying to understand. "It says his mother killed him."

"She wasn't his mother," Daddy says. "They got that right." He stops what he's doing and looks off into the distance for a moment. "Look, you're too young to understand."

"He was a friend of mine," I say, my eyes blurring with tears. I wish I hadn't seen those dreadful papers.

Daddy pauses, and for a moment I think he might tell me more, but then he picks up another carton and puts it on the table. He won't talk anymore. And I know it's no use asking Mother. She won't talk either. I blink, push up my glasses. The print on the spines of the books blurs. Brian will never get my goodbye present. I picture him stumbling across the room, supported by Mrs. Pierce. He was dying then. Poison making its way through his veins, draining his life. *Could I have saved him if I had cried out?* I turn away so Daddy won't see me wipe my eyes, and I try to think about something else: about my new room, the tiny garden that it looks out on, the thought of waking up there and getting dressed for a real school every morning in my crisp new white blouse with the notched collar and the new tunic with the crest in the middle. It helps a little.

This move is so different from last time. Then, Jonathan was here and we were surrounded by friends. It was cold outside, but everyone pitched in to help carry things under the naked trees, across the broad street, and up the stairs. We were moving into our haven. Everyone was so hopeful. Now it's Dominion Day, so it's hot, and the three people here are all strangers: Miss David's brother, Stefan, whom I have never met, and his two Polish friends from work. They have brought their dilapidated truck and loaded up the piano and the wardrobe trunk, the window boxes and a lot of cartons, with much shouting in their own language, and then driving away in the shimmering heat under the green archway of the Jarvis Street elms. Soon they will be back for the last load. Our new house isn't that far away. Mother points out that I'll be able to walk to school. I'd feel better about it all if Patricia weren't standing there, arms crossed, watching all the commotion as she leans against the wall just outside the O'Malley's back door, her round moon-face strangely expressionless.

Mother stands looking lost in the living room, now shorn of everything personal. Our dining table is gone, and so are the dining chairs, the wing chair, and even Jonathan's daybed, which will now be mine for my new room. Only the huge oak desk remains, waiting for the new people who will live here. The place looks lighter, smaller. And sad. It is not a haven anymore. I move close to Mother, and she puts her arm around me and hugs me.

"What a life," she says, shaking her head.

"Mummy, who was Mrs. Pierce?" I ask.

"I have no idea, dear," Mother says. "Come on. Let's wait for the men downstairs."

"What's going to happen to the harpsichord?"

"That is the least of my worries," Mother says.

Baggy Bones has closed her door. I think of her watering her plants in her dim greenish room, feeding her secret cats on the windowsill, talking endlessly to Marie. She will have enough gossip now to keep her going for years.

As we walk down the long hall, I take one last look at the tapestry. I try to look deep inside the forest as I used to, but now everything is flat. Colourless. Silent. Dead.

Like Brian.

Caro Soles' novels include mysteries, erotica, gay lit, science fiction and the occasional bit of dark fantasy. She received the Derrick Murdoch Award from the Crime Writers of Canada, and has been shortlisted for the Lambda Literary Award, the Aurora Award, and the Stoker Award. Caro lives in Toronto, and loves dachshunds, books, opera, and ballet, not necessarily in that order.

ACKNOWLEDGEMENTS

The picture of a writer toiling alone is true in a sense. But we are not alone all the time. We have a lot of help along the way from family, friends, first readers, and editors. I want to especially thank Inanna Publications for welcoming me into their literary family and being my first Canadian publisher. Thank you, Luciana Ricciutelli, for patiently switching all the American spelling I had worked so hard to use for my American agent and U.S. publishers, and for straightening out some of my more convoluted sentences. And thanks, too, to Val Fullard for the cover design which puts the piano front and centre, where it belongs in the story.